Sleigh Bells
AND
SNOWSTORMS

CLAIRE KINGSLEY

Always Have LLC

Published by Always Have, LLC

Edited by Michelle Fewer

Cover design by Lori Jackson

ISBN: 978-1-959809-23-4

www.clairekingsleybooks.com

For everyone who didn't know they needed a small-town/romcom/romantic suspense/Christmas romance. I didn't know I needed to write one either, but here we are!

Happy holidays!

About the book

From USA Today Bestselling author Claire Kingsley, the stand-alone small-town, romcom, romantic suspense, Christmas romance you didn't know you needed.

Handsome, charismatic, and charming, Jensen Lakes is an enigma in a designer suit. But his playboy reputation is a persona—one of many—that he uses in his unique line of work.

A priceless heirloom goes missing right before the holidays, and Jensen is hired to find it. Tracking down the perpetrator will be simple. He'll be in and out before Santa hits chimneys.

Natalie Thatcher needs a break. She's a dedicated sister, aunt, and nurse, but her life is no Christmas carol. Between bills, mounting home repairs, and holiday shopping still to be done, most days she feels like a tangled strand of lights.

Jensen follows his quarry to Tilikum, and the Christmas-clad town throws him for a loop. As does Natalie. He enlists her aid—who better to help him navigate the local quirks than the captivating woman next door? Despite their chemistry and sizzling banter, love isn't on his Christmas list. Or hers.

But as danger mounts, Jensen finds himself in an unexpected position—falling in love with his partner. And when her life is on the line, he'll risk everything to keep her safe.

And get her home for Christmas.

Author's note: A handsome charmer falls for a sassy small-town girl. Adventure, witty banter, Christmas coziness, and a holiday happily ever after that will leave your heart full.

CHAPTER 1

Jensen

Pretending to ignore the woman at the bar, I casually leaned against it and adjusted the cuffs of my suit jacket. As predicted, her eyes immediately moved to me, holding there as she shifted toward me. The change was almost imperceptible, but I was a master of my craft, deftly keying in on the subtle alteration of her posture, the openness in her body.

Still, I ignored her, checking my watch as if I were impatient for something, and cast a hard look at the bartender. She responded to that too—lifting her eyebrows and pressing her lips into the hint of a smile.

Her dark hair was sleek, in an elegant updo that matched the formality of her gown. Deep red with a hint of shimmer, thin straps, plunging neckline, a high slit up one thigh, and stilettos that reminded a man to be careful. She was beautiful, if you liked that sort of thing—sculpted features, thick lashes, full red lips, long manicured nails.

She looked expensive.

It fit. We were in one of the most luxurious hotels in New York City. It was decked out for the holiday season, with a

1

massive Christmas tree in the lobby decorated in silver and gold. Garlands, wreaths, and soft white lights were everywhere, and instrumental Christmas music played in the background.

I flicked my eyes in her direction, and she glanced away, feigning disinterest. I almost smiled. So that was how she wanted to play.

The bartender—she was young and pretty, dressed all in black—came over to take my order. She chewed her lip, and her cheeks flushed as I ordered a scotch, neat.

"I like your accent," she said.

"Americans usually do."

"You're British?"

I nodded and looked away, hoping to dissuade further conversation. Pretty as she was, I wasn't there to flirt with the bartender. I was angled so I could still see the woman in the red dress and noted a hint of jealousy flash across her face. She liked attention, and it was increasingly irritating her that I refused to give her mine.

Naturally, I continued to tease her with apparent indifference while the bartender served my drink. I took a sip, the amber liquid sliding pleasantly down my throat.

Finally, I deigned to take notice of her.

Turning, I let my eyes sweep up and down with exaggerated slowness. That pleased her. She gave me a similar once-over, and the corners of her mouth lifted.

"Evening." I looked her up and down again and moved closer. "Can I buy you a drink?"

Her eyes widened as if my offer surprised or maybe even offended her, and she answered in a French accent. "Pardon me, sir. How do you know I'm not here with someone?"

I didn't bother to look around. "If you are, I daresay he's unsuitable for having left you alone."

"Quite so. A woman can't be too careful."

"Indeed, she cannot." I continued moving closer and took another sip of my drink. "But I know you're alone."

"How do you know this?"

I met her eyes, my gaze intense. "Because I've been watching you."

She gasped as if that shocked her. I doubted it.

"That's terribly rude."

"Is it?" My lips turned up in a devilish grin. "And can you blame me? You must know what that dress does to a man."

"All right, a drink. It's the least you can do. That, and tell me your name."

"Arthur Kingston." The pseudonym came easily. It was one persona of many. "And you are?"

"Delphine Moreau. It's a pleasure to meet you, Arthur."

"I assure you." I held out my hand, and when she placed hers in mine, I lifted it to my lips and brushed a light kiss across her knuckles. "The pleasure is mine."

I signaled the bartender, and Delphine requested a martini. The banter that followed verged on boring—for me, at least. She engaged with increasing attention and not-so-subtle suggestion. I played the part she expected—the predator waiting for a chance to seize his prey.

Maple's voice, her accent matching mine, spoke quietly in my earpiece. "This is going well."

"Indeed," I said, managing to make the reply appear to be for Delphine.

The earpiece I wore was essentially invisible, but it gave Maple Exton, my trusty handler, a listen-in to all that went on.

"I thought she'd at least make you try," Maple said, her tone taking on a bit of a pout.

If I hadn't been in the middle of a rather important seduction, I would have rolled my eyes. Of course it was going well. I was Jensen Lakes. Women—especially women like Delphine —never made me work very hard.

So much the pity.

Interestingly, Delphine did seem to be alone—for the time being, at least. I was well aware of my surroundings, managing glances around the bar, and I hadn't seen anyone watching us.

Her minions were in the hotel. They had to be. But she'd apparently dismissed them for the evening.

Maple was right. It was going well.

"Delphine, I must say, I've noticed that no one is appearing to rescue you. I fear you really are alone."

She sighed. "Sad to say, I'm far from home in a city of strangers."

The corner of my mouth lifted. "That must be lonely."

Her eyes met mine, full of heat and suggestion. "Very."

"I can help with that. For tonight, at least." Licking my lips, as if anticipating the taste of her, I traced a finger along her jawline. "Shall we go upstairs?"

A flush hit her cheeks, and she hesitated before answering. "I don't usually do things like this."

I grinned. She was a good liar. "Neither do I."

"You tease me."

"Oh, yes. And I can assure you, I'll tease you more before the night is over." I leaned in so my mouth was close to her ear and lowered my voice. "Trust me. You'll love every second of it."

Her body trembled, and her breath caught.

"Are you going to make me regret this?" she whispered.

"No. You know you want this, Delphine."

As if I'd already found the spot to drive her crazy, she took a shuddering breath. With the way I stood close enough to devour her and she gazed at me with parted lips, we must have looked almost obscene.

She nodded. I smiled in triumph.

"Your room or mine?" she asked, her voice breathy.

"Yours."

"That was bold," Maple said in my ear. "She's not actually going to let you in her room, is she?"

Of course she was. I had the situation well in hand. Delphine had no idea who I really was.

With my hand on the small of Delphine's back, I led her to the elevator. No one followed, and the hall was empty when we emerged onto her floor. Her room was around a corner, and when she unlocked it, I followed her in.

As soon as the door shut behind us, I pushed her up against the wall. But I didn't kiss her. Attractive as she was, my desire for her was feigned.

And she was just as likely to put a knife in my back as return the kiss.

Instead, I caressed her jaw before moving my hand to wrap around her throat. Her eyes flashed with lust. She liked it.

"The things I'm going to do to you tonight," I said, my voice low, and her mouth lifted in a smile. "Do you know what I want?"

"What?"

"You, in the shower."

"What are you implying? That I'm too dirty for you?"

"On the contrary. I like it dirty." I tightened my grip on her throat, and she whimpered. "Can you be a good girl for me?"

Her smile was wicked. She was not a good girl, but she'd play one for me.

"Take your clothes off, get in the shower, and lather up that exquisite body so you're nice and slick. Then I'll join you. We're going to spend our evening doing unspeakable things."

"Is that a promise?"

"Call it a threat."

She bit her lower lip, and I let her go, taking a step back. With a sultry smile, she sauntered into the bathroom and softly shut the door.

Without a second's hesitation, I got to work. Pulling a small tool from an inside pocket, I used it to jam the lock on the bathroom door. It wouldn't hold her for long, but I only needed a minute.

"She fell for it, didn't she?" Maple asked.

The shower turned on. She hadn't noticed the door.

"We knew she would," I answered, speaking quietly as I went straight for the safe in the small closet. Our intel indicating Delphine had a weakness for assertive men in nice suits had proven out. "It's why you sent me."

"It could still be a trap."

"Everything in this line of work could be a trap." I took another device out of my pocket and attached the electrical probes to the lock. In a few seconds, it would reprogram the code, and I'd be in. If that didn't work, the small explosive I also carried would do the trick. It would make more noise—and make my exit more difficult—but it was a suitable backup plan.

"And you're more than happy to spring their traps, aren't you?"

"Just let me do my job."

Delphine's voice came through the bathroom door. "Arthur?"

The reprogrammed code flashed on the screen, and I entered it, disengaging the lock. My lips curled in a smile of triumph as I pulled out a carefully wrapped bundle and peeked inside.

It was an ancient Greek terra-cotta figurine—now worn with age—of a woman in a long dress. The priceless piece had been stolen from a private collection in Germany.

I worked for a secretive organization of thief hunters who tracked down stolen jewelry, art, and antiquities. Often the artifacts were priceless, like the Greek figurine I held in my hand. I was there to steal it back.

The shower turned off, but Delphine didn't call out again.

"I have it," I whispered to Maple as I pocketed my tools and slipped the figurine into my jacket.

"I have a strong suspicion you need to get out," Maple said. "Now."

Delphine rattled the door. "Arthur? What's going on?"

A second later, I was out the door.

"I'm out," I said, heading for the stairs. We were on the eighth floor, but I couldn't risk an elevator.

"Are you sure she's alone?"

"I didn't see anyone, but..."

Footsteps sounded behind me. Multiple people. They sped up, and I chanced a glance over my shoulder. Two men in suits.

"There they are," I said, sprinting for the stairway entrance.

The footsteps followed.

"What floor?" Maple asked.

I burst through the door to the stairs. "Eight."

"Go up first."

Sprinting, I took the stairs several at a time and slipped out onto the ninth floor. I doubted I'd evade my pursuers that easily, but I slowed to a walk as I made my way down the hallway past a pair of hotel guests bound for their room.

"Happy holidays!" the woman said, sounding a little tipsy.

I gave her a nod and hurried past, ducking down another hall. The woman greeted someone else—probably Delphine's minions—and a second later, I heard footsteps and low voices.

Still after me.

I went farther down the hall, hoping for another set of stairs.

"Where are you?" Maple asked. "I have a layout of the hotel."

"Passing room 9015."

"Keep going. There's a closet three doors down."

I reached the closet and tried the door.

"Locked."

"Stairs coming up on the right."

I was already running for the door, holding the figurine against my chest. My pursuers must have taken a different turn, but their voices grew closer again. I slipped through the door into the stairwell and started down.

"I'm going down."

The door above me opened, and heavy footsteps rang out. One of them said, "Lobby."

Someone would be waiting for me downstairs. Possibly several someones.

"Can't go to the lobby," I told Maple as I kept racing downward.

Making a snap decision, I exited the stairwell on the third floor. The door opened onto a wide-open space with a large, brightly lit Christmas tree. Well-dressed people milled around, many with drinks in their hands.

"Third floor. People everywhere."

"There are ballrooms on the third floor," Maple said.

"Looks like a party."

I slowed so I wouldn't attract too much attention and made my way toward the ballrooms. The stairwell door opened, and a few people exclaimed in surprise as the two men rushed out.

Outside the first ballroom, I glanced down a side hallway. A man dressed in red with a thick white beard was emerging from a room a few doors down.

I ran to him and grabbed his arm, pulling him back inside.

"What the...?"

"Apologies," I said quickly and blinked when I realized what he was wearing. A Santa Claus costume. The beard was fake. "I'll give you a thousand dollars cash for your costume."

"I'm supposed to play Santa out there." He gestured toward the ballroom.

"Does it pay a thousand dollars?"

"No. I get a hundred bucks."

"I'd say my offer is considerably more generous." Careful of the figurine beneath my jacket, I pulled out my wallet and showed him the cash.

His eyes widened, and he shrugged. "All right."

He took off the costume, including the beard. Moving fast, I handed him the money, then put everything on over my suit, including the beard and hat. It was too loose, so I grabbed a throw pillow from the couch and stuffed it under the coat.

Without a word, I turned to leave.

"Merry Christmas," he said, his voice a little bewildered as the door snicked shut behind me.

Dressed as Jolly Old St. Nick, I walked down the hallway toward the ballroom, waving at the partygoers. One of Delphine's men was standing among the guests, talking to someone on his phone.

"She probably brought him up to her room to get laid," he said.

I couldn't help but smile. That she had.

Revelers exclaimed that Santa had arrived as I waved at them and walked by, heading for the elevators.

"Santa has a stop to make to deliver gifts," I said in an American accent. I pointed at a rather attractive woman in a sleek green dress. "I'll be back, and you can sit on my lap."

She laughed. The man with her did not.

Delphine's man didn't even look at me.

I sauntered to the elevator and got in. "I'm in the elevator. Next stop, lobby."

"How?" Maple asked.

"I'm dressed as Santa Claus."

"I wondered what you meant about a costume. God, I wish I could see that."

When the doors opened to the lobby, the people waiting to go up smiled at me.

"Ho, ho, ho," I called out in character as I walked out.

Another man in a dark suit stood nearby, watching the elevators while he spoke to someone on his phone.

He hardly glanced at me as I strolled right by.

Waving to a few more people who shouted, "Santa," I made my way through the lobby and out the front door.

"I'm out."

"I have a car for you one block north."

"Might want to let him know how I'm dressed."

"He's aware."

Holding the pillow in place, I walked up the street and found my ride—a black SUV. I got in and nodded to my driver. He had Christmas music playing on the radio.

"Santa," he said with a hint of amusement.

I tugged off the hat and beard as the car pulled into traffic and started to drive away.

"That's better," I said to Maple. "The beard was awful."

She laughed. "Good work, Mr. Lakes."

"Thank you, Mrs. Exton."

"The car will take you to the rendezvous point. You're meeting Mr. Darrin to transfer the item."

"Understood."

I took off the rest of the costume and set the pillow aside. Then I drew out the figurine and carefully unwrapped it, ensuring it hadn't sustained any damage. It was aged and worn, but my rescue hadn't hurt it.

Another job in the books.

"Do I have a flight back to Seattle?" I asked.

"You do."

"Good. I'm quite looking forward to a holiday after this little adventure. I owe my sister and her family a visit."

"It is almost Christmas," Maple said. "But I have an alternative."

"What's that?"

"A new job has come in."

"I just finished one moments ago, and you want to put me to work again?"

Maple laughed. "I know. But it makes sense to send you. It's not far from Seattle."

"Well, that's something. What's the job?"

"Client is the Beaufort family. They have an old estate outside London. Their line goes way back in the aristocracy."

"They sound stuffy."

She ignored my comment. "Someone stole one of their family heirlooms. It's a jeweled necklace known as the Emerald Crown. The Beaufort family puts it on display for the Christmas season each year, hence the urgency to recover it. We've tracked the culprit, and we think he's hiding in or around Tilikum, a small town in the mountains a couple hours' drive from Seattle."

"Odd location. Is the thief someone we know?"

"No. But it appears to have been a solo job."

I paused, pondering. I'd been looking forward to some time off, but it made sense to accept. I was already headed for Seattle. Spending a week or so in the mountains wouldn't be a hardship. And another payday was never a bad thing.

"All right, I'm in. Send me the details."

"Already on it. I'll make the necessary local arrangements."

"You're such a gem, Maple. Whatever would I do without you?"

"Find yourself in endless amounts of trouble, no doubt."

I grinned. "Indeed. Although I do like trouble."

"I'm well aware."

I leaned back and watched the city go by as the driver took me to the rendezvous point. It was close to Christmas, and I did owe my sister a visit. But I wasn't concerned. I'd be in and out before then.

How hard could finding a jewelry thief in a small mountain town be?

CHAPTER 2

Natalie

Catching sight of my reflection in the rearview mirror, I winced. No wonder the cashier in Nature's Basket eyed me with concern while she rang up my groceries. I had a mascara smudge beneath one eye, and my dark circles made me look like I was recovering from the flu—or a bad hangover.

In reality, it was neither. I was simply an emergency department nurse who worked graveyard trying to function on my day off.

With a sigh, I tore my eyes from my less-than-perky reflection and looked again at the receipt. Had my three measly bags of groceries really cost that much? And why did my niece, Annabel, who was only six, seem to eat as much as me and my sister combined?

Probably because Annabel never stopped moving.

Just as I turned on the engine, Louise Haven walked by and caught sight of me through the windshield. She wiggled her fingers in a wave and scurried to the driver's side.

"Isn't this a lovely surprise," she said as I lowered the window. "Natalie Thatcher. So nice to see you."

Louise Haven was something of an institution in Tilikum, the quirky small town in the Cascade mountains where I lived. She had to be pushing eighty but had the energy of a puppy. Around town, she was known for three things: bringing food to neighbors—sometimes when they needed it and other times as an excuse to be nosy—her constant attempts to play matchmaker for her nephews, and her velour tracksuits.

Today, her tracksuit was forest green—appropriate for the holiday season—and she wore a necklace of blinking, multicolored Christmas lights.

"Hi, Louise. It's nice to see you, too. I like your necklace."

"Thank you, dear. Isn't this fun? I love being festive. Listen, do you have a minute? Because I was thinking..." She dug through her large handbag.

"Actually, I should get home and put away my groceries." As nice as she was, I didn't want her getting any ideas about involving me in her matchmaking schemes. I jerked my thumb behind me. "I have frozens."

She drew a small notebook from her handbag and flipped through the pages. "Here it is. I'm running out of single nephews, but the town has plenty of eligible bachelors. My friend Marie's grandson is an absolute catch. Works in finance. He doesn't live here full-time, but I think you two would really hit it off."

"Handsome businessman type?" I asked, not bothering to disguise the skepticism in my voice. "Plenty of money, always wears a suit?"

She smiled. "Oh yes, describes him perfectly."

"Hard pass, Louise. The last thing I need is a suit."

"Hmm." She went back to turning the pages of her notebook. "That's fine, dear. There's a firefighter who is inexplicably single, and—"

"Thanks anyway." I interrupted. "But I'm not dating right now."

"No? That's a shame. I'll keep thinking about it." She decisively shut her notebook. "How's your sister?"

"She's fine. Busy."

"Of course she is. The life of a single mother is full."

"Very full."

"Is she seeing anyone these days?"

My mind raced with excuses to keep my sister, Nina, off Louise's matchmaking radar. Maybe keeping it vague and pleading ignorance would be enough. "You know, there might be someone, but I'm not sure. We work opposite schedules, so I don't always know what she's up to."

"Because now that I think about it, Marie's grandson..." She tapped her lips.

"The suit? I don't think Nina needs a guy who's only in town part-time."

"That's fair. Well, the solution is bound to present itself, probably when we least expect it. Have a nice day, dear."

The solution is for me and my sister to both stay single, thank you very much Ms. Small-Town Matchmaker.

"You too, Louise." I smiled, keeping my thoughts to myself, and raised the window while she headed for the entrance to the store.

With no more meddling townspeople in sight, I left. A few snowflakes drifted from the low-hanging clouds. They wouldn't add much to the layer of white that already covered the town, but I hoped the flurries weren't the start of a bigger storm. I was used to getting around in the snow—mountain life—but the last thing I needed was one more complication. At least until after the holidays.

My phone rang, and the Bluetooth in my car picked it up. It was Rosa, one of my coworkers at the hospital.

"Hey," I answered. "What's up?"

Her voice was urgent. "Did you see the email?"

"No, I'm running errands. What's going on?"

"We're on strike."

My mouth hung open, and I hesitated for a second, not sure what to say.

"Natalie? You there?"

"Yeah, sorry. I didn't think it was actually going to happen."

"I know. Neither did I," she said. "Hopefully, they'll get everything worked out sooner rather than later."

"Fingers crossed."

"I wasn't sure if you were on the schedule for tonight and wanted to make sure you knew."

"Thanks. I appreciate the heads-up."

"No problem. I'll talk to you later."

"Bye, Rosa."

She ended the call, and I let out a heavy sigh as I drove. A nurses' strike. It was probably for the best. Things were tough in our field. Burnout was a huge problem, and there was a lot at stake in those negotiations. But man, the timing could not have been worse.

I didn't want to be selfish about it, but I had a family to think about. Not in the traditional sense, of course. But Nina, Annabel, and I were a family—a household. We shared a home, costs, responsibilities. And we did the best we could.

But lately, even being a two-income household was hard. We lived in our childhood home our mom left to us when she passed. Which was great, except it seemed like everything in the sixty-year-old house had needed repair, maintenance, or full-on replacement in the last year alone. Inflation was hitting hard, as were the mountain of home repairs. Not to mention, Nina's car died over the summer, mine had seen better days, and Annabel seemed to outgrow shoes every week.

A strike was not going to help, especially right before the holidays.

"Annabel, I hope you didn't put anything expensive on

your Christmas list," I muttered to myself. "Santa's on a tight budget this year. Again."

I drove home, pondering solutions. We'd been trying to save enough money to replace the furnace. It still worked, but if it went out in the dead of winter, that would not be good. Putting off that project would at least buy us some time. We had a wood stove. If worst came to worst, we wouldn't freeze. We'd probably have to move mattresses into the living room since the bedrooms would be cold, but Annabel would love an extended slumber party.

The bright side? If the strike went on long enough, I'd have Christmas off. And I hadn't been home for Christmas in years.

Everything would be fine. We totally had this.

I turned onto our street and blinked in confusion. Why was a van in our driveway? And why was Nina home?

Not just a van, but a water damage restoration service van. *Oh no.*

I parked, grabbed the groceries, and ran inside. "Nina?"

Her voice carried from the basement. "Coming!"

I took the bags to the kitchen and set them on the counter. Nina emerged from the stairway off the kitchen that led to the finished basement. She and I looked a lot alike even though she was ten years younger than me. Similar face shape, brown eyes, olive skin, and dark hair, although she kept hers shorter than mine.

"What's going on?" I asked. "Is someone here? And why are you home? I thought you had to work today." She was an aesthetician at a local spa.

"I was at work until Mr. Gardner called and said we had water shooting out of our hose bib on the side of the house."

"That's not good."

"Nope. And when I came home to check, I found that

water was not only shooting out of the hose bib outside, it was leaking into the basement."

I stared at her for a long moment. No words. I had no words.

"Obviously, I freaked out. Mr. Gardner saw me losing it in the backyard and came outside. He called the water restoration guys for me. They got the water to the house turned off, and they're down there now setting up a bunch of big fans and dehumidifiers to dry everything out."

I could imagine Nina freaking out on seeing the leak. My sister was many things, but calm in a crisis was not one of them.

"Thank you to Mr. Gardner, I guess," I said.

"He is a nice neighbor."

"But this also means we don't have water."

"Um, yeah, about that. The restoration guys said we need a plumber to fix whatever broke before we can turn it back on."

I let out a long breath. Water damage. A plumber. None of it was good news.

"Okay." I nodded a few times. "This is fine. We can figure it out."

Nina nodded along, her eyes wide and hopeful, looking to me for reassurance.

"Have you called a plumber yet?" I asked, and she shook her head. "Let's call Jason. He'll do a good job and won't over-charge us." One of the benefits of small-town life—being able to call someone you knew from high school when you encountered problems in the grown-up world.

"Good idea." Her shoulders dropped with relief.

Moving on autopilot, I started putting the groceries away. "Do you need to go back to work?"

"Yeah. I got someone to cover one client, but I have more appointments this afternoon."

"That's fine. I'll take over from here."

"You don't work tonight, do you?"

"I don't work at all for the foreseeable future. As of today, we're on strike."

"What?" Her face went ashen, and when she spoke again, the pitch of her voice rose with every word. "You're on strike? That means you can't work, doesn't it? Which means you don't get paid. And we have water damage and need a plumber, and oh my god, Natalie, it's almost Christmas. What are we going to do?"

"Don't panic."

Her voice came out in a squeak. "But the water and the plumber and the bills and—"

"Nina." I grabbed her by the shoulders and held her steady. "It's going to be okay. We'll figure it out."

"How?"

I let go. "We have the money set aside for the furnace. We can live on that for a little while."

"The furnace sounds like something out of a horror movie every time it turns on."

"We'll make it work. Even if we have to chop wood all winter and use the wood stove."

She ran her hands up and down her face. "How are you so calm? We're probably going to freeze."

I rolled my eyes. "We won't freeze."

"I know, but this sucks."

"What about the apartment?" I asked. Our house included a separate apartment above the detached garage we often listed as an Airbnb. When it was full, it brought in some extra income. "I've been thinking we might want to go back to renting it to long-term tenants instead of trying to capture the visitor market."

"I thought we made more money on the short-term rentals."

"We do, but it's also more work. And we haven't had a booking for what, a month? And nothing over the holidays?" My brow furrowed, and my lips turned down in a confused frown. "Wait a minute. We always have bookings over the holidays. The listing is active, right?"

"I think so?" She didn't sound very confident.

I got out my phone and navigated to the Airbnb dashboard.

Inactive.

"Well, that explains it."

"What happened? Is it not listed?"

"Nope. One of us must have deactivated the listing."

Biting her lip, she winced. "That could have been me. I probably messed it up the last time I made a change. I'm so sorry."

"It's okay, accidents happen. I'll turn it back on. Hopefully, we'll get someone in there, at least for a weekend."

"Fingers crossed." She grabbed her purse off the counter. "I have to get back to work. Are you still good to pick up Annabel?"

"Yep, I've got her."

"Thanks. And thanks for being the rational one. If I didn't have you, I'd be sobbing on the floor."

"Hey, you did a great job. Totally handled it."

"More like Mr. Gardner took pity on me and handled it."

"Still. We're in this together. We've got this."

She smiled and stepped in for a hug. I squeezed her tight. We were always in it together. Had been since we were kids.

"Okay, I gotta go," she said. "If you're on strike, the last thing we need is for me to get fired."

"Let's not pile more problems on this heap. Even my positivity has limits."

A few minutes after she left, the water restoration guys came upstairs. Explaining what they'd done to mitigate the damage, they told me the fans and dehumidifiers would need to run for at least a week to fully dry things out and make sure we didn't wind up with mold. The good news was, it could have been worse. And they promised to work with our homeowner's insurance to cover at least some of the cost.

The bad news was, I still needed a plumber before I could even flush a toilet. And I was all too aware of the fact that we'd opted for a very high deductible on said homeowner's insurance to save money on the premiums.

"It's fine," I said aloud. "This is fine. There's always a way."

With about half an hour before I needed to leave to pick up Annabel from school, I called Jason the plumber. He could come by that afternoon, and that bit of good news lifted my spirits a little.

Fortunately, I caught a glimpse of myself in a mirror before I left the house again, and my reflection reminded me to swipe beneath my eyes with a makeup wipe. I still looked tired, but that was basically who I was as a person. And it wasn't like I cared about impressing the people in the school pickup line at Tilikum Elementary.

When I got to the school, Annabel came running to my car, her pink-and-purple backpack bouncing up and down on her back, and she was carrying her coat instead of wearing it. Typical Annabel. She was basically allergic to coats and impervious to cold.

See, Natalie? If the furnace goes out, we'll be fine. The kid won't even notice.

"Hey, Anna-banana," I said as she climbed into the back. "How was your day?"

"Good." She untangled her arms from her backpack straps and set it on the floor at her feet. "I made something."

"Oh yeah? What did you make?"

With a triumphant smile, she produced a red and green

23

paper chain from her backpack and held it up. "It's a Christmas countdown. We take a loop off the chain every day until Christmas."

"How fun is that? I love it."

"I ripped it a little bit, but my teacher helped me fix it."

"It looks like it's in great shape." I pulled out of the pickup line and turned onto the street. "Where should we hang it?"

"In the kitchen."

"Good idea."

"Auntie Natalie, when are we getting a tree?"

"That's a great question." The cost dinged in my mind like an old-school cash register. "Maybe this weekend. We'll ask your mom when she gets home."

She fingered the paper chain in her lap. "Okay. Can I help decorate?"

"Of course."

"But you get the top. I'm too small."

"Deal. I'll hang the ones you can't reach."

"Mommy, too."

I nodded. "Yep. Mommy too."

"Auntie Natalie?"

"Yeah?"

"Will you be home for Christmas?"

"Well... that depends on work."

Her shoulders slumped. "Oh."

I glanced at her and my heart nearly broke. Her lower lip protruded, and she fidgeted with her paper chain. She'd never asked about me being home for Christmas before. Until the last year or so, she'd probably been too young to really notice.

"Are you sad about that?" I asked.

She nodded.

"Why?"

She took a deep breath. "Because Mommy makes pancakes, and we have sprinkles on them."

"That sounds yummy. And I'm sure Mommy will still make you special Christmas pancakes, even if I have to work."

"But Mommy said you might be home this year. And we have to open presents, and eat breakfast, and watch a movie."

I knew this wasn't about the pancakes, or the presents, or any of the little things she associated with Christmas. It was about being together on a holiday. She was old enough for those traditions to mean something to her, and knowing she was sad that I might not be there made my chest ache.

I had a feeling the strike would still be on, so it wouldn't matter anyway, but I had enough seniority to probably get the holiday off.

"Tell you what, kiddo. I'll be home for Christmas this year. No matter what."

Lifting her face, she gasped and gave me a big smile. "Really?"

"Really."

"Promise?"

Twisting in my seat, I reached back with my pinky sticking out. "I don't just promise. I pinky promise."

Her mouth opened in awe. We Thatchers took our pinky promises seriously. She offered me her pinky, and I wound mine around it.

"Annabel, I pinky promise that I will be home for Christmas."

"And we can have pancakes?"

I laughed, still holding her pinky. "You're being very specific. But yes, I'll be home for Christmas, and we can have pancakes."

She nodded, and we shook pinkies on it.

That was a promise I absolutely could not break.

CHAPTER 3
Jensen

L ight flurries of snow blew around my car as I navigated the winding highway through the mountains. The drive had been pleasant enough. Good weather, even over the pass, and the landscape had a certain rugged charm. Snowy slopes rose on either side of the road, with a few determined pine trees clinging to the rocks. Views of a river came in and out of sight as I drove, the banks crusted with ice.

It wasn't my first visit to the area. I'd never been to Tilikum, but my sister, Nora—half sister, if we were being precise—had gotten married at a winery not far from my assignment. I remembered the wine being excellent. I'd have to make time to swing through and pick up a case or two before heading home.

The entrance to the town was heralded by a *Welcome to Tilikum* sign, and the fact that it was the Christmas season was impossible to miss. Large red bows adorned the corners of the sign, and a very large wooden squirrel wearing a Santa hat and holding a present in its forepaws stood behind it.

That was... unique.

Large lit candy canes flanked the main road, wreaths adorned nearly every door, and the storefronts were awash in lights and greenery. I slowed as I drove by a park in the center of town. A parked fire engine on the grass had its ladder extended so someone could hang lights at the top of a massive tree.

I didn't mind the holidays, necessarily. I had nothing against Christmas or all the festivities that went along with it. I'd say I was more or less apathetic to it. Having spent holiday seasons working in places where they'd never heard of Christmas, I'd hardly missed it. So, while I wasn't about to bah humbug Tilikum's Christmas cheer, it did seem like a lot of trouble over nothing.

In any case, I wasn't in town for a holiday. I had a job to do.

"Where are you, sneaky thief?" I muttered as I glanced around the quaint streets.

Following the directions Maple had given me, I turned onto what could best be described as your quintessential small-town Main Street. A sign that read Angel Cakes Bakery caught my attention. That probably deserved a visit. Farther up the road, a large statue of a well-endowed pinup girl stood in front of a barbershop. She was clearly designed to look provocative, but for some reason, she had a white Santa Claus beard on her face.

That wasn't something one saw every day.

Not quite sure what to make of the town, I kept driving. Maple's directions led me into a residential neighborhood. I pulled up at the address, although it must have been a mistake. I was in front of a house, not a hotel.

But Maple never made mistakes.

She'd clear things up. I brought up her number and called.

"Is there a problem?" she answered.

"This address can't be right."

"Why?"

"I'm in a neighborhood, and this is someone's house."

"That's right."

"Excuse me?"

"Look for the garage. There's a flat above. It was the only thing I could find on short notice."

"Doesn't this town have any hotels?"

"They do, actually. A beautiful one called the Grand Peak."

"Then why am I not staying there?"

"Half of it is closed for renovations, and the other half is booked."

"So I'm to stay in someone's flat?"

"There's an outside entrance, and you have the entire place to yourself. The owners live in the main house, but you'll have all the privacy you need."

"Hmm. Privacy, but no room service."

She laughed. "I'm sure you'll survive. You've lived in more primitive conditions than someone's spare flat."

"True." I let out a breath. "And I suppose I won't be here long. I'll make do."

"There's a good boy."

"Good boy? You know I'm nothing of the sort. Too bad you can't travel with me."

"You know how Mr. Exton would feel about that, Jensen."

"It's such a pity you're married."

"Hardly a pity. Now go get settled. You have a thief to catch."

"Indeed, I do. Good night, Maple."

She ended the call. With an eight-hour time difference, I wondered if she was in bed, rolling over into Mr. Exton's arms. Marriage. It was a bit like Christmas. I didn't understand people's fascination with it.

I left my car parked on the street and turned off the engine. Snow covered the yard, but unlike the shops in town, my host hadn't put up any Christmas decorations. Not outside, at least.

I eyed the place with skepticism. The house itself looked a bit sad—worn and outdated. The garage had probably been added later. It looked newer and didn't quite match.

Maple sent me the code to unlock the door, so I went up the staircase on the side of the garage that led to the second floor. Inside, I shut the door behind me and took stock of my lodgings.

It was surprisingly nice, considering the outside of the building hadn't been anything to write home about. I'd been half expecting something old and musty, but the flat was bright and well decorated. Homey in a way a hotel couldn't be.

Even without room service, I could make do.

I took a quick tour. Two bedrooms, one with an attached bath. A small kitchen. Laundry in a closet. The living room had a TV and a shelf with games and books. It was clean. Perfectly acceptable.

My bags were still in my car, so I went down to retrieve them. I opened the passenger door when an accusatory voice behind me caught my attention.

"Who are you?"

I turned to find a small child wearing a purple shirt and chunky snow boots. Her nose and cheeks were pink from the cold, and she looked up at me with big brown eyes.

"Jensen Lakes. Who are you?"

"Annabel Thatcher."

I'd never been quite sure what to make of children. They puzzled me. Obviously, I'd been one, but I had few memories of that. I'd only recently discovered I could develop affection for a small child after my sister had one of her own. My niece,

Raina, was the cutest, most lovable baby who ever existed. But all other children seemed like loud, undersized humans who mostly got in the way.

"Pleasure to meet you, Miss Annabel."

"You talk funny."

"Do I?"

"That's okay. I do, too, sometimes. I lost a tooth." She opened her mouth wide and pointed at a gap.

"I see that. Do you expect a new one will grow in?"

She giggled. "Yeah, a grown-up tooth."

"That's good."

"Are you a bad guy?"

"I suppose that depends on who you ask."

"You kind of look like a bad guy."

"Hmm." I rubbed my chin. "Well, I don't plan on doing anything bad while I'm here. Does that help?"

"Yeah. And I probably shouldn't talk to you because you're stranger danger. But Mommy said we have a guest in the apartment, so does that count?"

"You're asking if I'm stranger danger?"

She nodded.

It was one of the oddest conversations I'd ever had. But the little girl was so straightforward. I liked her honesty.

"We just met, so I'm a stranger in that sense," I said. "But I'm not a danger to you."

"Good. Do you want to have a snowball fight?"

I opened my mouth to tell her perhaps another time when the side door to the house opened, and a young woman poked her head out.

"Annabel, don't bother him."

"I'm not bothering him, Mommy. I'm talking."

"Sorry." She stepped out onto the porch and hugged her arms around herself against the cold. "I promise she won't bug you. She knows she's not allowed over there. She just plays out here in the yard sometimes."

The corner of my mouth lifted. "Don't worry, love. She's not a bother."

The woman bit her lip and giggled softly. She was pretty—beautiful, even—with thick, dark hair and expressive brown eyes.

"Um... okay... good." Looking me up and down, she bit her lip again. "Do you need anything?"

"I don't think so, no."

"Are you sure?" She fiddled with a lock of her hair. "Because if you do, I can bring it right up. It's no problem."

"Much appreciated." I winked at her and glanced at Annabel. She was looking back and forth between me and her mother, her expression either disgusted or confused. I couldn't quite tell. "Miss Annabel, it's been lovely. I'm sure I'll see you again before my stay is over."

"Bye. I'll see you later, and we can have a snowball fight then."

Annabel's mother licked her lips as she watched me get my bags from the car. I grinned at her again and gave her a nod. She opened her mouth as if she were about to say something else, but Annabel interrupted her.

"Mommy, why are you acting so weird?"

I pretended not to hear as her flustered mum tried to explain that she was acting normal, and Annabel needed to come inside.

I was well aware of the effect I had on women. I'd meticulously cultivated my playboy persona for years. He wasn't the only part I knew how to play, but that personality was so deeply ingrained, sometimes even I thought he was real. Seduction had been a device in my toolbox for so long, wielding it was pure instinct.

Of course, it was more than a cultivated habit. I enjoyed

giving women attention. Loved watching them light up, glowing with the pleasure of male admiration. Whether or not it led anywhere was irrelevant. It was the chase I craved, whether the prey was a beautiful woman or a thief who thought he could get away with stealing a priceless heirloom.

Life was a game, and one I enjoyed playing.

CHAPTER 4
Natalie

My body was still a little confused about my sudden return to the land of the living—a.k.a. not working nights. I woke up Saturday morning feeling a bit like I'd napped too long in the middle of the day. The good news was, a cup of coffee and a hot shower could apparently work miracles, and I no longer looked like a sleep-deprived panda.

After getting dressed and throwing a load of towels into the washing machine, I went in search of breakfast. The low hum from the fans in the basement had become our constant companion. It was mildly annoying, but at least we had water. Jason the plumber had fixed the problem, and Annabel's cheerful suggestion that we all pee outside had not become necessary.

The green and red paper chain hung from a magnetic hook on the refrigerator. I had a feeling Annabel was not going to need any reminders to remove a link each day. She also had an Advent calendar that was the highlight of her morning, and this year's didn't even have candy in it.

I grabbed some eggs out of the fridge and glanced into the

living room. Annabel was curled up next to Nina on the couch while they read a book together. It made me smile. I helped out with my niece as much as I could, and we had a special bond, but I was happy to play second fiddle to my sister.

Nina had gotten pregnant with Annabel when she was only seventeen, and her boyfriend had bailed as soon as he found out. Spending her senior year growing a baby hadn't exactly been the plan. But she and I had already learned the hard lesson that life is full of uncertainty.

We'd always been close, and the hardships we'd faced had only brought us closer. And even though Nina was young, she was a great mom.

After scrambling my eggs, I took them to the living room and sat in the armchair next to the couch. We'd scored a great deal on new-to-us furniture a few years before, finally replacing the worn-out couch we'd jumped on as kids. A few family photos hung on the wall and a wood stove sat in the corner.

"Wow, look at you," Nina said.

"Look at me, what?"

"Awake and looking all bright and chipper. Are you wearing concealer?"

I scowled at her. "No. But thanks for reminding me that I usually look like garbage."

"I didn't mean it like that. It's actually unfair how pretty you are even when you keep vampire hours."

"What's a vampire?" Annabel asked.

"They're pretend monsters who only come out at night and drink people's blood," Nina said, making her voice sound spooky.

"Ew." Annabel wrinkled her nose. "I don't like blood."

"Tell me about it, kiddo," I said. "Once, at work, a patient came in with a gash on his forehead. It was only about two inches long, but the amount of blood coming out of his head was incredible. It—"

I stopped. Nina winced with horror, and Annabel's eyes were wide. Both looked a little pale.

"Sorry." I took a bite of my eggs. "He was fine. Just needed stitches."

"Anyway," Nina said. "How about another story?"

Annabel shut the book and hopped off the couch to take it to the shelf.

"Any plans today?" I asked.

"I have a bunch of errands to run."

"Can I come?" Annabel asked, bringing another book to the couch.

"Of course," Nina said. "What about you, Auntie Natalie? Any plans?"

"I don't know. Probably more laundry. And I should clean up some of the mess in the basement."

"It's a thrilling life we lead."

I smiled despite feeling a hint of sadness. I had a good life. I didn't want to complain. But the way she'd said *thrilling* reminded me that mine was anything but.

I finished my breakfast while Nina read Annabel another book. Then I cleaned up the dishes and went upstairs to check the towels. Still damp. I had a load of clothes to do, and the towels were going to take forever. Our dryer wasn't exactly top-of-the-line. But we had a second washer and dryer in the apartment. If I washed my clothes over there, I'd get through everything faster.

Stepping outside with my laundry hamper, the shock of cold air made me shiver, and I hurried up the stairs on the side of the garage. I should have put on a sweater over my T-shirt. Balancing the hamper on my hip, I punched in the code to unlock the door and rushed inside.

My heart almost beat right out of my chest, and I

screamed, dropping the hamper, as a man walked out of the bedroom.

Not just a man. An almost naked man.

Nothing but a white bath towel slung low around his hips. And when he startled in surprise, the towel loosened and fell to the floor.

"Oh my god." I clapped a hand over my eyes and turned away. But not before I'd gotten a glimpse.

Okay. Wow. That was a thing that existed in the world.

Anyway.

"I am so sorry." I kept my hand over my eyes. "I didn't know anyone was over here."

"That's all right, love." His deep voice, smooth as dark chocolate, wrapped around his British accent. "No harm done."

I stood still, like I was frozen to the floor, and kept my eyes squeezed shut.

"It's safe to look," he said.

Peeking through my fingers, I checked. He'd re-wrapped the towel around his waist and held it in one hand. His thick, dark hair was damp, and his crooked smile called attention to his stubbly chiseled jaw. The cut of his musculature was as shocking as his presence. They really made men who looked like that? They weren't just photoshopped fantasies?

The light dusting of chest hair and dark happy trail did add some realism to his physique.

Not that I was looking.

Slowly, I lowered my hand. "Well, this is mortifying."

His gaze swept up and down, the corner of his mouth lifting in an amused smile. He adjusted his grip on the towel, and my eyes were drawn inexorably downward before I could regain control of myself and look up.

"Sorry," I repeated quickly. "I didn't know you were here.

I'm guessing my sister dealt with your reservation and apparently forgot to tell me."

"I'm a bit of a last-minute guest. And where are my manners?" He walked toward me and held out his hand. "Jensen Lakes."

I reached out and slid my hand into his. "Natalie Thatcher."

Instead of shaking my hand, he lifted it to his lips and kissed the backs of my knuckles. If any other man had kissed my hand upon our first meeting, I probably would have smacked him. But something about this guy made it seem like the most natural thing he could do.

The brush of his lips across my fingers sent a tingle down my spine, and he paused, looking at me with the most intense dark eyes I'd ever seen.

"Nice to meet you," I said. He didn't offer any resistance when I pulled my hand away, but I caught the flash of surprise that crossed his features. "I should get out of your way."

Tilting his head slightly, he gazed at me with an almost puzzled expression. "It's nice to meet you, too. Very nice."

Why did he sound like that surprised him? Had he expected to run into the owners of the property and find them abhorrent?

"Okay, well, this has been... an experience. I'll just—" I was about to turn and escape out the door when I noticed my laundry scattered all over the floor. He'd stepped over one of my bras to take my hand, and his foot was right next to my hot-pink boyshort underwear.

Pressing my lips together and hoping my face wasn't flushed red, I crouched down to scoop my clothes back into the basket. Everything would have been fine, but he did the same. We both reached for my underwear and wound up lifting it together, our hands touching.

They were dirty. A mysterious and very handsome British man was holding my dirty underwear.

I pulled them out of his grip, and they snapped against my fist. He didn't say a word. Just licked his lips and pushed some of my laundry closer to the basket.

"Thanks," I muttered, wondering how I hadn't already died of awkwardness.

It wasn't that he was gorgeous—although he was—that had me wishing I could snap my fingers and disappear. He was a guest in my Airbnb, and I'd walked in on him unannounced, dumped my dirty laundry on the floor, and surprised him so much he'd dropped his towel.

Unprofessional didn't even begin to cover it.

I finally got my clothes under control and stood, balancing the hamper on my hip. He straightened, still holding the towel around his waist. I opened my mouth to apologize for being the worst host in the history of ever, but he spoke first.

"Would you have dinner with me tonight?"

"I... what?"

"Dinner. A meal, usually takes place in the evening. Pleasant when shared with good company."

I looked at him like he'd just suggested I jump out of an airplane. "Are you asking me out?"

His mouth twitched in that subtle grin again. "Is that so shocking?"

"I just..." I sputtered, not sure what to say. "No. No, I can't."

His eyebrows lifted. "No?"

Something about his apparent astonishment at being turned down snapped me out of my awkward daze. "That's right. I said no. Is that so shocking?"

"It is a little bit, actually."

I laughed softly. "Sorry, not sorry. I'm not available."

"Of course not." He shook his head. "I could hardly expect a woman like you to be single."

"Oh, I'm single. Very single. And staying that way. I don't need a boyfriend to be unavailable."

His dark brow furrowed. I didn't understand why he seemed so puzzled. I was being very straightforward.

"Anyway, sorry again for walking in," I said. "It won't happen again. Enjoy your stay."

"Goodbye, Natalie." The hint of awe in his voice—was that awe?—sent another shiver down my spine.

I hurried out before I could make things worse.

"Oh my gosh, oh my gosh, oh my gosh," I said in time with my steps as I descended the stairs.

I flew in through the side door and shut it behind me with a relieved exhale. Nina was in the kitchen. Because of course she was.

She shot me a confused glance. "What were you doing outside?"

"I was going to do a load of laundry in the apartment."

Her eyes widened. "Oh no. Did I forget to tell you it's booked, and we have a guest?"

"Yes. Yes, you did."

"I could have sworn I mentioned it. Or texted you. Didn't I?"

"No. And I walked in on him right when he came out of the shower."

She put a hand over her mouth to stifle a laugh. "Oh no."

"Oh yes."

"Well, I mean..." Grinning, she raised her eyebrows. "Did you get a good look?"

I set the laundry basket down. "I don't want to talk about it."

"You did, didn't you?"

"He's a guest, Nina. We're not having this conversation."

"Yeah, but I saw him fully clothed and—"

"Mommy?" Annabel came in. "Is it time to put shoes on?"

Nina pressed her lips together and gave me a knowing smile before replying. "Did you go potty?"

"No."

"Okay, go potty first, and then we'll get shoes on."

"I don't have to go."

"Are you sure? Remember how sometimes you think you don't need to go, but when you try, you really do?"

"Actually, I have to go big potty." Annabel spun around and scurried toward the bathroom.

"Why are six-year-olds so opposed to going potty?" Nina asked. "If you have to go, just go."

"It's a good thing you asked."

"Believe me, it's a required question before we leave the house these days. So about our guest over there." She waggled her eyebrows at me.

"Fine." I rolled my eyes. "He's attractive. But that's not the point. Can we focus on the fact that I just humiliated myself?"

"I'm sorry. That does suck."

"Thank you."

"How did he react? Was he mad?"

"No," I said, confusion plain in my voice. "Actually, he asked me out."

"What?" Nina shrieked. "He asked you out? When, tonight?"

"I guess, but I said no."

If she'd looked surprised before, she looked positively shocked now. "You said *no*? To *him*?" She stuck her arm out to point at the apartment.

"Of course I said no. I'm not going out with the random guy who rented our Airbnb for a few days."

"Sure, I can totally see why you'd say no to the insanely hot guy with the sexy accent. Makes perfect sense."

"Why would I go out with him? A man who looks like that, and is only in town for a short visit, is only after one thing."

"I know," she said vehemently. "And you could be the one to give it to him."

"I'm not having a fling with a guest."

"Why not? You deserve a fling with a hot British man."

"No."

She groaned. "Fine, but you're no fun. And I think you're missing out."

Annabel bounded into the room. "Ready, Mommy!"

"Let's get coats," Nina said.

"I don't need a coat."

"Wear it or carry it. Your choice."

"Carry it," Annabel answered decisively.

"Have fun, ladies," I said. "I'll see you later."

"Bye, Auntie Natalie."

I waved goodbye and watched them go, then picked up my laundry basket. A fling with the hot guy staying in our Airbnb? No, thank you. I didn't care what Nina said. I wasn't missing out on anything.

Jensen Lakes was exactly the sort of complication I did not need.

CHAPTER 5
Jensen

Natalie.

Mesmerized, I stood for a long moment, gazing at the door she'd just gone through. Something about her had left me in a daze, half hypnotized.

Never in my life had I experienced such a deep, visceral reaction to a woman. It was as if she'd glowed with an ethereal light. Her scent had been intoxicating, her magnetism irresistible.

It wasn't just that I found her attractive. I did—she was beautiful—but that didn't explain what she'd done to me. Her exit had sucked the air from the room, and I had the strangest desire to follow her, just to bask in her presence.

Of course, I was wearing nothing but a towel, and it was freezing outside. Not exactly the time to give chase.

"Natalie." I said her name aloud, savoring the taste of it. I went to the window and looked toward the house, but she'd already gone inside. "We'll meet again, darling."

The fact that she'd turned me down was a conundrum. No was not a word I was accustomed to hearing when it came to dinner invitations.

I went to the bedroom to get dressed. I wasn't annoyed or even terribly disappointed. My mouth twitched in a smile as I buttoned my shirt. She hadn't melted into a puddle the moment I'd kissed her hand, and I found that intriguing. I liked it. And her voice had betrayed a hint of stubbornness. I liked that, too.

Natalie Thatcher was a puzzle. A beautiful puzzle. I was going to enjoy finding out how her pieces fit.

But first things first. I was there to catch a thief, not ruminate on the woman next door.

After dressing—dark blue suit, no tie—I left and headed back into town in search of breakfast and to take another look around.

Dangling snowflake lights crisscrossed the main street, and the large tree in the city park sparkled with Christmas lights, even in the daylight. I circled through the small downtown area, looking for a place to eat. The Copper Kettle Diner caught my eye, and I parked out front.

The wind cut through my wool overcoat, and my Italian leather shoes weren't exactly ideal in the snow. But inside the diner was warm, and it smelled like buttery toast and coffee.

A young woman with a blond ponytail—Heidi, according to her name tag—came to the front. She opened her mouth, presumably to ask me if I'd like to be seated, but all she could get out was a flustered giggle.

"Um, hi." She giggled again. "Would you like to... I mean, do you want..."

The corners of my mouth lifted. "Breakfast."

"Right, yes. Of course." She fanned herself. "Sorry. Is it hot in here?"

I didn't reply. Just waited for her to continue.

"Do you want to sit at the breakfast bar?" she said, finally. "Or would you like a booth?"

"Booth."

"Okay. I can do that." She grabbed a large, laminated menu. "Right this way."

I followed her to a booth and took off my overcoat, laying it on the seat next to me. I sat facing out, where I had a good view of the rest of the dining room. Blushing furiously, Heidi handed me the menu. She spun to go back to the front and almost crashed into a server heading for my table with a carafe of coffee.

I didn't comment. Just watched with an amused half grin.

"Coffee?" the server asked. She had short gray hair and smile lines around her eyes.

"Absolutely, love." I pushed the white coffee mug closer to the edge of the table. "Thank you."

She gave me an I-know-your-type grin and poured. "Do you need a minute to look over the menu?"

"What do you recommend?"

"Our holly jolly snowflake eggnog scones are popular at Christmas. They're filled with red currant jelly and dusted with powdered sugar."

"I'm sure they're delightful, but they sound rather sweet."

"My favorite is the eggs Benedict."

"I'll take that."

"Sounds good. I'll get that going for you."

"Thank you, love."

She shook her head slightly as she took the menu and left, heading for the kitchen.

I sipped my coffee and glanced toward the front. The hostess watched me while whispering excitedly to one of her coworkers. Customers glanced in my direction as well. One woman at the breakfast bar stared at me with her mouth open.

And there I was, not even trying to cause a stir.

I knew how to get attention when I wanted it. Eye contact, a subtle smile, a well-placed wink. And body language could speak volumes. But in this case, it didn't serve my purposes to be noticed. I didn't have any reason to believe the thief would know who I was, but I didn't want to tip him off that I was on his trail, either.

Ignoring the curious glances and whispering townspeople, I focused on the job.

Maple had sent over the dossier compiled by my associates. Local law enforcement had told the client there wasn't much they could do, but they'd keep the case file open. That was where we came in. Using our resources, my associates had traced the thief to a commercial flight into the States. He'd then boarded a plane that had landed at the small, private airport in Tilikum.

Suspect was believed to be a Caucasian male, mid-thirties. He'd almost certainly traveled under an assumed identity. That meant he wasn't a total amateur. But he didn't appear to be someone we knew. He was either a new player and this was his first big score, or he was someone who'd evaded our notice until now.

The latter was possible, although the former more likely.

My question, as I reviewed the evidence they'd gathered, was one of motivation. In my experience, two types of thieves stole the sort of high-value items I was hired to find—wealthy private collectors who wanted rare items for their collection and typically paid someone to get them, or those hoping for a big payday by selling the contraband on the black market.

I gazed at the fuzzy security cam image of the thief. Which type was he? Had someone hired him? Or was he hoping to offload the necklace and take home a suitcase full of cash?

The server brought my breakfast, and I thanked her. My disregard for the curious stares of the other patrons seemed to be working. I didn't encourage their attention, so most of them went back to their meals.

Breakfast was surprisingly good, and I pondered my first move while I ate. If the thief had been hired and brought the necklace to Tilikum, the person behind the theft might have been local. My first order of business was to find out if there were any wealthy collectors in the area.

As a place to start, I'd pop in to the local antique stores. Antique dealers were usually aware of locals with an interest in the rare and valuable.

Not far from the diner was an antique store, so I decided to go there first. With that settled, I finished my meal and paid the bill. When I left, I turned down my swagger, using my body language to deflect, rather than attract, attention. It didn't work as well as it should have, and several sets of eyes still followed as I walked out the door.

The sun had come out, but it was still bitterly cold. After slipping on a pair of sunglasses against the glare as I got in my car, I brought up directions to the antique store. The Treasure Chest. Hoping it wasn't a pirate-themed junk store, I drove over and parked in front.

There were no black flags, skulls and crossbones, or nautical items outside. In fact, the building was in good repair, and the window displays were uncluttered and tasteful. Seemed like a good sign.

A bell above the door jingled when I went in. The air smelled stale—a combination of dust with a hint of decay— and the lack of clutter in the windows gave a false impression. The interior was packed. Furniture, faded paintings, vases, and statues were everywhere. Shelves were filled with dishes, candlesticks, teacups, and various trinkets.

And why on earth were there so many squirrels?

Taking slow steps, I wandered through the cramped aisles, my bewilderment growing. There were wooden squirrels, ceramic squirrels, glass squirrels, painted squirrels, realistic squirrels, and cartoonish squirrels with unnervingly large eyes. One case held a collection of squirrels encrusted with crystals, holding colored gems in their forepaws.

An elderly woman with white hair and cat-eye glasses came out to greet me. She was wearing a Christmas sweater with a squirrel dressed in a red-and-white Santa costume. "Can I help you?"

Time for a little charm. Meeting her eyes, I lifted the corners of my mouth. "Hello, there."

The effect was immediate. She smiled and batted her eyelashes. "Well, aren't you a handsome one? Can I help you find something?"

"Perhaps." I glanced around. "This is quite the collection of squirrels."

"Oh yes. They're an important part of Tilikum culture."

I raised my eyebrows. "Are they?"

"Of course." Her voice was cheerful as if she enjoyed this topic. "You must be a visitor?"

"Yes."

She turned and started down the aisle. Apparently, I was meant to follow because she kept talking. So I did.

"We're known for our large squirrel population," she said, talking over her shoulder as she walked. "And ours are particularly smart and well-organized. Naturally, that gives rise to a demand for squirrel decor."

"Naturally."

She stopped and gestured to a wood carving on the wall depicting a squirrel with a large, bushy tail. "That was carved back in the late eighteen hundreds. Very important historical artifact."

Without waiting for my response, she kept going. Slightly bewildered—and beginning to regret my casual observation about the squirrels—I followed her to a glass jewelry case in the center of the store. A glance didn't reveal anything of note.

"If you'd like me to take out anything for you, of course let me know. This is one of our most treasured items." She pointed at a rather unremarkable silver necklace. A pendant hung from the chain, engraved with the image of a squirrel.

"This is one of your most treasured items?" I asked.

She nodded gravely. "It's one of the friendship pendants worn by Sarah Montgomery and Eliza Bailey. At least, we think it's an original. It's not for sale."

"Am I meant to know who those women are?"

"Silly me." She waved her hand in front of her face. "You're a visitor. Of course you don't know our history. The Montgomerys were one of the founding families of our town. It was long believed that Ernest Montgomery had hidden his treasure somewhere in the mountains. And of course there was the feud between the Baileys and the Havens. They're two more old Tilikum families. That's all settled now, but it went on for generations."

I had no idea what she was talking about, or how my question about squirrels had brought us to hidden treasure and town feuds.

"Fascinating," I said. "Your charming town must have quite a rich history."

"Oh, it does." Her voice was laced with solemn enthusiasm.

"I have an interest in history myself," I said. "Especially when it comes to artifacts and family heirlooms. I'm something of a collector."

Her eyes brightened. "Then you'll want to see this."

She led me through racks of clothing and down an aisle of stools and chairs in various states of disrepair. At the back of the store was a wall displaying what might have been described as art. Some framed photographs and paintings were interspersed with what appeared to be old business signs, including a large, rusty *Haven Timber Company* sign right in the center.

The wall of so-called art and oddities wasn't where she led me, but where she had made me stop in my tracks.

"Is that a mummy?" I asked, gazing at what appeared to be a desiccated body in a narrow glass display case.

"Yes, that's Bernard."

"Bernard? Is it real?"

"Of course he's real," she said with a slight laugh. "One of the Baileys was an explorer in the late nineteenth century. Came back to town with all sorts of interesting things."

"He brought back a mummy? Where on earth did he get it?"

"Oh, I have no idea. But we named him Bernard, and now he lives here. Been here for decades." She adjusted her glasses. "He's not for sale."

"Isn't that a shame."

"But right over here, we have an amazing family heirloom." She moved on from the mummy and stopped in front of a massive bronze statue of a human-like figure.

"Is that... Bigfoot?" I asked.

"Sasquatch," she answered proudly.

I had to admit the craftsmanship was good and the scale was impressive. It had to be at least seven feet tall and quite detailed. It even had squirrels sitting around its large feet.

Because of course it did.

"This is a family heirloom?" I asked.

"Yes. We're incredibly lucky to have gotten our hands on it. It was passed down through the Haven family for generations."

"An old Tilikum family?"

"One of the originals," she said. "Plenty of them still live in Tilikum today, but this beautiful piece ended up in our keeping."

"Can't imagine why none of them want it."

"That's what I always say." Gazing up at it, she shook her head. "Almost doesn't seem right."

My hope of finding any hints about a local collector was

fading—quickly. It wasn't that I'd been expecting to find a store full of rare china and priceless paintings. But hundreds of squirrels and a Sasquatch statue that was considered a family heirloom weren't exactly in the same category as a centuries-old emerald and ruby necklace.

And there was a mummy.

"This has been very enlightening," I said. "You have quite the establishment."

"Why, thank you."

"As I said, I'm something of a collector. Art, antiquities, that sort of thing. I heard there's someone in the area who is as well."

"Hmm." She pressed her lips together and furrowed her brow. "There is the Tilikum Historical Society. They have a nice little museum."

A local museum wasn't what I was after. "Ah. How nice."

"Of course, there was the fire some years back. But they've reopened since."

"But you don't know anyone who's more of a private collector?"

"Actually, yes. Rich Pine. He collects all sorts of things. But now that I think about it, the county might have gotten involved and made him clean up his property. And I'm not sure he had anything that was very historical. He mostly just never threw anything away."

A hoarder. No.

"Thank you for your time." I gave her a slow grin. "It's been lovely."

Her cheeks flushed, and she put a hand to her chest. "It's been nice having you. Come back anytime."

I winked at her. "Enjoy the rest of your day."

"Goodness," she said, fanning herself.

I navigated my way through the cluttered store and left.

Disappointing. As far as I'd seen, it was the only antique store in town. And it had turned up absolutely nothing.

Or maybe there simply wasn't a collector in the area—not the type I was looking for, at any rate.

Mildly frustrated, I got back in my car and headed for my temporary lodgings to regroup.

CHAPTER 6

Jensen

Maple called right as I parked outside the flat.

"Any updates?" she asked, her tone cheerful.

"This town is dripping with Christmas decorations, and they have a very odd fascination with squirrels."

"Well, it is December. Decorations are appropriate. Not sure what to say about a squirrel fascination."

"I went to an antique store. There's only one, in this town at least, and their prized family heirlooms included a squirrel necklace and giant Bigfoot statue."

Maple laughed. "That's unique."

"I was hoping to find out if we have a collector in the area. One with the resources to pull off a heist. So far, all I have are squirrels."

"And Bigfoot."

"And a mummy."

"Excuse me?" she asked. "Did you say a mummy? In the antique store?"

"His name is Bernard."

She laughed again. I wasn't nearly as amused.

"There's something odd about this town," I said. "People stare at me like they've never seen a well-dressed man before."

"You love it when people stare at you."

I rolled my eyes. "Only when I want them to. I wasn't trying to attract attention."

"You're in the real world, Jensen. No wonder it's throwing you for a bit of a loop. You're accustomed to dealing with wealthy aristocrats and business tycoons. Even the thieves who steal from them travel in certain circles."

I thought back to my last job. Delphine Moreau had led me to a high-end hotel in New York City, and we'd both been perfectly at home there.

That was typical. I'd infiltrated luxury hotels, celebrity parties, private resorts, and exclusive events. I knew how to blend in among the rich and powerful—attract notice when it suited me and fly under the radar when it didn't.

But after only half a day in the small mountain town, I was at a bit of a loss.

"Do you want my advice?" Maple asked.

"Only if it's good."

"You need a local. Someone who knows the town well and can give you insight."

I was about to remind her that I worked alone—on the ground, at least—when the door to the main house opened, and Natalie emerged.

My lips turned up in a grin. "Natalie."

"Who's Natalie? You make me nervous when you use that tone."

"She's my local."

"Don't go causing trouble."

My smile widened. "I would never."

"You would always." She sighed. "Be careful, Jensen. I have an odd feeling about this job."

On any other occasion, the concern in Maple's voice

would have caught my attention. Trusting her instincts, I would have pressed her on what was bothering her. But Natalie was about to get in her car, and I wanted to catch her before she left.

"I'll check in later," I said, ending the call.

My eyes locked on Natalie as I exited my vehicle. She was hunkered down in a thick winter coat, and her long hair spilled out from a knit hat as she paused to take a phone call.

"I really don't know," she said, and I didn't miss the impatience in her voice. This wasn't a call she wanted to continue. "That isn't my business."

She caught sight of me walking toward her, and I paused, waiting for her to finish her call.

"No, I'm not asking him that," she said with a roll of her eyes. "Yes, I have, but only in a professional capacity. I have to go, okay? I'll see you around."

With a sharp exhale, she jabbed her finger onto her phone screen to end the call. It took her a few tries before she managed it.

I couldn't help but smile. She was so feisty. I liked it.

"Hi, Mr. Lakes," she said. "Do you need something?"

"It's Jensen, darling," I said. "Is everything all right?"

"Yes, fine. It's just Tilikum being Tilikum." She hesitated. "You kind of set the gossip line on fire."

"How did I manage that?"

"Somebody saw you in town this morning and told someone else—I'm not really sure how it started—and then word got around that you're staying here. I've had three neighbors just *happen*," she said, using air quotes, "to stop by with Christmas cookies."

My brow furrowed. "They brought dessert? What does that have to do with me?"

"It's an excuse to come over. Mostly so they could get a look at you or ask me what I know about you—or both. And

Mrs. Dallas just called, insisting I tell her everything I know. But at least she was straightforward about it."

"Isn't there tourism in this town? You must have visitors."

"We do. But this time of year, it's mostly people into winter sports or families coming for sleigh rides and Christmas Village. Not men traveling alone who look like... you. You don't look like a typical tourist."

Perhaps Maple's idea was a good one, and not simply as an excuse to get to know Natalie. I did work alone, but there was something to be said for getting help from a local who understood the town's ins and outs.

Something I certainly didn't. Not so far, at least.

"I can't help how I look," I said, "but I'm not keen on this sort of attention."

"Don't worry. I'm not saying a word to anyone. Not that I have anything to tell."

"I appreciate your discretion."

Her expression turned suspicious. "You're not here doing something illegal, are you? I guess you wouldn't tell me if you were."

"The small child did ask if I'm a bad guy."

She laughed. "That would be my niece, Annabel. Sorry about that. Kids don't have filters."

"No need to apologize. She was actually quite delightful."

"Yeah, she's a great kid."

"I see that you're about to leave, but before you go, could I have a bit of your time? Perhaps indoors where it's warm?"

Her suspicion was back. "Why?"

"You're right, I'm not a typical tourist. I'm here on business, and I could use your help."

"Why me?"

Because I find you intriguing, and I'd love an excuse to get closer to you.

"I need the perspective of a local. Preferably one who won't feed into the... what did you call it? The gossip line?"

"Yeah, town gossip is basically a sport here." She hesitated, looking me up and down. "All right. I guess if you have questions, I can try to answer them."

The corners of my mouth lifted. "Wonderful. I wouldn't dream of asking you to invite me into your space, so would you come up to the flat?"

She glanced at her phone—probably checking the time. "All right."

I led the way up the stairs and opened the door, stepping aside so she could go in.

"Can I take your coat?" I asked.

"Thanks." She unzipped, and I stepped in to take it as she slid her arms out.

I had to resist the urge to bring it to my nose and inhale her scent. A coat tree was by the door, so I hung it for her, then took off mine and did the same.

"Coffee?" I asked. "Or tea?"

"No thanks."

I gestured to the couch, and she took a seat, still wearing her hat. My instincts told me not to crowd her, so I sat in the adjacent armchair.

"So what do you want to know?" she asked, folding her hands in her lap.

Trust her.

The voice in my head was a gentle whisper. Somehow, the lack of force made me inclined to listen.

"I'm here to catch a thief," I said. "It's what I do."

"What did they steal?"

"A necklace. But not any necklace. A priceless family heirloom known as the Emerald Crown. It was stolen from an estate outside London, and my associates tracked the thief here."

"Are you with the police?"

"No, I work for a private organization."

"A private organization that catches thieves?"

"In a sense. My job involves recovery of stolen items."

"What kind of items?"

I leaned back and crossed my ankle over my knee. "We're hired to track down stolen art, antiquities, priceless heirlooms, that sort of thing."

"So you're telling me you're a thief hunter, and you came to Tilikum to track down a stolen necklace?"

"The Emerald Crown, yes."

She nodded slowly, but her skepticism was clear as she started to get up. "And I'm supposed to believe that?"

"Wait." I put up a hand. "Let me call Maple. She'll verify my story."

She lowered herself back onto the couch. "Who's Maple?"

"My handler." I got out my phone and called, putting her on speaker.

"Yes, Jensen?" Maple answered.

"Maple, I'm here with my new friend, Natalie." I met her eyes. "She's understandably skeptical about my reasons for being in town. Would you explain to her what it is we do?"

"Well, this is a new one," Maple said. "Hello, Natalie. Lovely to meet you."

"Hi?" she said, sounding confused. "Nice to meet you, too."

"I assume Jensen filled you in on the fact that he's tracking a stolen necklace?"

"He did say that."

"Brilliant. Yes, we traced the thief to your town, which is where Jensen comes in. He's there to recover the stolen item."

"Why would a thief who's good enough to steal a priceless heirloom come here?" she asked. "What's in Tilikum?"

"We don't know. But we're confident in Jensen's ability to

recover the item." Maple paused. "I almost hate to say this where he can hear me, because it will inflate his already enormous ego, but he's the best at what he does."

Natalie gazed at me. "I guess you're either both in on some kind of elaborate prank, but I can't really think of why, or this is real."

"It's quite real," Maple said. "But your questions are understandable. We keep what we do out of the public eye as much as possible."

"Thank you, Maple," I said.

"Of course," she said. "Keep me apprised as the situation develops."

"I will." I ended the call and set my phone on the armrest. "Does that help?"

"I think so?" Natalie's voice was still tentative, but she settled back against the couch cushions. "I have a feeling I'm going to regret this later, but now I'm curious."

"For you, darling, I'm an open book. I'll tell you anything you want to know."

"Is Jensen Lakes your real name?"

"It is."

"Why didn't you use an alias?"

"I often do. But in this case, it didn't seem necessary."

She nodded slowly. "Well, if you want to stay on the down-low in this town, you need to use the gossip line, not be in the gossip line."

"And how does one do that?"

"Good question." She paused, glancing away, and when she turned back toward me, her eyes brightened. "I know what we do."

"What?"

"Keep them talking, but point them in the wrong direction. I assume you were hoping to lay low so the thief doesn't know why you're here?"

"Precisely."

Her mouth lifted, and I found myself mirroring her smile.

"So we throw them off," she said. "Spread a rumor that's wild enough to catch on but completely untrue. Then if the thief does hear about the mysterious British man in town, he won't suspect who you really are."

"Brilliant. What's my story?"

"How about... you're the son of a wealthy businessman who arranged a marriage between you and his rival's daughter, hoping to form a partnership worth billions. You're in hiding to escape the wedding."

"Rather sounds like something I would do if my father was inclined to such machinations. A bit outlandish, though, don't you think?"

"Oh yeah. They'll eat it up."

"And you can plant this rumor?"

She nodded as she pulled her phone from her pocket. "Like a seed in the garden in spring. Hold on."

I watched while she made a call and waited for the other person to answer. A buzz of excitement swept through me. I was enjoying our little collaboration.

"Hi, Mrs. Dallas, it's Natalie. I just ran into my guest again. Yes, him. I actually found out why he's in town, and it's not what everyone has been saying." She paused, grinning at me. "No, they have it all wrong. Get this. His father is some kind of wealthy businessman, and he arranged a marriage for him with his rival's daughter."

The squeal on the other end caused Natalie to move the phone away from her ear.

"I know, right?" she continued. "He doesn't want to marry her, so he's hiding out here until everything blows over. Can you imagine?"

Our gazes met, and she paused while Mrs. Dallas talked. Natalie's dark eyes sparkled with amusement, and the way her lips twitched upward did strange things to me. I felt the electricity sparking between us, to be sure, but there was more. Something that wasn't purely sexual.

"You're welcome," she said. "But don't spread it around, okay? I think he wants this to stay quiet."

I chuckled softly at that. Probably the best way to get a rumor to spread.

"Anyway, I should go, but have a good afternoon." She ended the call and set her phone down. "That should do it."

"I'm impressed."

"Thanks," she said, and her smile infused a strange sense of warmth in my chest.

The phrase "*trust her*" ran through my mind again.

Where was that coming from? Did I want to trust her because I found her so alluring? Or were my instincts pushing this agenda?

I decided to go with my gut.

"It's not just the rumors that could be a problem for me. Your town has a certain way of life that's a bit outside my experience."

"It's quirky." Her tone was matter-of-fact.

"Indeed. I always work alone, but in this case, I could use a partner."

"Isn't Maple your partner?"

"In a sense, but she does her work behind the scenes. I was thinking of you."

Natalie's eyebrows lifted. "You want me to be your partner? To help you recover a stolen necklace?"

"Yes." I gave her a nod. "And I'll give you a cut of my fee. It's quite substantial."

Her lips parted, and she gazed at me for a long moment. "What would I need to do?"

"Help me navigate a town that's oddly fascinated with

CLAIRE KINGSLEY

squirrels and has a statue of a pinup girl wearing a Santa Claus beard in the middle of town."

She laughed. "That would be Lola. She gets bearded all the time."

My brow furrowed.

Natalie waved her hand as if that didn't matter. "Never mind. Weird town lore. And yes, the squirrels are a thing. Keep an eye on your wallet. They like to steal things."

"See? You're already providing me with vital intelligence."

She took a deep breath. "Okay, Jensen Lakes. I'll help you find the necklace. If I can. I have no idea what I'm doing."

"That's all right, darling." I winked at her. "I'll be by your side every step of the way."

A subtle shift in her expression betrayed her skepticism. Or maybe it was distrust. And one thing ran through my mind.

Who hurt you?

Because it was clear that she'd been hurt before. And whoever he was, I wanted to do murderous things to him.

I stood and offered her my hand. She took it, and I helped her to her feet. As much as I wanted to kiss the backs of her knuckles again, I didn't. Charm wasn't going to reach her. I wasn't sure what would, but turning up the charisma wouldn't win me any points.

So I shifted my grip to shake her hand instead. Businesslike.

"I look forward to working with you, Natalie."

"You too, Jensen." She slipped her hand from mine. "Where do we start?"

"I'll show you what we know so far."

And just like that, I had a partner.

CHAPTER 7
Natalie

Being an ED nurse, it was hard to surprise me. I'd seen things. But a British thief hunter who wanted my help to track down a stolen heirloom in my small town? I had not seen that coming.

He got out his laptop and set it on the dining table. I was getting warm, so I took off my hat, set it on the couch, and ran my fingers through my hair. I'd been planning to run a few errands while Nina and Annabel were out, but those could wait.

My skepticism remained. Was Jensen's story actually true? There were a lot of unanswered questions, and the distinct possibility that he was not who he claimed to be.

But when he'd said he was an open book—that he'd tell me anything—I sort of believed him. And he got a few points for not asking me out again. He wasn't hitting on me, so I didn't have the sense that this was some elaborate ruse to get in my pants.

And the excitement buzzing through my veins was hard to resist. My job had its share of intensity, but this was different.

It felt like an adventure. And that stirred something deep inside me—a flurry of almost-forgotten dreams.

"What does this necklace look like?" I went over to the table and took a seat next to him.

He clicked on an image to expand it. "This is it."

I gazed at the screen. I'd never seen anything like it. The necklace was displayed on a black velvet jewelry mannequin stand, and I couldn't fathom how much it weighed. It looked huge. Diamonds set in gold created a netlike effect, with red rubies set in the middle of each square. A large teardrop emerald draped in the center. It reminded me of a crown, only worn around the neck.

"I can see where it got its name," I said. "It's all real, isn't it?"

"Of course."

"How much is it worth?"

"Hard to say for sure. On the black market, I'd expect at least five million."

"Wow. That's a lot of money." I touched my collarbones. "I can't imagine wearing something like that."

"This piece doesn't get worn. The family brings it out each year at Christmas and puts it on display."

"It does look Christmassy, now that you mention it."

"Originally, it was a Christmas gift to the Countess of Beaufort in the eighteenth century. The family has had it ever since."

"For five million dollars, no wonder someone stole it. Are you sure the thief didn't already sell it?"

"We can't dismiss that possibility, although it's unlikely he would have had time. He also could have handed it off to someone else en route. But we have no evidence of that, so for now, we search here."

Jensen brought up another screen with a few grainy security photos.

"Is that him?" I asked.

"He's our thief. I don't suppose you recognize him."

Scrutinizing the photos, I shook my head slowly. "There's not much of him to see."

"No, he was careful. We don't think he's a known entity, so either he's new to this, or he's experienced, but we've never caught sight of him before. Hard to know at this stage."

"Do you think he stole it for himself? Or did someone hire him?"

Jensen's mouth turned up in a smile. "Excellent question. You're already good at this."

"I'm an emergency nurse. We're problem solvers."

His eyes held mine for a second, and the intensity in his sent a tingle down my spine. "It's possible he's working on his own and plans to sell the necklace. It's also possible he was hired. It wouldn't be the first time a wealthy collector was behind a heist."

"What if someone hired him, but he's double-crossing them and plans to sell it himself? That's a lot of money."

"Always a possibility, but I don't see that as often as you'd think. Gets messy if the thief thinks he can demand more money or decides to make off with the goods himself."

"I guess there's not a lot of trust among thieves."

"Not at all."

"Have you found anything so far?"

He let out a frustrated breath. "No. I went to the antique store, hoping to find out if there was a wealthy collector in the area. Usually people who deal in antiques are aware of that sort of thing. But no luck there."

"You went to the Treasure Chest?"

He nodded.

"Was there a little old lady with cat-eye glasses?"

"Yes."

"That's Dottie McNess. No wonder the gossip line is

going wild. She probably made ten phone calls before you left the parking lot."

"Lovely," he said, his voice laced with sarcasm. "She was very enthusiastic about her store's collection of important local artifacts."

"Like Bernard?"

"The mummy." His tone shifted from sarcasm to distaste. "Yes, we're acquainted."

"I used to love that thing. I'd go to the Treasure Chest just to stare at him. I found him fascinating."

Oddly, he didn't look at me like I was strange. He gazed at me with a hint of bewilderment but with no indication he was judging me.

I shrugged. "But nothing really grosses me out. That's probably part of why I became a nurse. Anyway, I don't think Dottie would know any wealthy collectors. She's not exactly dealing in high-end antiques. Unless it's by accident."

He smiled, and my heart skipped. That thing was a deadly weapon. And I had a feeling he knew it. I needed to be careful with him. He was dangerous.

But looking at him made me think. "Do you have anything else to wear?"

He looked down at his clothes. "Why?"

"You look very... expensive."

"This was expensive."

I laughed. "Exactly. It's part of why you stick out. Not the expense, necessarily. No one would notice if you were dressed in thousands of dollars of winter gear. But this makes you noticeable. And those shoes can't be good in the snow."

"All my clothes look like this. What do you suggest?"

"Let's stop by Friendly Farm and Feed."

His brow furrowed in confusion. "Farm and Feed? I thought we were talking about clothing."

"You've clearly never been to a small-town farm store. They have everything."

"Apparently, I need your help more than I realized."

"Trust me," I said. "You're going to look great."

"Of course I will. I always look great."

With a slight shake of my head, I rolled my eyes. "And you know it, too."

He just grinned at me.

This guy was going to be a handful.

❄

We pulled into the parking lot at Friendly Farm and Feed, and Jensen found a spot. An old tractor parked out front was draped with multicolored Christmas lights, and a scarecrow with a Santa hat sat in the driver's seat. Half a dozen holiday inflatables lined the front of the building, including a snow globe, a smiling Santa Claus, and a twelve-foot reindeer.

Jensen gave me a skeptical glance. "You're sure about this?"

"Yeah, they'll have everything you need. At a good price, too."

We got out, and our feet crunched on the crusted-over snow. I paused as a vintage fire engine with a snowplow on the front drove by. Speakers mounted on top blared a lively rendition of "Santa Claus is Coming to Town."

"Who, and what, is that?" Jensen asked.

"That's Woody Blankenship. He restored that old fire truck and now he uses it to plow the roads in winter. He also plays Santa Claus every year. The kids love him."

Woody leaned out the window and waved. His white beard was as real as it came, and he looked a lot like Santa, even without a costume.

"Brilliant," Jensen said. "Of course there's a man who

looks like Santa Claus driving a vintage fire engine playing Christmas music. Why wouldn't there be?"

I waved at Woody as he passed. "That's Tilikum for ya. Come on. Let's go inside."

The wide entrance was open, and large overhead heaters blew warm air. We passed a stack of chicken feed and a cart unceremoniously filled with winter hats and gloves. I grabbed two hats and two pairs of gloves as we walked by and handed them to Jensen.

"When am I going to need these?"

"I don't know, but when you're in the mountains, it's good to be prepared."

"Fair enough. Lead the way."

I led him to the clothing section. He took slow steps through the racks, eyeing everything dubiously. There were coveralls, jeans, thick coats, and four racks of flannel shirts.

He plucked the sleeve of a red-and-black buffalo-plaid flannel and held it out. "This is... interesting."

"Yeah, I'm not really feeling that on you. Maybe something more subtle." Pressing my lips together to hide my smile, I picked a bright orange plaid shirt and held it up. "What do you think?"

"How is that subtle?"

"Fine, I'm kidding." I put it back and chose a dark green. "What about this one?"

His brow furrowed. "I suppose that isn't terrible."

"Great. I think a blue as well." I kept shuffling through the shirts. "And this gray is nice. Why don't you find some jeans in your size."

Jensen went to the wall of jeans, organized in cubby shelves. He held up a pair and tilted his head, regarding them as if denim was a foreign concept.

We grabbed several more things, then I led him to the back where a curtained-off square with an upside-down bucket for a stool functioned as a fitting room. He went in and shut the curtain, although it left a crack on one side.

I moved so I wouldn't be tempted to peek.

Customers wandered by while I waited, some pushing carts and others carrying armfuls of items. The Christmas inflatables seemed to be popular. I saw several people with the big, brightly colored boxes in their carts.

The curtain swished open, and Jensen stepped out. It was hard not to gape at him. How did he make a green plaid flannel and jeans look like they belonged on a runway?

"What do you think?" He turned in a circle.

The shirt accentuated his biceps, and the jeans hugged him in all the right places. It was like they'd been tailored to his body.

"Looks good," I said, careful with my choice of words. I didn't want to blurt out something embarrassing, like *you're a Greek god in flannel*.

But seriously, he was.

With a subtle grin, he glanced down at himself and adjusted the shirt. "I could grow to like this."

"It'll help you fit in."

"Then mission accomplished."

He returned to the fitting room and tried on a few more things, settling on two pairs of jeans and a few flannels. I suggested he get some white T-shirts to go under them, and we found socks and a pair of boots that would do much better in the snow than his sleek leather shoes. We also grabbed a dark blue winter coat.

As we walked to the front of the store to check out, I could see why he'd lit up the gossip line so fast. Everyone seemed to notice him. Heads turned, mouths opened, and he left a trail of wide eyes and whispers in his wake.

Hopefully, his new look would calm things down. I wondered if my story about him being a runaway groom had already made the rounds, and people in the store were realizing it was him.

But that was fine. In fact, I could probably use it. If I dropped a few well-placed hints that we'd gone to Farm and Feed to disguise him as a local so he could evade the evil machinations of his father and arranged bride-to-be, it would lend more credence to the rumor. And if we played things right, Tilikum would develop a maternal protectiveness toward the handsome visitor.

Maybe that would lower the chances of the thief realizing who Jensen really was—and what he was doing in Tilikum.

And we'd be more likely to get the necklace back.

CHAPTER 8

Jensen

On the drive back to the flat, my mind should have been on one thing—my next move. Instead, I was thinking about how to convince Natalie to have dinner with me.

A voice in the back of my mind—one that sounded suspiciously like Maple—reminded me I had a job to do. And it was not Natalie Thatcher.

"What happens now?" she asked.

"Well, since I don't have a solid lead yet, my usual strategy is to keep my ear to the ground. Listen, observe, talk to people. See if I can spot anything that will point me in the right direction."

She nodded slowly as if she were thinking. I paused, but she didn't say anything.

"Do you have an idea?" I asked.

"I do, actually. I was thinking ear to the ground makes total sense. And if there is a jewelry thief in town, or someone who hired him, or even a buyer, there might be hints of that in the gossip line. So we should go somewhere that allows us to listen in."

"And where would that be?"

She hesitated. "There are several options. The Steaming Mug, the coffee shop downtown, could be a good place. Especially if Louise Haven and her band of little old lady friends happen to be there. But for this, I think we need to go to the Timberbeast."

"The timber what?"

"Timberbeast Tavern. It's a local hangout."

"Sounds charming."

She laughed. "It's a small-town bar. Nothing fancy, but the drinks are good. It caters more to locals than visitors, so townspeople tend to congregate there."

"All right. Drinks at the Timberbeast." I glanced at her and winked. "It's a date."

"Not that kind of date."

"If you say so."

"I do say so."

The corner of my mouth lifted in a smirk, but I didn't argue. She rolled her eyes.

I pulled up outside her house and parked. "What time shall we depart this evening for drinks that is not a date?"

"How about four?"

"Four? Isn't that a bit early?"

"We're looking for the 'grabs a beer before dinner and probably goes to bed by nine' crowd."

"Fair enough. I'll pick you up at four."

"Still not a date, Jensen."

"Of course not, darling."

With a soft laugh, she shook her head, then got out of the car.

Perhaps it wouldn't be a date. But there was always next time.

❄

Standing in front of the full-length mirror in the bedroom, I took a hard look at my reflection. Something wasn't right.

I'd donned the dark green flannel, and the jeans were a good fit. My stubble wasn't exactly a thick beard—I'd seen many of those around town—but that would take a bit of time to grow if I wanted to really embrace the lumberjack aesthetic. And I wasn't sure that was necessary.

But there was something I didn't like.

The sleeves. That was the problem. I unbuttoned the cuffs and rolled them up to my elbows. Much better.

Decked out in my new Tilikum wardrobe, I put on the boots and coat Natalie had selected. It made me wonder what my sister would think if she saw me. No one in my family knew what I did for a living, and they were used to a much more sophisticated Jensen Lakes. My behavior was particularly outrageous when I was with my sister. Pretending to shamelessly flirt with her friends had long been one of my favorite pastimes.

I decided it would be fun to keep Nora guessing. I took a selfie and texted it to her, asking how she liked my outfit.

Nora: What are you wearing???

    Me: Do you like it?

    Nora: I would love to make fun of you, but you wear that too well. How do you do that?

    Me: All part of my charm. How is my precious Raina?

    Nora: Busy stealing my husband from me.

    Me: As it should be.

    Nora: Exactly. She's sitting up on her own now.

    Me: I knew she was the world's smartest little girl.

    Nora: Of course she is. She's mine. I don't suppose you're going to tell me what you're up to?

    Me: Probably not.

Nora: Fine. Stay out of trouble.
Me: Where's the fun in that?

I slipped my phone into my pocket and went next door to pick up my not-date for the evening.

Natalie answered wearing her winter coat, and her face lit up with a smile. "You look great. Very Tilikum."

"Thank you. Shall we?"

I led her to my car and held the door for her while she got in. She smelled amazing—a hint of vanilla that was warm and inviting. Like a Christmas cookie. It made me want to get closer to her. Touch her skin. Bury my face in her neck and breathe her in.

Of course, I couldn't. Not unless she wanted me to, and she'd had her guard up since the moment we met.

She gave me directions, and like everything in the small town, it was close and easy to find. We parked outside as the streetlights went on. The sun set early in December. A Christmas wreath hung on the door and inside we were greeted by a string of multicolored lights lining the bar.

Christmas really was everywhere in that town.

The bartender looked like he probably spent most of his free time chopping wood. He had a thick beard and even thicker arms, straining the seams of his red-plaid flannel shirt. He gave us a chin tip as we entered.

Several tables were filled, and about half the seats at the bar were occupied. One rather grizzled gentleman at the bar had turned on his stool and was engaged in a lively conversation with several men at an adjacent table.

I gestured for Natalie to choose our seats, and she selected a table near the conversing men.

"What can I get you to drink?" I asked. Her insistence that

it wasn't a date was fine, but I wasn't letting her pay for her own drink.

"You don't have to buy me a drink."

"Don't worry. It's a business expense."

"Okay, a Christmas ale if he has them."

Natalie took her seat, and I went to the bar, catching bits and pieces of the surrounding conversations as I waited. Two men on stools behind me were discussing golf. Several couples sat at a nearby table and appeared to be talking about the weather—whether or not there would be more snow before Christmas. Nothing of note in either case.

The bartender took my order—a Christmas ale for Natalie and a scotch for me. He brought them to me, and I took them to our table.

I slid Natalie's drink toward her and took my seat. "Hear anything interesting?"

She shook her head. "Not yet."

"Me neither. Just golf and the weather."

"I don't know why we discuss the weather so much here. It's December. There will probably be snow."

"In London, it's usually rain."

"Is that where you're from?"

"Originally. I spend more of my time in the States now."

She took a sip of her drink. "Where in the States?"

"I have a place in Seattle."

"How'd you end up there? You seem like the type who'd live in Manhattan or something."

"New York does have its appeal. But my sister lives in Seattle. If you meet her, don't let on, but I actually quite like her."

"How did she end up in Seattle from London?"

"She's American, actually. My half sister. Our family is a bit... complicated. We have the same father, but my mother was the other woman."

Natalie winced. "Ouch."

"Not ideal. I suppose I can give my father a little bit of credit. He's still with my mother. But my origins aren't exactly honorable. Nora and I were born a month apart."

"Did you grow up knowing about each other? Or did you find out as adults?"

"We always knew. Nora spent summers with us, at least some of the time."

"Was that awkward for your mom?"

"I suppose it was. But to give my mother credit, too, she was always kind to Nora." I took a sip of scotch. "Tell me about you. How did you come to live with your sister and her daughter?"

She took a deep breath. "That's kind of a long story. Nina is ten years younger than me, so I was always like a second mom to her. Our dad died when we were still kids, and then our mom died when Nina was in high school. I moved home to take care of her. Then she got pregnant with Annabel."

"That must have been difficult."

"Yeah, it was a lot at first. The jerk she was with bailed as soon as he found out. Didn't want to have anything to do with her."

"Well, now I hate him. But at least she had you."

She nodded, and a smile lit up her face. "Since then, we've just done our best. I'd already finished nursing school, and Nina became an aesthetician. We work opposite schedules so one of us is always available for Annabel. We make it work."

I gazed at her. What about her was so intriguing? I was awed by her, but I couldn't explain why. Her story was admirable—she'd obviously sacrificed a great deal for her family. I respected that. But something deeper, something behind those dark brown eyes kept me captivated.

"How did you become a thief hunter?" she asked.

I hesitated, feeling a strange sense of vulnerability. I didn't usually share things about my life with... anyone. Especially things from my past.

"I started out as a thief."

Her eyes widened slightly. "You did?"

"Not stealing art and antiquities, of course. I started young, nicking sweets when I was nine or ten. When I got a little older, I discovered I could steal things and sell them—cigarettes, booze, small electronics. I had quite the business going."

"So mostly shoplifting?"

"At first, yes. Then I started targeting my father's friends. Wealthy people had such interesting things. From there, I branched out and started breaking into other posh houses."

"Why? For the money?"

"I suppose I liked the money. It certainly made me popular. I also liked the thrill of it. The risk. Getting in and out without being seen. Or charming my way out if I was caught. That happened more than once."

"That doesn't surprise me."

"And if I'm being honest, I was angry with my father. Adultery was not the only of his sins. He was difficult, to say the least."

"And that was your way of getting back at him?"

"I wouldn't have said so at the time, but yes, it was."

"But how did you go from stealing things to this?"

"I got caught by the wrong man. Or the right man, as it were. He worked for my organization and recognized that I had amassed quite a set of skills. He made me a deal. He could turn me in, or I could work for him. I chose the latter."

"Are you glad you made that choice?"

"Always have been. I'd matured enough by that point to realize I needed to stop. My life was heading in a dark direction, but I didn't know how to change it. He gave me a chance. I'm grateful for that." I took a sip of my drink. "And now, here I am."

"And your organization is legit, right? You follow laws and everything?"

"For the most part." I winked at her. "We have people who routinely interface with law enforcement. Especially if there are... messes to clean up."

"But—" She stopped, as if something had caught her attention, and held up a finger. Tilting her head, she seemed to be listening.

"I heard that, too," the man at the bar was saying. His voice was rough and gravelly. "Where do you suppose he got the money for that?"

"Probably stole it," a man at the adjacent table grumbled.

Natalie raised her eyebrows.

"He didn't steal that car," the man at the bar said. "I heard he ordered it straight from the factory, and they brought it to him with a helicopter."

"What the hell are you talking about? That's not how they ship cars."

"Sure they did. Brought it in hanging from a big harness."

The man at the table waved his hand. "Bah. Don't believe everything you hear. And I meant he stole the money to buy it, not the car."

Another man spoke up. "I don't trust that guy any farther than I can throw him. Never trust a man with statues outside his house. Pretentious as all hell."

"I heard he got those from overseas," the man at the bar said. "They were originally outside some hoity-toity mansion in France or something."

"Did they bring those in on a helicopter too?"

He shrugged. "Hell if I know. But I hear they're made of marble. Not the kind of thing you get around here."

I leaned across the table and lowered my voice. "Do you know who they're talking about?"

"I'm not sure," she whispered. She twisted in her chair and cut in on their conversation. "Are you guys talking about Rich Pine?"

I flinched a little at her directness. But maybe she knew what she was doing.

"No, no," the guy at the bar said with a wave of his hand. "He doesn't have statues."

"I didn't think so," she said. "Who does?"

"You know, the odd duck who lives on the north side. There are two flanking the walkway to his front door. Fancy ones. Like something you'd see in a museum."

"Guy has more money than he knows what to do with," one of the men said. "New cars. Fancy clothes."

"And statues," Natalie added.

Statues could mean anything. After all, the local antique dealer had described a seven-foot Sasquatch as a "family heirloom." But it was also possible they were talking about an art enthusiast. Maybe even a wealthy collector.

"See?" The man at the bar pointed at Natalie. "She gets it."

"I heard he moved here from New York," one of the men said.

"I thought it was San Diego," Natalie said.

"No, no," the man at the bar said, waving his hand again. "We're talking about Julian Myers."

"Oh, Julian Myers," Natalie said, turning to give me a subtle smile. "You're right. He's not from San Diego."

I raised my eyebrows and gave her a subtle nod. Impressive. She'd been right about listening in on town chatter. It wasn't much of a lead, but it was better than nothing.

She'd been right about my clothes, too. No one in the bar seemed interested in me.

We sat for a while longer, sipping our drinks and casually eavesdropping. At one point, Natalie rose and wandered to an old jukebox. I watched with a barely concealed smile as she pretended to peruse the song selections, all the while turning her ear to the group of couples at the nearby table. I made a trip to the bar, ostensibly to get a napkin, and paused to listen in on a few of the patrons.

Neither of us heard anything else that seemed relevant. Just more talk about the weather, some griping about a neighbor, and concern over whether the squirrels had enough sustenance for the winter.

There they went with the squirrels again.

Satisfied with our reconnaissance, we decided it was time to go, and I led Natalie out to my car. She gave me a wary look as I opened the passenger door for her. So guarded. She got in, and I couldn't help myself. I leaned in and inhaled deeply, filling my nose with her scent.

A wave of heat swept through me. It was as if Natalie was a woman created to be my ultimate weakness. If I didn't know better, I might have wondered if she was a lure, sent by an enemy to trap me.

CHAPTER 9
Natalie

I left the Timberbeast feeling mildly intoxicated. And it had nothing to do with the drink. Or Jensen Lakes.

Okay, maybe Jensen had a little bit to do with it. It was hard to imagine any woman spending time with a man like him and not feeling the force of his masculine charm.

But it wasn't the alcohol or the company. It was the thrill of hunting a thief.

Honestly, it was silly. All we did was go to the tavern for a drink and eavesdrop on the locals. That was a typical Saturday night in Tilikum. But it had felt like more.

When I'd gone over to the jukebox and pretended to look through the songs, I'd imagined myself somewhere else—in a fancy hotel or a swanky party, like a scene from a spy movie. Then I'd turned to see Jensen watching me with that hint of a smirk on his lips and almost blushed with pleasure.

I needed to be careful or I was going to get carried away. I wasn't a spy. I wasn't a private detective or a thief hunter or whatever Jensen called himself. I was an ED nurse on strike, struggling to make ends meet right before Christmas.

Still, it had been fun. And where was the harm in that?

Jensen cast a glance at me as he drove, and the corner of his mouth lifted. That subtle grin of his was dangerous.

He was dangerous. And not because he chased art thieves for a living.

I turned toward the window, taking a deep breath to clear my head. Every time he looked at me, I felt the same thrill. Like we really were partners on an adventure, not strangers from different worlds.

But we were, and I couldn't forget that. The last thing I needed was another hotshot in a suit to swoop in and screw up my life. Even if this one did look just as good in a flannel and jeans.

I was not going there. No matter what those dark eyes did to my insides.

"I'd call that a success," he said. "A man with a pretentious reputation isn't necessarily our suspect, but it gives us someone to look into."

"It makes me want to drive by his house and see what they're talking about with the statues. But I'm not actually sure where he lives."

"What do you know about this fellow?"

"Not much. I vaguely remember when he moved to town. People were talking about him. He was single, so I think that had a lot to do with it. This place turns into a Jane Austen novel when a single man of means moves into the area."

"Or when one is visiting and has the audacity to be British."

"Very true. Your outfit seemed to help. Did you notice a difference?"

"I did. That was good advice."

I smiled and made the mistake of meeting his eyes. My heart skipped at the intensity in his gaze. It was like he had a dial and knew exactly how to turn up the heat.

He broke eye contact—after all, he was driving—and I looked out the window again.

"So how do we find out if Julian Myers had anything to do with the theft?" I asked.

"I need to meet him."

An idea popped into my mind. The Snowflake Ball. When was that? It seemed like the sort of thing a guy like Julian might attend. I took out my phone and searched.

"Looking for something?" he asked.

"Yes. The Snowflake Ball. It's a big charity thing they have every year. All the well-to-do people in Tilikum and the surrounding towns attend. Especially the ones who want everyone to know they're fancy."

"Sounds perfect."

"Here it is. Tuesday night at the Grand Peak Hotel. But I have no idea how to get tickets." I cast a glance at him. "In case you haven't figured it out, I'm not one of the fancy people in Tilikum."

"Don't worry, darling. I'll take care of it. Will you text me that link?"

"Sure. But I don't have your number."

"That's an easy fix."

He gave me his number, and I put him in my contacts, then texted him a link to the event. I was well aware that meant I'd just given him *my* number. And I could tell by the return of his smirk that he'd done it on purpose.

Well, we were working together while he was in town. It made sense for him to have my number.

We turned onto my street, and he parked in front of the house. With my hand on the door handle, I hesitated, oddly reluctant to get out. Once I stepped out of his car, I'd be back in the real world.

"Thank you again for your help," he said, his voice disarmingly soft.

"You're welcome. It was kind of fun, actually."

"I enjoyed it as well." He paused, and there was that hint of surprise in his tone again. "Have a good evening."

"You too."

I got out, and the real world hit me along with the cold night air. My brief fantasy of espionage faded, and I was back to being... me. Sister, aunt, nurse. Broke.

Boring.

I went inside, hoping Jensen did somehow get tickets to that event. Not because I cared about rubbing elbows with a bunch of small-town snobs in designer labels. Because infiltrating an event that required a dress and heels sounded deliciously adventurous.

And doing so with Jensen at my side? Dangerous or not, that idea was irresistible.

❄

Going back to working nights when the strike was over was probably going to kill me. Rolling over in bed, I stretched my arms above my head. I was getting used to sleeping at night all too quickly.

When I went downstairs, signs of Annabel's breakfast were all over the kitchen table. Nina must have made her eggs and toast. She'd also made coffee, so I helped myself to a cup.

The house was quiet, even for so early in the day, and I wondered if they'd gone somewhere. We didn't have a Christmas tree yet, so maybe they'd gone to get one.

I decided I could help by bringing up the decorations from the basement. I went down the stairs where the fans and dehumidifiers still roared. At least everything looked dry, and condensation wasn't building up anywhere.

Trying not to think about what it was costing us to rent those huge fans, I went to the closet where we kept our decorations. We didn't have a lot—just a few bins of lights and ornaments. Fortunately, nothing on that side of the basement had gotten wet. Losing our Christmas decorations would have made a bad situation that much worse. Some of our ornaments were from when Nina and I were growing up.

I brought the bins upstairs one at a time and set them in the living room. Still no sign of Nina and Annabel, so I figured I'd test the lights. One Christmas, we'd forgotten to do that and didn't realize half the strands were dead until they were already on the tree. I didn't want to make that mistake again.

The first bin was filled with ornaments. I was about to push it aside when one of them caught my eye. Sitting right on top, half covered with a scrap of torn tissue paper, was an old, homemade salt dough ornament in the shape of a stack of pancakes with a pat of butter and green and red sprinkles on top.

I hadn't thought about it in years, but Christmas morning pancakes had been a Thatcher family tradition since Nina and I were young. It was the red and green sprinkles that made them special. Mom would mix them into the batter, and we'd scatter more on top, adding a sugary sparkle to our holiday breakfast.

Nina had made the pancake ornament when she was a kid. I couldn't believe we still had it.

And it hit me. No wonder Annabel was so insistent on me being there for Christmas. Nina had continued the sprinkle pancake tradition, and Annabel wanted us all to be there for it. Together.

Nina's car pulled up outside. Sniffling, I set the ornament back in the bin and swiped beneath my eyes. That had been an unexpected rush of feelings from an old ornament.

The door flew open, and Annabel rushed in. She kicked off her boots and dropped her coat on the floor.

"Auntie Natalie, I got coffee!"

Nina came in behind her and shut the door. "Where does your coat go?"

"Oops. Forgot." She spun around and skipped back to the entry to hang her coat on the low hook just for her.

"Coffee?" I asked. "Because she doesn't have enough energy?"

Nina smiled. "It was a hot chocolate, but it was from the Steaming Mug, so it was in the same kind of cup as Mommy's and Auntie's coffees. She was very excited."

"Is that where you guys went?"

"Yeah." Nina plopped down on the couch. "Miss Early Riser over there woke up before the sun did. I figured you could use some sleep, so we got out of the house. The coffee shop is open early, and for obvious reasons, I needed the caffeine. Win-win."

"Thanks. I did need the sleep. It's going to be a rough transition when I go back to work. It's like we're made to sleep at night."

"Who knew?"

"Mommy, can I go play outside?" Annabel asked. "I put my boots back on."

"Yes, but stay in the yard and put on your coat."

"I'm not cold."

"At least take it with you."

"I will!"

Annabel scurried outside, slamming the door behind her.

"I thought you might have been out getting a tree," I said.

"Yeah, we were going to do that yesterday."

"Why didn't you?"

Pressing her lips together, she glanced away. She only did that when she had something to hide.

"What's that look for?" I asked.

"What look?"

"That one. The one that means you're trying to keep a secret from me."

"I don't have a look." Her lips turned up. She was totally trying not to smile. "Or a secret."

"Liar."

She blew out a breath. "Fine. But don't make a big deal out of this. Because it's probably nothing, and I don't want Annabel to think something is going on."

It was hard to contain my impatience. "Tell me while she's still outside."

"Okay, so, there's this guy."

I gasped.

"I know, I know. There's never a guy. Except now..."

"Now there's a guy."

"Maybe. I mean, there is. But I'm not sure what's going on yet."

"Who is he? How did you meet? Tell me everything."

"He's a single dad, and his daughter is in Annabel's class. We've met at school stuff, so I've seen him before, but I didn't know much about him. The other morning, we were both early for drop-off, and somehow it came up in conversation that we're both single." She tucked her legs beneath her. "I don't know. It felt like we had a moment. But then it was time to go, and nothing happened."

"I'm so invested in this. Go on."

"Annabel and I went to Christmas Village yesterday, and out of nowhere, she shrieks and runs off. I was about to freak out, like where the heck are you going, kid? But she'd spotted her friend Lucy."

"Let me guess. The cute single dad's daughter? He is cute, right?"

"So cute," she said on a sigh. "Anyway, yes, it was them. So we kind of hung out together all day. Never made it over to the trees."

"Are you guys going to see each other again?"

"That's the thing, I don't know. We didn't make any plans. He didn't even get my number. So obviously, I'm doubting that he even likes me."

"What's wrong with him?"

"I don't know. He seems very reserved. Not shy, but like he's... careful. Does that make sense?"

"It does."

"We also got interrupted when we were saying goodbye. Another one of the school moms showed up. She's very much not single, but she acts like it." She rolled her eyes. "She flirts with him every time they're around each other. It's so gross."

"Oh my gosh, I think I know who you're talking about. Is she the one who gives off mean girl vibes?"

She nodded. "That's probably her."

"Well, that sucks. Hopefully, you'll see each other at drop-off, and he'll ask you out."

"I hope so, too. At least, I think I do. I don't exactly trust my taste in men."

"Come on, you were seventeen last time. Who has good judgment then?"

"I guess. I just don't want to get my hopes up."

I didn't blame her. I didn't want her to get her hopes up, either. Not that I was opposed to her dating someone. But if he hurt her, I'd have to plan a murder.

"Don't stress about it. You'll see him this week, and I bet he asks you out."

She smiled. "Thanks. If he does, you can watch her, right?"

"Obviously. Just not Tuesday. I might have a thing."

"What thing?"

I hesitated. I wasn't going to lie to my sister, but I knew Jensen needed me to be discreet. I'd wait and tell her the whole story—every detail—when it was over. Then I'd only be keeping it from her for a little while, and only because it was necessary to get the job done.

Besides, it wouldn't have been the first time one of us kept a secret from the other. We were close, but we didn't share everything.

"Work thing. For the strike."

She made a face. "Yuck."

"Yeah, it's fine."

A happy Annabel shriek carried through the window.

"What is she doing out there?" I asked.

"I don't know." Nina got up and went to the window. "Oh... my... You have to come see this."

"Why? What's going on?"

"Just look."

I stood and joined her by the window. And I couldn't believe what I saw.

Annabel was having a snowball fight. With Jensen Lakes.

He had his back to a small tree—it didn't provide much cover—while he packed snow in his hands. Annabel threw a snowball that crumbled when it landed about a foot away from him. Then she ducked behind her blue plastic sled, using it as a shield.

Jensen threw his snowball and clearly missed on purpose. It hit the side of the house with a splat.

"Missed!" Annabel yelled and laughed.

Holding her sled in front of her, she crept closer. Jensen didn't bother standing behind the tree. He watched her come, a bewildered smile on his face.

"You know I can see you." He leaned down and scooped up another handful of snow.

She laughed again.

"All right. You asked for it." He threw the snowball at her sled.

With another shriek, she let it drop and grabbed snow in

both hands. Jensen pretended to be stuck to the ground as if his feet had frozen in place, while she made a snowball.

"Oh no!" he said, half laughing. "She's going to get me."

When Annabel tossed the snowball at him, he twisted so it tagged him on the shoulder. Grabbing his arm, he cried out as if in pain and toppled to the ground.

"I wouldn't have pegged him as a kid person," Nina said. "But he's been really sweet to her."

I gazed at him as Annabel ran over to see if he was okay. He tossed a little bit of snow in the air. It wasn't enough to hit her, just made her laugh.

That smile of his was so... genuine. It wasn't the cocky smirk or self-assured grin I'd seen before. It was just a smile—a man having fun with a little kid. It was strangely wholesome.

And unbelievably sexy.

Blinking away my daze, I realized I hadn't replied to Nina. "Yeah, he's full of surprises."

"You should have gone out with him."

I stepped away from the window. "Still no."

"Okay," she said, her tone skeptical.

I turned and went to the kitchen, hoping that would end the conversation.

Yes, Jensen Lakes was handsome beyond reason. And seeing him be sweet with Annabel did terrible things to my ovaries. But I couldn't start indulging in feelings for a man I'd just met—a man who was never going to stay.

I couldn't take that risk.

CHAPTER 10
Natalie

A buzz of anticipation made my stomach tingle and my heart race. Jensen had actually scored tickets to the Snowflake Ball, which meant we were on.

Fortunately, I'd been able to dig a black cocktail dress out of the depths of my closet. Even more fortunately, it still fit.

I paused in front of the mirror in my bathroom. Was that me? I hardly recognized the woman in the reflection. No dark circles, nice makeup, red lipstick. The sleeveless sheath dress hugged my curves, and my hair was up in a simple but pretty style that left my neck and shoulders bare.

That woman looked nothing like the sleep-deprived hot mess in scrubs with a bedraggled ponytail I was used to seeing.

Jensen Lakes was certainly an interesting side story in the usual monotony of my life.

Annabel had dance that afternoon, saving me the need to explain my outfit or sneak out of the house without being seen. I might have to sneak in when I got home, but I'd cross that bridge when it came.

There was a knock on the door, so I grabbed the little

clutch I couldn't remember ever using and went downstairs to answer it.

I'd seen Jensen morph from sophisticated in a suit to charming in a flannel and jeans. But nothing could have prepared me for Jensen Lakes in a tux.

It fit him perfectly, the sleek lines hinting at the toned body underneath. But it wasn't the tux, it was the way he wore it—comfortable and confident, as if he could network with the rich and powerful before blowing up a building and making a daring escape by helicopter, all without getting his tux dirty.

Looking at him made me wonder if he had ever blown up a building. Or made a daring escape by helicopter. It wouldn't have surprised me.

His eyes swept up and down, and the corner of his mouth lifted. "Darling, you look absolutely gorgeous."

My cheeks warmed, and I ran my hands down my hips. "I've had this dress forever. I can't even remember the last time I wore it. It's amazing it even fits."

He met my gaze. "Don't do that."

"Do what?"

"Deflect my compliment. I mean it. You look good enough to eat. Don't try to explain it away."

Hesitating, I pressed my lips together. "All right. Thank you."

"Much better. Shall we?"

I grabbed a trench coat I also hadn't worn in ages, and Jensen helped me slip it on. His proximity made my skin prickle. And how did he smell so good? I couldn't have named the scent if I'd tried, but it woke up my hormones and made them take notice.

We left and went to his car. He opened the passenger door, and I got another whiff of him as I got in. It was hard not to imagine what it would be like to get closer—to feel the warmth of his body pressed against mine, that masculine scent surrounding me.

He got in, and I resisted the urge to fan myself. This was getting ridiculous. We weren't on a date. We had a job to do.

"This should be a date," he said, turning on the engine.

"What? No. It's not a date. It's a… mission."

He grinned. "Indeed. But we should behave as if we're on a date."

"Oh, for cover. That actually makes sense."

He glanced at me again, and those intense dark eyes smoldered. "Don't worry. I'll behave."

The flush of heat crept from my cheeks and raced downward to burst between my legs. That man could probably give a woman an orgasm from across the room.

When we arrived at the Grand Peak Hotel, he parked in the outer lot, far from the entrance. I didn't mind walking, but it seemed like an odd choice. What if we had to make a quick getaway?

Besides, Jensen seemed like a valet parking sort of guy.

Before I could ask any questions, he reached into his pocket and pulled out a small black case. He opened it and handed me what looked like a very small earbud.

"What's this?" I asked.

"We'll be able to hear and talk to each other through these."

Pinching it between my thumb and forefinger, I held it up. "It's so tiny."

"Strictly speaking, we're not supposed to have these."

"Where did you get them?"

"The less you know, the better. It fits right into your ear."

I pushed it in, and although I could feel it, it was surprisingly comfortable. "Am I going to be able to get it out?"

"Shouldn't be a problem. And they're almost invisible."

He put one in his ear, and he was right. It was almost totally hidden.

"Can you hear me through the earpiece?" he asked.

His voice was soft in my ear. "Yes. Can you hear me?"

He smiled. "I can, and I daresay I'm going to enjoy having your voice in my ear tonight."

"What's the plan?"

"I don't suppose there's much need for an elaborate cover story. You're my beautiful date, and we're here to have a good time. Once we get in, we'll wander a bit, see what—and who—we see. When I have a feel for the room, we'll probably split up. Make conversation and get names."

"Okay. I can do that."

"And remember, Julian Myers is a possibility, and I certainly want to get a look at him if he's there. But anyone could be involved."

"In other words, be on the lookout for anything suspicious."

"Absolutely anything. You never know where the smallest hint will lead."

He backed out of the parking spot and drove around to the front of the hotel. He got out and held up a hand so the attendant wouldn't open my door for me. As he came around the front, I shrugged my coat off, deciding it would be easier to leave it in the car.

Opening the door, he offered his hand. I took it and noticed it wasn't smooth like his tux. Even with his gentle touch, I could feel his strength, and his skin was calloused.

Full of surprises.

The intensity of his gaze as I stood sent a pleasant shiver down my spine, and I hoped he couldn't hear my heart racing in his earpiece.

He offered me his arm, and I slipped my hand in the crook of his elbow as we walked inside.

The lobby was decked out in a beautiful array of lights and decorations. A huge tree stood in the center, covered in red and green ornaments and white lights. A sign pointed to the Snowflake Ball in the ballroom.

"We're going to cause a stir when we walk in," Jensen said, pitching his voice low so I could hear him through the earpiece.

"What do you mean?"

"I'm going to attract their attention on purpose. I want every person in that room to want to talk to me or be seen with me."

"How are you going to do that?"

"You'll see. It's all part of the game. Just play along."

I took a deep breath as we entered.

The entire room seemed to sparkle with twinkling lights. At least a dozen Christmas trees decorated the perimeter, and lit snowflakes dangled from the ceiling. Icy-blue linens and silver centerpieces adorned the tables. And a pianist in a white suit played Christmas music on a shiny grand piano.

Heads turned the moment we walked in. The man beside me seemed to morph into someone else. I couldn't explain how he did it—how the subtle shift in the way he moved had such a dramatic effect. But suddenly, nearly everyone was looking at him.

Some eyed him with interest or curiosity. Others gaped openly, their eyes wide and mouths hanging open. Women licked their lips, men furrowed their brows, and whispers swept through the room.

"Wow, you weren't kidding," I said.

He flexed his bicep, subtly squeezing my hand, and kept strolling into the ballroom. A server brought a tray of champagne. Jensen handed a glass to me before taking one for himself.

Watching the crowd, I sipped my drink. Most men wore

dark tuxes, and several had opted for white or silver bow ties. The women, however, seemed to have all known something I didn't—the dress code.

Every woman—at least that I could see—wore pale blue, silver, or white. Apparently, it was expected to dress to the snowflake theme.

"I'm wearing the wrong color," I whispered.

"No, you're not." Jensen sipped his champagne.

"Yes, I am. They're all wearing winter colors."

He turned and met my eyes. "You look amazing. I wouldn't have it any other way."

His gaze flicked to my mouth, and for a second, I thought he might lean in and kiss me. My lips parted, and my heart raced. What would I do if he did?

Kiss him back and enjoy every second of it—that's what I'd do.

But he didn't. His eyes lifted, and he moved his hand to the small of my back.

He approached a man with salt-and-pepper hair and said good evening. The way the other man's back straightened and his chest lifted made it obvious he was pleased to be the first to garner Jensen's attention.

I played the part of arm candy for a while as Jensen worked the room, moving from person to person. He'd introduce himself, obviously to get the other person's name, and engage in small talk before offering a nod and moving on.

His ability to make it all seem so natural was impressive. He held eye contact in such a way that everyone he talked to probably felt—for a moment, at least—like the only other person in the room. And no one seemed to suspect he was anything other than a guest.

After a while, he glanced at me with a look that seemed to say, *go ahead.* With a little thrill running through me, I moved away and set my empty champagne glass on a table.

"Just talk to a few people," Jensen said softly in my ear. "Make it natural."

A pair of women probably in their sixties stood nearby, and although they were talking, they didn't seem too engrossed in conversation. Smiling, I made eye contact and complimented their dresses.

It took a minute of chatting with them to get used to tuning out Jensen's conversation heard through the earpiece and concentrate on the people in front of me. But as I moved around the room, introducing myself and greeting people, I found it easier to focus, letting his voice pass in the background.

I glanced back at him. Several young women surrounded him, and he was clearly enjoying the attention. Jealousy flared hot, and I had to stop myself from glaring daggers at them.

As if he could feel me looking, his eyes flicked toward me. He lifted his drink to his lips and spoke just before taking a sip. "Easy, darling. It's all part of the game."

Apparently, I hadn't stopped the glare.

With a sigh, I went to get another glass of champagne from one of the servers.

"There's a bloke near the piano who's been watching you," Jensen said. "Turn right and wander. Look lost."

I did what he suggested and turned, then looked around while I took a few more steps. I caught sight of the man he meant. Jensen was right. He was watching me. Was that Julian? He looked familiar, but I couldn't place him. If he lived in town, he might have been someone I saw out and about. Or maybe he'd been a patient. That was always a possibility. I tended to know who people were based on their medical emergencies.

"Do you notice what's different about him?" Jensen asked.

"No."

"That Brioni suit he's wearing probably cost ten grand."

"Seriously? I didn't know they made suits that expensive."

"It certainly makes a statement. Especially here. He wants to show off."

The man in the expensive suit moved toward me, and I glanced away, pretending not to notice. My heart raced with excitement. What if that was him, and I was about to break Jensen's case wide open?

"Natalie?" an all-too-familiar voice said behind me.

A surge of dread swept through me as I turned to find Tucker Ross—my ex-boyfriend.

He was dressed in a tux with a silver bow tie. A few years before, I'd made the mistake of falling for his charm and breaking my rule to never date coworkers. And it had gone spectacularly wrong.

"Hi." My tone was a bit chilly, but I couldn't help it. "I didn't know you'd be here."

"I didn't know you'd be here, either."

"It was kind of a last-minute thing."

He looked me up and down with an appreciative smile. "You look great."

I drew my eyebrows in. What was he doing? "Thanks."

"I haven't seen you in a while. How have you been?"

Haven't seen me in a while? More like you stopped noting my existence. We work in the same hospital, dumbass. "Fine."

"It's kind of strange that you're here," he continued. "I've been thinking about you lately."

"Who is this?" Jensen asked in my ear, his tone suspicious.

I wasn't sure how to answer him with Tucker standing there, so I took a sip of my champagne. "Why would you be thinking about me?"

Glancing away, he shrugged. "You know, life goes on, but we can always look back and wonder if we did the right thing."

"Oh god, he's your ex, isn't he?" Jensen asked.

"Mm-hmm," I said.

"You were always one of the good ones, Natalie," Tucker said.

"One of the good ones? What does that even mean?" I asked.

"I'm just saying, you've been on my mind. And seeing you tonight feels like fate."

"Fate? We weren't pulled apart by the tides of history. You cheated on me with one of the medical assistants at work."

"All right, he's done," Jensen said in my ear.

"I know, I made a mistake. But you can't hold that against me forever."

"Actually, I can."

When he opened his mouth to say something else, Jensen's hand slipped around my waist, and he drew me close.

"There you are, darling. So sorry to leave you alone."

Looking up, I met his eyes. He gazed at me with an intensity that made my breath catch and my heart flutter.

"It's all right," I said.

He turned slightly to look at Tucker. "And you were just leaving."

It wasn't a question or a mere suggestion. Tucker's eyes narrowed in anger, and for a second, I wondered if things would get ugly. Jensen moved his hand from my waist and took a subtle step in front of me. But his body remained relaxed. If he was worried, it didn't show.

With a glare, Tucker turned and stalked off.

To my surprise, he didn't head for the bar or find someone else to talk to. He walked right out of the ballroom as if Jensen's command held the force of law.

"Well, that was unpleasant." Jensen softly brushed a strand of hair off my face. "Are you all right?"

His gentle touch made my skin tingle. "Yes, I'm fine."

"Good."

The piano player began a new song—"White Christmas"—and it seemed to catch Jensen's attention. He slipped his arm around my waist, drawing me closer, and took my hand in his. With his eyes on mine, he shifted his feet, and we started to dance.

"Would you like me to ruin his life?" he asked. "After all, it's almost Christmas, and I hardly know what to get you."

I laughed. "Tempting, but no. Guys like him usually make themselves miserable enough."

"The bloody prick actually cheated on you?"

"Yep. One minute he was all, let me whisk you away and give you an amazing new life. And the next, he was bending some MA over his desk."

Jensen shot a glare toward the door. "Now I really want to ruin him."

We swayed to the music and the feel of his body against mine was intoxicating. I'd wondered what it would be like to be this close to him, and it was headier than I'd imagined. I wanted to lean into his neck and get lost in his scent. Maybe even let my lips graze that tempting stubble on his jaw.

His eyes moving around the room as he turned me in a slow circle brought me back to reality.

We're here for a job, Natalie. A job.

But with his hand splayed on my lower back, pressing me to him, it was hard to keep my head.

CHAPTER 11

Jensen

Natalie felt good in my arms. No one else was dancing, but I hardly cared. I liked the feel of my hand on her lower back, her body close to mine. I wanted to press her against me. Lean in and trail my mouth down her bare neck.

But we had a job to do.

More importantly, I didn't think she'd let me.

If I was going to have a shot at getting my mouth on this woman—which I certainly wanted—it would be on her terms. Not mine.

For a second, I thought about making a move. Putting my mouth next to her ear and asking if I could kiss her. If she said yes, the teasing could begin. I'd softly kiss her neck. Nothing outrageous or obscene. Certainly nothing that would make her uncomfortable or draw undue attention.

But enough to tempt her. Make her want more.

Except I caught sight of the man in the Brioni suit heading for the doors to leave. And I still wanted to talk to him. Something about him made my instincts light up. Maybe he wasn't our guy, but our infiltration would be a failure if I didn't have the chance to get a feel for him.

"Be right back, darling," I whispered.

With a nod, Natalie stepped away. I didn't like letting her go, but I didn't have much choice.

On my way toward the man, I deftly picked up a full glass of champagne from a server's tray. I wouldn't have time for subtlety. Striding fast, as if I were in a hurry, I pulled out my phone and pretended to focus on the screen.

Nothing to see. Just a man on his way out the door to take a phone call.

I got close and collided into him, making sure to tip my hand so my drink spilled all over that very nice bespoke suit.

"Fuck." I stepped back and lifted my hands as he whirled around to face me. "So sorry, mate."

I watched his face carefully. He looked surprised. And who wouldn't if they'd just had a full glass of champagne dumped on them? But there was something else. Alarm. And possibly... recognition?

Did he know who I was?

That was an interesting twist.

"Can I get you a napkin?" I asked. "Actually, no. Let me pay to have it cleaned."

He glanced over his shoulder—most of the champagne had gone down his back. "That's all right. I'll take care of it."

"No, I insist. It's entirely my fault." I slipped my phone back into my pocket and held out my hand. "Jensen Lakes."

He hesitated before taking my hand. "Julian Myers."

It was him. Imported statues and a very expensive Italian suit. It didn't prove anything, but it certainly made him a person of interest. Especially because he kept looking at me like our interaction concerned him.

Who are you, really? A new player?

I was going to find out.

"Are you sure I can't make it up to you?" I asked.

"No. It's fine. Accidents happen."

"That's generous of you." I tipped my chin and stepped back. "Cheers."

His eyes flicked behind me, to something—or someone—in the ballroom, before he turned and walked out through the double doors.

"Well, now we know who Julian Myers is," Natalie said in my ear. "Should we follow him?"

"No. I want to have Maple look into him. Plus, I think he suspects me. I don't want to show my cards just yet."

I set my empty champagne glass on a side table and spotted Natalie as she came toward me. It gave me the chance to enjoy the sight of her in that dress. The way her hips swayed made my blood run hot.

What was it about this woman?

"Have I mentioned you look delicious?" I asked as she approached.

She shook her head. "Stop."

"If you think that's just a line, it's not. I could eat you for dessert."

"Jensen," she scolded.

"All right. I'll behave. For now." I winked at her.

She glanced away, but I didn't miss the playful smile on her lips.

Getting under her skin was fun.

"What do we do now?" she asked.

"I think our work here is done." I offered my arm. "Shall we?"

She tucked her hand in the crook of my elbow, and I led her outside. I took the liberty of putting an arm around her to keep her warm while we waited for the valet to bring the car around. She didn't resist.

On the way back to her house, we chatted about our

evening. What people wore, who was from Tilikum versus the neighboring towns, our theories about Julian. I did wonder why he'd been watching Natalie. According to her, they didn't know each other. Was it simply the magnetic draw of a beautiful woman who'd caught his eye?

Hard to say. But I didn't blame him. I couldn't stop looking at her, either.

I pulled up outside the house and parked.

"You don't have to walk me to my door," she said. "I'm kind of hoping to sneak in without Nina noticing. I don't want to have to explain the dress."

"Fair enough."

"I'll see you tomorrow?"

I nodded. "Looking forward to it."

Her smile sent a tendril of warmth through my chest. We both got out, and I went up the stairs to my flat. When I got to the top, I glanced down, making sure she got inside before I went in.

On a whim, I sent her a text.

Me: You were magnificent tonight.

Natalie: I hardly did anything.

Me: I disagree. You played your part perfectly. And I quite enjoyed having you as a partner.

Natalie: Thanks.

Picturing the curl of her lips as she smiled sent another surge of warmth spreading through me. It was an odd feeling—not something I was accustomed to. The heat of attraction was familiar enough, and I felt that too. But I experienced a different type of pleasure when I was with Natalie. One I couldn't name.

I checked the time. Maple wouldn't be up for a while yet, so I decided to get some sleep. I'd ring her first thing in the morning.

❋

My phone woke me. I sat up, instantly alert, and answered.

"Bloody hell, Maple, what time zone do you think I'm in?"

"Sorry. It's important."

"I was going to ring you first thing anyway. I have someone I need you to look into."

"Jensen—"

"Bloke by the name of Julian Myers. It might be a dead end, but my instincts tell me something is off. He could be a new player."

"Jensen," she said, her voice insistent.

"What?"

"We just got word that Archer Prince resurfaced."

That got my attention. I'd been hunting Archer Prince for years. He was a prolific black market art and antiquities dealer, and we'd connected him to a number of major heists. Catching him had become something of an obsession. But he'd gone completely dark in the past year as if he'd fallen off the face of the earth. Maple and I had begun to wonder if he were dead.

"Where?"

"We're not sure where he is now, although some reports say Cairo. But it's not where he is now that's important. It's where he's going to be. We have reliable intelligence that he has a deal planned."

"What sort of deal?"

"We think he's going to sell the *Storm on the Sea of Galilee*."

"You're fucking joking."

"I'm fucking not."

The *Storm on the Sea of Galilee* was a Rembrandt and one of the most famous pieces of stolen art in modern history. Two thieves posing as police officers had stolen it and a dozen other paintings from a museum in Boston more than three decades earlier. The crime had never been solved.

Had Archer been behind one of the biggest art heists in decades?

"Do we know he has it?" I asked.

"We don't have confirmation. But Jensen, this is your chance. Our informant tells us he's heading to Paris to close the deal."

I rose and paced across the room, my body thrumming with excited energy. "Paris. That's an interesting choice. Who's the buyer?"

"We're not certain, but there are several possibilities. Known entities. We'll have a plane waiting for you in Seattle. You need to get there as quickly as possible."

I stopped in my tracks. "I'm in the middle of a job."

"We'll handle it. You need to leave now. There's a winter storm headed your way."

I hesitated. Why was I hesitating? The choice was clear.

"All right."

"Good. I'll send over what we have. You can review it en route."

The call ended. I went over to the window and looked out at Natalie's house. It was dark.

"Fuck."

But what did it have to do with her? I wasn't in Tilikum for Natalie. I was there to do a job. And sometimes, in my line of work, plans changed. As for our agreement, I'd be sure she was compensated even if I wasn't the one to bring in the necklace.

I packed my things but decided to leave my Tilikum attire in my car. I wouldn't need flannels or jeans where I was headed. After a quick sweep through the flat to ensure I hadn't forgotten anything, I was ready. Maple texted to ask if I was on the road yet. I needed to get ahead of the weather.

I couldn't just leave without a word to Natalie. But I didn't want to wake her—or her sister and niece. After a moment's hesitation, I settled on a note. I wrote it out quickly, folded it, and left it on the kitchen counter.

Trying to ignore the odd sense of dread in the pit of my stomach, I carried my things out to my car and left.

CHAPTER 12
Natalie

You were magnificent tonight.

The fact that I woke up with Jensen's text running through my mind should have been a warning sign. Instead, I lingered on thoughts of the evening with him as I got up, showered, and dressed for the day.

His gentle touch on the small of my back as we worked the room. The intensity in his eyes. The display of protectiveness when he'd so effectively confronted my ex. Dancing to soft music with my body pressed against his.

Had it all been a dream?

I'd spent my evening in a cocktail dress, infiltrating an event I was pretty sure we'd crashed without tickets. Jensen had been vague about how he'd get tickets, and it occurred to me as I thought back on the evening, we hadn't stopped to check in. We'd walked right in as if we belonged, and no one had questioned us.

The heady thrill had been intoxicating. Even more than our strategic eavesdropping at the Timberbeast.

But was it the excitement of the hunt that had swept

through me? Or Jensen's touch, presence, and undeniable allure?

I paused and took a deep breath before going downstairs. I was in big trouble. Because I was starting to think things I shouldn't have been thinking. And giving in to feeling things I shouldn't have been feeling.

Attraction, yes. I couldn't lie to myself and claim I wasn't physically attracted to him. But it was more than that. It was as if he were awakening something in me I hadn't realized I'd lost.

He made me feel alive.

I went downstairs, wondering what he had in store for us next. Was Julian involved in the heist? Or were we following a lead that was destined to go cold?

What was our next move?

Nina was bustling in the kitchen while Annabel ate her breakfast at the table.

"Morning," I said.

"Morning." Nina didn't look up from what she was doing.

"Hi, Auntie Natalie," Annabel said around a mouthful of food.

"Don't talk with your mouth full, honey," Nina said.

She made a show of swallowing. "Sorry."

"Do you need help?" I asked. "You look stressed."

"I'm fine. I just woke up late, and now I'm frazzled. Thank goodness for dry shampoo, am I right?"

"One of modernity's great inventions. Do you want me to take Annabel to school?"

"No, that's okay." She closed Annabel's lunch bag. "I've got it."

"Are you sure?"

"Yeah, it's not a problem. Hurry up, kiddo. We need to get going."

I glanced at the time. They weren't in danger of being late. Then I realized why she was in such a rush. She was hoping to see the cute single dad at drop-off. Maybe even spend a few minutes alone with him before the other parents arrived.

"Are you done?" I asked Annabel, and she nodded. "Go get your shoes and coat. It's time to go."

Nina glanced at me with a smile. I winked at her. I had her back.

"Oh, before I forget, the apartment needs to be cleaned and turned over," she said. "Mystery man had to leave. I can help when I get home."

It felt like I'd just been punched in the stomach. The air rushed from my lungs, and it took me a second to get a word out.

"He left?"

"Yeah, there's a message from his assistant. Something came up, and he had to check out."

I poured a cup of coffee so I had an excuse to turn away from her. She didn't know about the time I'd spent with Jensen. For all she knew, I'd hardly spoken to him since I'd refused his dinner invitation. And I wasn't ready to tell her what had actually been going on. My feelings were a mess.

Not even a mess—it was like an emotion bomb had gone off.

"I'll take care of it," I said. "I think I should also stop by the picket line at the hospital for a while. Do my part."

"The weather is supposed to suck today. More snow."

"I'll bundle up."

"Sorry, I don't need to tell you to wear a coat. I'm just used to my little penguin child." She raised her voice. "Annabel? Are you ready to go?"

"Yes, Mommy!"

"Okay, I'm off. I have clients until four, so are you good to pick her up?"

"Yep, not a problem."

"Thanks. Stay warm out there."

"I will. Drive careful."

Annabel shouted goodbye before she and her mom left. I stayed in the kitchen for a long moment, frozen by the shock of Jensen's abrupt departure.

I should have known better. Of course he left. He was never going to stay.

But he hadn't even said goodbye.

Groaning in frustration at myself, I put my coffee down and went to grab my boots out of the closet. He'd gone in the middle of the night—or early in the morning—so he'd obviously been in a hurry. What did I expect? A romantic goodbye on the front step while delicate flakes of snow drifted around us?

This was real life. It had felt like a fantasy for a minute, but it was never meant to last.

I went out into the falling snow and trudged across to the apartment. Inside, it was almost pristine—the rumpled bed and used towels the only signs anyone had been there.

That and the hint of his scent left behind in the air. Knowing I shouldn't, I picked up one of the pillows and inhaled. Groaning, I tossed it back on the bed. Why did he have to smell so good?

Although I was trying to convince myself that I wasn't upset, being in the apartment—especially with it so empty—was not putting me in a good mood. There was still cleaning to be done to get it ready for the next guest, but I'd come back and do it later.

On my way out, I glanced into the kitchen. Something was on the counter. I was going to leave it—it was probably nothing—but a spark of curiosity flared to life.

It was a folded piece of paper with my name on the outside.

With my heart beating hard, I opened it and read.

Darling Natalie,

It is with deepest regret that I depart. Please accept my apologies for not saying goodbye in person. I've been called away to another job, and time is of the essence.

Jensen

Well, there it was. He was off, probably to chase another thief. A bigger one, if I had to guess.

It was better this way. The longer he stayed, the more tangled my emotions would have become. I'd have started daydreaming about a different life—a life I could never have.

A life that had him in it.

Which was as stupid as it was impossible. It had been fun, but he and I were from different worlds. And no matter what I'd imagined in his eyes, he'd only been doing his job. The touches, the looks, the dancing—none of it had anything to do with me.

I took the note with me and went back to the house. The picket line sounded like an even better way to spend my morning. That was my life. I was a nurse who happened to be on strike, and I needed to show my support. Eventually—hopefully soon—I'd be back to vampire hours, treating patients in the emergency department.

Nina had been right, I did need to bundle up. I put on some layers—a wool long-sleeve shirt, sweater, jeans, and thick socks. I donned my snow boots, then grabbed my knit hat, scarf, gloves, and winter coat, and headed out.

I gave the driveway a quick once-over with the snow shovel before I left so too much wouldn't accumulate. I'd been dreaming of an electric snowblower for years, but it never made it into the budget.

If only Santa Claus were real. I'd work pretty hard to stay on the nice list if a snow blower was the prize.

The side roads were bound to be slick, but the main roads would be plowed regularly. And I'd grown up in the mountains—I was used to driving in the snow. I left my house, taking it easy around the corners, and headed toward the hospital.

I'd tucked Jensen's note in my purse. Maybe that had been a mistake. I was so aware of its presence in my car as if I carried a piece of him with me. Was I feeling the sharp pang of regret, or did I just miss him?

I couldn't miss him. I barely knew him.

But I did. In the short time we'd known each other, he'd opened a piece of my heart that I'd firmly closed. And no matter how many times I told myself none of it had been real, the emptiness he'd left behind still ached.

I turned on my Christmas playlist, hoping for a cheerful distraction. "White Christmas" came on.

Because of course the song we'd danced to would shuffle in first.

I slowed to a stop at an intersection, then pulled forward to turn left. And out of nowhere, all hell broke loose.

Another car slid down the hill opposite me. I saw it coming—going too fast and clearly not stopping. But there was nothing I could do. My car was in control, but theirs was not, and I didn't have time to get out of the way.

And in the split second before the other car slammed into

me, I wondered with horror what Nina and Annabel were going to do if I died.

CHAPTER 13
Jensen

Frustrated and brooding, I drove toward Seattle.

Snow chased me until I crossed the mountain pass. Then it turned to rain. Heavy gray clouds hung low, and my windshield wipers had a hard time keeping up.

The oppressive sky matched my mood.

Maple called to update me on the intel we'd gathered. The information was solid. There was a good chance I'd be able to intercept Archer in Paris before he did the deal. I'd be a fucking hero—the one to take down a notorious criminal and restore a priceless work of art to its rightful place.

It made sense to go. I followed jobs wherever they took me, all around the world. And I'd been waiting for the right opportunity to confront Archer Prince for years.

So why did I want to turn around?

Torrents of rain beat down on my car as the elevation descended on the west side of the mountains. Endless forests of evergreen trees stretched out on either side of the freeway and tendrils of fog snaked through their branches.

Soon, I'd be on a plane, heading east. I wondered if the

flight path would take me over Tilikum—and the missing necklace.

"What is wrong with you?" I asked aloud. "A chance to recover a famous Rembrandt, and you're worried about a fucking necklace?"

But it wasn't the necklace. True, I didn't like leaving a job unfinished. But it wasn't the job that made me want to turn around and drive straight back to Tilikum.

It was Natalie.

Why? Why was I so preoccupied with a woman? That had never happened to me before. Relationships were transient things—fine while they were mutually satisfying, but for a man like me, never meant to last. I'd known Natalie for a matter of days, and she was so deeply lodged in my head, I couldn't stop thinking about her.

Not just my head. My chest—in a place that felt suspiciously like my heart.

There was only one thing to do. Call my sister. Nora and I had a lot in common. She'd also resisted long-term relationships for years. Yet she was married—to a hulking tattoo artist, no less—and living a blissful family life with her teenage stepdaughter and new baby.

How had she done it? How had she known?

One way to find out.

"Hi, Jensen," she said, her voice lifting like it was almost a question.

"Nora, I need your help."

"I'll try. What's going on?"

I let out a breath. "God, where do I begin? I've been in a small town pursuing a business opportunity. In so doing, I met a woman."

"And this is news because...?"

"I don't know. That's why I'm calling."

"Okay, go on."

"Another business opportunity arose, and I had to leave town abruptly. I'm on my way to Seattle to catch a flight to Paris."

"What did you do? Sneak out of her bed and leave her behind?"

"No, nothing like that. I've not been in her bed. Or had her in mine."

"Oh."

"Don't sound so surprised. I'm not nearly the manwhore you think I am."

She laughed. "Sure, Jensen."

"Anyway, that's not the point."

"What is the point? If you didn't sneak away, I'm assuming you told her why you had to leave. And if the problem is you want to see her again, can't you just go back when the new business deal is finished?"

"Yes. That's a very reasonable way of seeing it."

"You don't sound convinced."

"That's the problem. I'm not, and I don't know why."

"Uh-oh."

"What?"

I could almost hear her smiling. "You like her."

"Of course I like her. Isn't that obvious?"

"No, I mean you *really* like her. You don't want to leave because you're going to miss her. You probably already do."

"I like her, and I'll miss her," I mused aloud. "Which is why I'm strangely reluctant to leave town?"

"Tell me this. You said you had to leave abruptly. Did you say goodbye?"

"I didn't want to wake her, so I left a note."

"Then call her, dummy. You're probably worried that you left her with hurt feelings. We'll gloss over how surprising that is. I didn't know you had feelings, let alone cared about them in others."

"Am I such a monster?"

She laughed again. "No. But have you ever cared about a woman enough to call me for advice?"

"No. This is a first."

"See? Just call her. And be honest. Tell her you're sorry you had to leave. You're going to miss her and will come see her again as soon as you can."

"You're brilliant," I said. "Thank you."

"You're welcome," she said, her tone cheerful. "And Jensen?"

"Yes?"

"Thanks for calling."

"Give my niece kisses."

"I will."

I ended the call and pondered what she'd said as I kept driving. I liked Natalie and I was going to miss her. That was why I felt like I had a hole in my chest. And Nora was right. Once I had the business in Paris under wraps, I could go back. There was no reason not to.

Unfortunately, it wasn't likely this job would be an in-and-out situation. It was entirely possible I was about to embark on a game of cat and mouse that could span the globe. I'd been close to him before, and he'd always eluded me.

A call came through, and I had the fleeting hope that it was Natalie. But it wasn't—it was Maple.

"Go ahead," I answered.

"Just wanted to update you that we're sending Deacon to Tilikum. Can you put him in touch with your asset there so he can pick up where you left off?"

What was that scorching heat burning through my veins? Grinding my teeth, I gripped the steering wheel, irrationally angry. I'd felt the same way when I'd listened to Natalie's ex-boyfriend at the Snowflake Ball. I hadn't understood it then, either. Why was I so filled with rage?

Wait. Was that jealousy?

"Jensen?" she asked.

"Sorry." I loosened my grip on the steering wheel. "Yes, I can do that."

"Good. I'll let him know."

I didn't reply, and a second later, she ended the call.

Shock reverberated through me. Jealous? I'd never been jealous of another man in my life. I always had what they wanted, not the other way around.

But the thought of Deacon waltzing into Tilikum and laying his eyes on Natalie—my Natalie—had me seeing red.

Or was it green?

"Bloody prick," I grumbled.

Maybe I just needed to take Nora's advice and call Natalie. Hearing her voice would put me at ease. I brought up her number and called.

No answer.

That was odd. She couldn't be at work; they were on strike. Had she left her phone elsewhere and hadn't heard it?

Her voicemail greeting ended, and I decided to leave a message.

"Natalie, darling..." I wasn't sure what else to say. "Give me a call when you get this."

Well, that had been bloody stupid. Jealous and tongue-tied? What the hell was wrong with me?

And why hadn't Natalie answered?

I kept driving, resisting the urge to ring her again. I was being irrational. Natalie wasn't the type to be glued to her phone. The fact that she hadn't answered didn't mean anything.

Except what if it did? What if she'd ignored my call

because she was angry with me? What if I had hurt her feelings?

How could I live with myself?

Feeling like I had a concrete block crushing my chest, I gave in and tried her number again. Still no answer. Fortunately, I stopped before I made an even bigger fool of myself on her voicemail.

My sudden fear of having hurt her was not a good reason to abandon what might turn out to be a once-in-a-lifetime opportunity. But my fear of having hurt her combined with concern over why she wasn't answering *and* mind-numbing jealousy?

That did it.

I rang Maple.

"Yes?" she answered.

"I have to go back."

Heedless of the legality of the maneuver, I cut across an open spot in the median and flew onto the eastbound freeway.

"I'm sorry, what?" she asked.

"I have to go back to Tilikum. I can't go to Paris."

"What on earth are you talking about?"

"My reputation is at stake. I can't leave a job unfinished. If word got out that I abandoned a client for a bigger fish, what would people think? We're trusted because we're reliable."

It wasn't a bad argument. I almost believed it myself.

Maple sputtered for a second. "Well... Perhaps... I guess you have a point, although Deacon is very good."

My lip curled with distaste at hearing his name. Not good enough to work with my Natalie. "Still. I have to see this through."

"Are you sure? You realize what you're giving up?"

"I know exactly what I'm doing."

She took a deep breath. "All right. I'll get things worked out on my end."

"Brilliant. I'll touch base when I'm back in Tilikum." I ended the call.

A weight lifted from my shoulders as I sped through the rain. Did I know exactly what I was doing?

Despite what I'd said to Maple, not in the slightest.

CHAPTER 14

Jensen

T he drive back to Tilikum was frustratingly slow. Snow fell steadily and traffic moved at a glacial pace.

I tried ringing Natalie one more time. Still no answer. Tempting as it was to keep calling, a dozen missed calls from me would send the wrong message. I wasn't stalking her. I was simply concerned.

Finally, I turned past the Welcome to Tilikum sign. Snow clung to it, making it largely unreadable, but the large Christmas squirrel still beamed his odd greeting at the passing cars.

The town was rather idyllic, decked out for Christmas and covered in snow. I passed snowmen being built in the park and the large tree sparkled with lights.

But where was Natalie?

Tension rippled through me as I made it to her street. I pulled up to her house and didn't see her car. Did she park in the garage? She hadn't before, but maybe she'd done so to get it out of the snow.

I parked and got out, heedless of the new-fallen snow on

the walk up to the front door. I knocked, then stepped back and waited.

No answer.

I knocked again, harder. Still nothing. It was a weekday, which probably meant school for Annabel, and I assumed Natalie's sister would be at work. But where would Natalie be?

Turning, I was about to return to my car—if I had to drive all over town, I was going to find her—when a thought hit me. What if Julian was behind the heist, and I hadn't imagined his look of recognition? Everyone in that room, including him, had seen me with Natalie.

Had he done something to her?

Fuck.

After a glance around, I pulled a lock-picking tool out of my wallet. Standard issue. It only took me a second to unlock the door. I eased it open and went inside.

"Natalie?"

All was quiet. Small shoes and, child-size socks, and gloves were scattered around the entryway. I took a few steps inside and came upon what looked like signs of a struggle. A box of Christmas ornaments had been knocked over and lights trailed over the coffee table and onto the floor.

"Natalie, are you home?"

Still no answer, so I rushed around the house. A chair was tipped over in the dining room and a collection of ginger-bread family pillows seemed to have been thrown down the stairs.

What had happened there?

I raced upstairs, but the bedrooms and bathrooms were empty. No sign of Natalie or her family. The little girl's room looked like a fight had broken out. Discarded clothes and toys were everywhere.

Bloody hell, had he gotten to all of them?

Another stairway off the kitchen led to a finished basement. Large fans hummed loudly, but it was empty.

Trying to stay calm and think it through, I returned to my car. She could have been out running errands or doing whatever she usually did when she wasn't at work. I needed to eliminate the other obvious possibilities.

Work. She'd said they were on strike, but that could mean a picket line. I brought up the hospital on my GPS and headed across town.

It was easy to find—as hospitals generally are—and sure enough, a small group of men and women bundled up against the cold stood outside, holding up signs. I slowed as I approached, narrowing my eyes as I looked for Natalie.

I didn't see her, so I stopped and lowered the passenger side window. A woman in a red-and-green stocking cap leaned closer.

"Hi," she said. "If you're looking for the emergency department, it's open. Just follow the signs."

"Actually, I'm looking for Natalie Thatcher. Do you know her?"

"Yeah, of course I know Natalie. But I haven't seen her today."

"Could she have been here earlier?"

"I don't know." She straightened and tapped the person next to her. "Have you seen Natalie?"

He shook his head, and the first woman leaned down again. "I thought she was coming today, but I don't think she's been here yet."

"Thank you." I gave her a polite nod and raised the window.

Fuck. Again.

I kept going and headed back toward town. If I had to circle through every street, I was going to find her.

My sense of panic rising, I rang Maple.

"Go ahead," she answered.

"I can't find Natalie."

"Your asset?"

I bit back a sharp reply. She wasn't just a fucking asset. "I'm back in town, but I don't know where she is."

"Is there a reason to be concerned?"

"Yes," I said, my voice vehement. "I left her a bloody note instead of saying goodbye. What if I hurt her feelings?"

"I'm sorry, what?"

I knew I wasn't making sense, but it was too late for that. Somewhere along the way, I'd lost my damn mind. Recalibrating, I offered Maple something more relevant to her helping me find Natalie. "We encountered a possible suspect last night. He might have done something to her."

"That makes more sense than hurt feelings. Who is he, and why do you think he took her?"

"Julian Myers. And fuck if I know. I don't know what game he's playing."

"Jensen, I'm not hearing a lot of rationality in your voice at the moment. Are you ill?"

I growled in frustration. "No. I just need to find her."

"All right. I assume you checked her house."

"She wasn't there. And it was a mess. Signs of struggle everywhere."

"Okay. Is she at work?"

"She's a nurse, and they're on strike. I just checked the picket line."

"Do you know anything else about her schedule or routine?"

I pinched the bridge of my nose. "Not really."

"Did you call the hospital?"

"I told you, she's on strike."

"No. To see if she's a patient. If something happened to her, she could be there."

"What the fuck is wrong with me?" I glanced around. I was the only vehicle in sight, so I did a U-turn in the middle of the street. My tires slid as I went around, but I managed to straighten out. "Why didn't I think of that?"

"I'm not really sure what you're thinking."

"I'll update you later." Without waiting for Maple to reply, I ended the call.

Following the signs to the emergency department, I passed the picket line again—searching for her among her coworkers one more time—and parked outside. Snow kept falling as I got out, and I held the lapels of my coat together as I ran inside.

A woman in blue scrubs looked up from the front desk as I approached. "Do you need to be seen?"

"Is Natalie Thatcher here?"

"Are you a family member or friend?"

"Friend."

"I can't give out any specific medical information, but she is here being treated, yes."

I put a hand on my chest. A mix of relief and renewed alarm filled me. "I need to see her."

"Just give me a minute. I'll find out if she can have visitors." She stood and disappeared into the back.

I paced around the waiting room, clenching my fists, rage burning hot in my veins. What had he done to her? I'd make him pay. I was going to tear him limb from limb.

He had no idea who he was messing with.

"Sir?" The woman was back. She pushed a clipboard across the counter. "If you'll sign in here, I can take you to see her."

Grumbling at the delay, I signed in. She disappeared again, and a moment later, a large automatic door swung open, and she gestured for me to come through.

My heart raced, my body thrumming with urgency. The woman brought me to a room, and I braced myself for the worst. What would I find behind that curtain? Bruises? Broken bones? Was she conscious?

I was going to fucking kill him.

When I stepped around the curtain, relief almost made my legs buckle. Natalie was there, sitting up in bed—alive.

And then she did the most remarkable thing. She smiled at me. And my heart cracked wide open in my chest.

CHAPTER 15
Natalie

In a day already filled with shocking events—no one expects to get sideswiped, even when the roads are icy—nothing could have surprised me more than seeing Jensen Lakes appear in the emergency department.

He paused just inside the curtain and stared at me, his expression filled with raw emotion. No cocky smirk. No intense eye contact. He let out a long breath, and his shoulders dropped as if a wave of relief washed over him.

I opened my mouth to answer what I thought would be his first question—are you all right—but he didn't say a word. With a look of determination, he came over to my bedside, cupped my face, and pressed his lips to mine.

I'd been wrong. Something *could* surprise me more than his appearance. His kiss.

The shock of his lips on mine was so astonishing that at first, I stiffened. But a heartbeat later, my eyes fluttered closed, my lips softened, and I melted.

His mouth was warm and inviting, working magic on mine while my mind went blank. He teased my lips apart, brushing them with his tongue. I opened for him, and he took the kiss deeper—still gentle, but with a passion that sucked the air from my lungs and made my entire body tremble.

He didn't stop devouring me. It was as if he couldn't get enough. As if I were oxygen and he needed me to live. Our tongues tangled, velvety soft. Deep to shallow, then deep again. Heat surged through me, and I gripped his arms, hanging on for dear life while he consumed me.

Eventually, he pulled back and rested his forehead against mine. My head swam with euphoria, and my swollen lips tingled. We held there for a long moment, noses brushing, breathing together.

And I knew one thing with utter certainty—Jensen Lakes had just ruined me.

Never in my life had I been kissed like that. So passionately. So thoroughly. Every kiss I'd ever experienced had been nothing compared to what he'd just done to me.

I was never going to be the same.

"What happened to you?" he whispered, and the concern —maybe even fear—in his voice almost undid me. "Who did this?"

"Just some tourist. The road was icy, and he couldn't stop."

"What?" Still cupping my cheeks, he pulled back slightly, and his eyes roved over my face. "A car accident?"

I nodded. "I'm okay. Just banged up. They brought me in as a precaution."

Smiling slightly, he shook his head and lowered his hands. "Bloody hell. I thought it was Julian."

"What?"

"I tried to call, but you didn't answer. And when I went to your house, not only were you not home, there were signs of struggle everywhere."

"Signs of struggle? What are you talking about?"

"Christmas lights strewn about, and a dining chair was knocked over. Chaos everywhere."

I laughed. "Jensen, I live with a single mother and an energetic six-year-old. That's just what our house looks like." Pausing, I drew my eyebrows in. "Wait, how did you see all that?"

He glanced away. "I broke in."

"You what?"

Meeting my eyes, he touched my cheek. "I guess I lost my mind for a minute. I was worried about you."

I gazed at him, not sure what to think.

He leaned in to kiss me again, and I reveled in the roughness of his stubble and the softness of his lips. Moving my hands around the back of his neck, I slid my fingers through his hair. He tilted his head and slanted his mouth to cover mine more fully, and a low groan rose in his throat.

I was in so much trouble.

He pulled away, and reluctantly, I let him go. Of course, I was not only in the emergency department but I was also in my workplace. Getting caught making out—even though I was there as a patient—was probably not in my best interest.

"Who's the fucker who hit you?" he asked. "Do you need me to ruin him?"

"No. I'm sure he has enough problems."

"What about you?" He brushed my hair back. "You said banged up. What's wrong? Can you walk?"

"Yes, I can walk." I bent my knees to demonstrate. "Nothing's broken. Just bruising, and I'll be sore for a while."

"Are they holding you hostage, or are you free to go?"

"I haven't been discharged yet. I'm sure the covering nurses are just behind, what with the strike and everything." I paused, absently tracing my finger over the back of his hand. "I'm so glad you're here. I wasn't sure how I was going to get home."

"Don't worry, darling."

A fresh wave of dismay washed over me, and I pressed my palm to my forehead. "My car is probably totaled. And I'm supposed to pick up Annabel from school. Nina's at work, and I don't know what happened to my phone. It must be in my car, but I don't even know where that is."

"It's all right." His voice was soft but firm with confidence. "I'm here now."

"I know, but none of this is your problem."

"I needed a partner." He gave me a soft kiss. "That goes both ways. You don't have to handle this alone."

My lips parted, and I stared at him as tears stung my eyes. I did not want to cry in front of him, but it had been a hard day.

"Thank you," I said and dabbed the corners of my eyes. "Sorry. Today has been a lot."

He kissed me again. How did that feel so natural? It was as if suddenly there was nothing more normal in the world than Jensen kissing me.

I decided not to think too deeply about that. I had enough on my plate. For the moment, I'd simply enjoy it.

Enjoy him.

"Are you hooked up to anything?" He glanced around the bed and peeked beneath the blanket.

"No. I just have to wait for my discharge paperwork."

He rolled his eyes. "I hate paperwork. Let's be on our way."

I laughed. "Jensen, I work here. I can't walk out without being discharged."

"Fine." He stood. "Who do I need to talk to?"

"No, just wait." I took his hand and tugged on it, nudging him to sit. "She'll get to it as soon as she can."

He lowered himself onto the edge of the bed again. "Are we in danger of being late for Annabel?"

I checked the clock on the wall. "No, she doesn't get out of school for another hour."

"And you're sure you're all right? No internal bleeding or anything?"

"I'm sure. If I were bleeding internally, I'd have a lot more pain, especially in my abdomen. Plus weakness, dizziness, rapid bruising or swelling at the impact site, cold clammy skin, and nausea and vomiting."

"I suppose you do know what to look for."

I nodded and glanced around the room. "I've actually never been a patient here. It's weird. I think this is the room where we treated the guy who'd nailed his hand to a two-by-four a few weeks ago. He didn't want to pull out the nail himself, so he sawed off the end of the board and brought it with him."

"You mean he came in with a nail through his hand, still attached to the wood?"

"Yep."

"Well, good on him for thinking on his feet."

"That's what I thought. We were able to get it out and it didn't do any permanent damage."

The nurse came around the curtain and thankfully, she had my discharge paperwork. No one likes having to spend time in emergency, but I felt especially awkward, considering my coworkers were all outside picketing.

Once she left, Jensen stood. I was in a hospital gown and my clothes had been set aside, so I hesitated, clutching the blanket that covered me.

"I need to get dressed," I said.

The corners of his lips turned up in a wicked grin. "Go ahead."

"The first time you see me naked is not going to be here."

His smile grew, and his tongue slid across his lower lip. "Is that an invitation to see you naked later?"

"I don't know," I said decisively. "I haven't decided about you yet."

"All right." That smile was going to kill me. "What about dinner, then? Have I convinced you of that?"

He turned up the heat, his dark eyes smoldering with suggestion. But I wasn't giving in that easily, no matter what his kiss had done to me.

"How about this? You can come to dinner at my house. With Nina and Annabel there."

"I'd love to," he answered without hesitation.

"And it will probably be pizza."

"I love American pizza."

"On paper plates."

"If you're trying to talk me out of it, you're failing miserably. Can we also wear pajamas?"

"Don't threaten me with a good time. I love a pajama pizza party."

"Are you up for it tonight? Or should you rest?"

"I think I can rest while having pizza. Even with you there."

"Brilliant. It's a date."

"All right. A date." I looked him up and down. "Do you own pajamas?"

"No, I sleep naked."

I laughed.

"Can I find them at the... what was it?" he asked. "Farm store?"

"Knowing them, they probably have some. But you could try a few other places."

"Easy enough. I'll be properly attired. And I'll pick up the pizza."

I smiled. "Thank you. Now turn around so I can change."

He put his back to me, and to his credit, he didn't peek—not even to tease me. Bending over hurt, and when he knelt to help me with my shoes, I almost swooned to the floor. He looked up at me with that sexy grin, making my cheeks flush and my spine tingle.

That man. I didn't know what he was doing to me or what it all meant. But whatever was happening between us, wherever it was going to lead, I was powerless to stop it.

CHAPTER 16

Natalie

J ensen and I picked up Annabel from school, and she was oddly lacking in questions as to why our Airbnb guest was driving. I waited outside his car so she'd see me, and when she climbed in the back seat and sat in the extra booster seat we'd picked up at home, she simply said hi and launched into a story about the puppy book her teacher had read.

He took us home, and although he planned to leave again —after all, he needed pajamas—he insisted on walking us in. He closed the front door behind us as Annabel dumped her things in the entry and ran straight for the kitchen. I didn't have the energy to worry about her mess, so I stepped over her discarded backpack and shoes.

She'd already removed the day's link in her Christmas chain, but she counted them again, finishing with a twirl.

"Getting closer," I said.

"Can I have a snack?" she asked.

"Something you can get yourself, okay? Auntie Natalie is tired."

She grabbed a string cheese out of the fridge and brought

it over to Jensen. With a curious glance at me, he took it and opened it for her.

"Thank you," she said, then marched into the living room.

"She's awfully excited about that," Jensen said, gesturing to Annabel's Christmas countdown.

"Oh yeah. She can't wait for Christmas."

He brushed a lock of hair from my face. "Are you sure you're all right?"

"Sore and tired, but yes."

"You're not going to develop a life-threatening complication and die if I leave you alone, are you?"

I laughed a little. "No. I can be left alone, and I'm pretty sure I won't die."

"All right." He slipped his hands around my waist and gently drew me against him. "Does this hurt?"

The new level of contact left me slightly breathless, and I draped my arms over his shoulders. "No. Doesn't hurt."

"Good." He leaned down and kissed me, then pulled away and licked his lips. "I rather enjoy doing that."

"Does that surprise you?"

"Not in the least." He kissed me again. "You taste delicious."

"Shh," I said, trying not to laugh, and lowered my voice to a whisper. "I don't want Annabel to hear things like that."

He put his mouth next to my ear, and his deep voice sent pleasant tingles down my spine. "I'll be quiet. But you do taste good." He kissed my neck and grazed my earlobe with his teeth.

Suppressing a giggle, I scrunched my shoulders. It sent a stab of pain across my back, and my body stiffened. "Ow."

"Sorry." He pulled away, and concern crossed his features. "Did I hurt you?"

"No, I just moved wrong."

"I'll be more careful." He pressed his lips to my forehead. "I should go. I have a date tonight."

"Sounds exciting."

"I'm looking forward to it."

That made me smile. "Me too."

"The rest of you better be in pajamas when I get back," he said.

"Who's wearing pajamas?" Annabel asked.

Startled by her voice, I stepped away from Jensen.

Without missing a beat, he turned around. "We are. For dinner. Your auntie Natalie invited me over for pizza in pajamas. Is that all right with you?"

Her eyes widened. "I get to come too?"

"Only if you're dressed properly."

"Can we wear Christmas pajamas?" she asked, the pitch of her voice rising with every word.

"Seems like the obvious choice," he said.

Throwing her arms overhead, she jumped up and down. "Yay! Pizza and Christmas jammies!"

"I think you just made her week," I said.

"I do love to make the women in my life happy." He seemed to want to step in for a kiss, but Annabel was still dancing around the kitchen, so instead, he winked.

He crouched down, and Annabel stopped jumping.

"Miss Annabel, I have a very important job for you."

She nodded, her expression turning serious.

"Your auntie hasn't had the best day. Could you take good care of her for me while I'm gone?"

Her nodding turned vigorous. "Okay, Mr. Jensen. I'll take care of her."

"There's a good girl."

He stood, gave me another brain-melting smile, and left.

It took me a second to come out of my daze, but the pain

from being banged around inside a moving car did it. I needed to sit down.

Fortunately, Annabel was used to entertaining herself. She grabbed a box of crayons and a coloring book and took them to the table. I carefully lowered myself onto the couch and did my best to get comfortable.

Nina got home soon after. The door opened, and she walked in already talking. "Is your phone off? I tried to call you to see if you wanted me to pick up dinner, but you didn't answer. Hi, Annabel. How was your day?"

"Good," Annabel answered without looking up from her coloring. "I got to ride in Mr. Jensen's car, and we're having pizza, and can I put my Christmas pajamas on now?"

Nina paused with her coat half off and her mouth open. "That was a lot in one sentence."

I chimed in. "It's a long story, but it starts with, 'Don't worry. As you can see, I'm okay.'"

"Obviously not a good story if it starts like that. What happened?"

"I got sideswiped, and they took me in. Minor injuries. I'm bruised and sore. The car... I don't even know yet. I lost my phone, too. It's probably in the car. And then..." I hesitated, not sure how to explain the next part. "Jensen came to the hospital, and we picked up Annabel. I invited him over for pizza, and somehow, it became pizza in pajamas."

Nina gaped at me, her coat still hanging from one arm. "I have so many questions."

"I know."

We both looked at Annabel, then back at each other.

"Hey, kiddo," Nina said, "you can go put on your Christmas pajamas now. That's a great idea."

A crayon rolled onto the floor as she scrambled off the chair. A second later, she was thundering up the stairs.

Nina slid her arm from her coat and let it drop to the floor

—like mother, like daughter—then rushed over to me. She sat on the floor next to the couch. "What is going on? Car accident? Jensen?"

"Yeah, it's a lot. I was heading for the picket line this morning, and some dude couldn't stop on the ice and slid into me. It sucked, but I'm okay. I was taken to emergency to get checked out, just as a precaution. And then, out of nowhere, Jensen showed up at the hospital."

Her brow furrowed. "You're going to need to explain that because I am obviously missing something."

"You're missing the part where I've secretly been hanging out with him."

Eyes widening, she gasped. "What? Why didn't you tell me?"

"I was going to. I just hadn't yet."

"So the wickedly hot guy has a heart," she said. "Who knew? But why are we having pizza?"

"I invited him over for dinner but said it would probably be pizza. Because, you know, car accident. And somehow, that turned into wearing pajamas. I don't know. A lot happened and my head is kind of fuzzy."

"Do you have a concussion?"

"No. But he kissed me, and it basically melted my brain."

She squealed. "This is the best early Christmas ever."

"Don't get the wrong idea. It's not like he's going to stay."

"I'm not even worried about that. You never do anything for yourself. Have some fun. Make out with the hot guy and let him kiss all your boo-boos."

I pressed the heels of my hands over my eyes. "Stop. And what are we going to do about my car?"

"Nope. We're not discussing that tonight. Your date is coming over, and we're going to have a nice evening."

"But—"

"It's not like you have to drive to work. See? Bright side."

I let out a long breath. "Okay, I'll face reality tomorrow."

"Good. Do you need help getting up? We need to get you ready for your date."

"It's barely a date. I invited him to have pizza with my sister and niece."

"I know, and the fact that he accepted makes me like him." She held out her hands. "And you can still look cute. Even in pajamas."

She helped me to my feet, and we went upstairs to get ready.

❄

The three of us had matching Christmas pajamas from the previous year, but when I dug them out of my dresser, the tags were still attached. I held them up, feeling a sting of sadness. Like usual, I'd worked Christmas Eve, well into Christmas morning. When I'd come home, I must not have bothered with them.

The gray shirt had a festive Christmas tree on the front and red-and-black buffalo-plaid sleeves. The plaid pants were soft and matched the sleeves. I put them on, and for the first time that December, I felt a tiny spark of real holiday excitement.

My problems—and there were many—tried to crowd into my mind. The basement, the furnace, my job, my car. I didn't know if we could afford to get a tree or what I was going to get Annabel for Christmas.

"It's going to be okay," I said quietly to myself. "We'll figure out a way. We always do."

It wasn't in my nature to put my worries out of my mind —I wanted to jump into problem-solving mode—but Nina was right. A very hot man who was the world's best kisser was coming over. I could put real life on hold for one night.

I contemplated dabbing on more makeup and doing something with my hair, but I didn't have the energy. Besides, Jensen had seen me in the hospital, and I certainly hadn't been looking my best. Grateful the airbag hadn't deployed, and my face wasn't bruised, I brushed the tangles out of my hair and put on some lip gloss. It would have to do.

Downstairs, Nina and Annabel were moving the lights and totes filled with decorations so they weren't in the middle of the room. Christmas music played in the background, and Nina had set out paper plates on the dining table.

"Sit down," Nina said, pointing at the couch. "We've got this."

"It looks great in here." Trying not to wince, I sat and tucked my legs under me.

She paused, resting her hands on her hips, and looked around. "No one is going to accuse us of having a pristine house, but at least it no longer looks like a bomb went off."

A knock on the door made all of us freeze. Annabel's eyes lit up with excitement.

"Don't get up," Nina said. "I'll get it."

Annabel scurried over while Nina answered the door.

"Welcome," Nina said, stepping back.

"Hi, Mr. Jensen!" Annabel exclaimed.

He came inside, carrying two large Home Slice Pizza boxes with a grocery bag on top. His onesie pajamas were dark green with red-and-white candy canes. But he hadn't stopped there. He topped it off with a Santa hat.

I was speechless.

"You look like Santa," Annabel said.

"Do you like it?" He handed the pizzas to Nina and took something out of the bag. "I brought one for you."

He helped her put a red-and-white Santa hat on her head. It was a little big, draping low on her forehead.

"Thank you." She spun and rushed to the kitchen. "Mommy, look!"

Jensen grinned at me, and the hat didn't make it any less sexy.

Shaking my head slightly, I laughed. "This is amazing." I gestured up and down. "You definitely understood the assignment."

"I don't do things halfway." He came over to the couch and sat beside me, then produced another Santa hat from his bag. "I brought them for all of us."

Gently, he put the hat on my head and leaned in to brush my lips with a soft kiss.

"Gorgeous," he said. "Very Christmas chic."

Putting my hands beneath my chin, I pretended to pose. "Thank you."

"Stay here. I'll bring your dinner." He pulled a bottle of red wine from the bag. "Would you like a glass?"

"I'd love one. Thanks."

He took the wine into the kitchen, and a moment later, Nina—wearing a Santa hat—set up the pizzas on the dining table. She helped Annabel get a slice while Jensen brought me a plate and a glass of wine.

After dishing up, we all settled in to eat in the living room. Annabel and Nina sat on the floor, using the coffee table. Jensen sat next to me on the couch, and I shifted so he had room to get closer.

Right as we were about to start eating, "White Christmas" began in the background. Jensen glanced at me and winked.

"You seem to be lacking a tree." He gestured at the boxes of lights and ornaments.

"We still need to get one," I said.

"Can we go back to Christmas Village?" Annabel asked.

"Probably," Nina said. "We definitely need a tree. Even just a small one."

"Miss Annabel, how's your pizza?" Jensen asked.

"Good," she said around a mouthful.

"How's yours?" I asked.

"Everything pizza ought to be," he said.

"So Jensen," Nina began, and I widened my eyes, imploring her not to ask too many questions and make things awkward. "Where do you live? In the UK?"

"Seattle, actually," he said. "Most of the time. I do keep a flat in London, but I spend most of my time in the States."

"That's interesting." She met my eyes. "Seattle isn't very far."

"Not at all. My sister lives in the area. And the weather reminds me of home."

"And you are, in fact, single."

"Quite."

"Do any women *think* they're dating you?"

"No."

"Have you ever been married?"

"Nina," I scolded.

Jensen didn't seem bothered. "No, never married."

"Why?"

"Nina," I said, more forcefully.

"It's a valid question," she said.

"It's all right." He gave me a subtle smile, then turned back to my sister. "I suppose I've never seen myself as the settling-down type."

"Hmm." Nina narrowed her eyes a little. "How long are you going to be in town?"

"Will you be here for Christmas?" Annabel asked.

He opened his mouth but closed it again, his brow furrowing as if he needed to consider his answer.

"He has his own family, kiddo. He'll probably be with them on Christmas." I glanced at him. "Although if you're still in town, you're welcome to spend it with us."

He met my eyes and gave me that look again—the one that almost seemed surprised. "I would love to."

"You'll come for Christmas?" Annabel asked.

"Yes, Miss Annabel. I'll come for Christmas."

"Do you promise?"

"I think that's a promise I can keep."

Her expression grew serious. She got up and came around the coffee table to stand in front of him, then thrust her hand toward him with her pinky finger sticking out.

"Do you pinky promise?"

Nina gasped, and I almost stopped him. Pinky promises were solemn in our family, and Annabel would take it as seriously as a blood oath—if she'd known what a blood oath was. Before I could get a word out, he wrapped his finger around hers.

"I pinky promise," he said.

With fingers clasped, they shook on it.

She threw her hands in the air. "This is going to be the best Christmas ever!"

He went back to his pizza and gave me a subtle wink.

And maybe Annabel was right. Maybe it was going to be the best Christmas ever.

CHAPTER 17

Jensen

I was accustomed to wearing a mask. Even slight changes in behavior, body language, and speech patterns could produce the desired effect. Hide who I really was. Conceal my true intentions.

Those masks were easy to slip on and off. Except one.

My real self.

Sitting on the couch with Natalie and her family, dressed in the gaudiest Christmas pajamas I'd been able to find with a Santa Claus hat on my head, I felt more like myself than I had in ages.

We ate pizza until we were stuffed. Watched Annabel put on a little Christmas show, singing "Rudolph the Red-Nosed Reindeer." And played a board game.

A bloody board game. And it was fucking delightful.

When Nina told Annabel it was time to get ready for bed, the crocodile tears commenced. I had a feeling the situation would be easier to manage if I left, so I said goodbye to the small child and asked her to be a good girl for her mum.

Natalie rose from the couch and walked me to the door as Annabel's despondent wails disappeared up the stairs.

"Thank you," Natalie said.

"You're welcome." Leaning down, I pressed my lips to hers, and I realized one of the reasons I felt so at ease. I didn't have an agenda.

Maple had referred to Natalie as an asset, and in a sense, she was. But that had nothing to do with why I'd spent the evening with her. I wasn't trying to get anything from her.

I didn't need to play games.

"Come have a drink with me," I said.

Rubbing her lips together, she searched my face. "I don't know if I should."

"No pressure. I very much enjoy kissing you, but this is not a ploy to get you naked." I brushed her lips with another kiss. "You're safe with me."

She hesitated another moment before answering. "Okay. I'll come over."

I retrieved the rest of the wine while she put on a pair of boots, then we walked through the freshly fallen snow to the flat.

Inside, we took off our shoes. I invited her to sit and brought the wine to the kitchen where I found wineglasses in a cupboard. I poured and brought our drinks to the living room.

"How are you feeling?" I sat next to her on the couch.

She shifted, and a spasm of pain crossed her features. "Like I was hit by a car."

The desire to ease her hurts was almost overwhelming. I still wanted to ruin the idiot who had hit her. But more than that, I wanted to make her feel better.

"What can I do? Do you need ice?"

"No, I'm okay. I iced everything a lot this afternoon." She took a sip of her wine. "Can I ask you something?"

"Of course."

"Why did you have to leave so suddenly?"

"We received intelligence about an art thief I've been chasing for years. There might have been an opportunity to catch him."

"Then why did you come back?"

"I wanted to finish what we started. And call it instinct, but I knew I needed to get back to you." I reached over and caressed her cheek. "I'm sorry I left without saying goodbye."

"It's okay. It all worked out."

One corner of my mouth lifted. "Did you miss me?"

"I was a little busy getting in a car accident." She smiled. "But yes. Kind of."

"Kind of? I'll take that."

"Who's the art thief you've been chasing?"

"His name is Archer Prince. He's been operating for decades. Always manages to elude us."

"Is there a lot of money in this kind of thing?"

"Oh yes, millions. But I have a theory about Archer. I don't think he does it for the money. Maybe he did at first, but now I think he does it for the challenge." I took a drink. "Speaking of thieves, we still have work to do here."

Her eyes lit up. "You're right, we do. I want to know more about Julian."

"As do I. I'd love to get a look inside his house."

"You aren't planning to break in, are you?"

"No. Not yet, at least. Usually, I'd contrive a way to be invited, but I suspect that isn't going to work. It's possible he recognized me."

"You think he knows who you are?"

"I can't be certain. But it's why I thought he might have gotten to you."

She shook her head. "I haven't seen him."

"We'll have to do some reconnaissance."

"Do you mean spy on him?"

I lifted a shoulder in a slight shrug. "Essentially. But only if you're feeling up to it. You need to rest."

"I'll be fine. Although if it involves running to make a quick getaway, I might have regrets."

"We'll see how you feel tomorrow. How's that?"

"Probably smart. Although I don't want to hold you up."

"Don't worry about that. I'm not in a hurry to leave. Besides, I made a certain little girl a promise I'd be here for Christmas."

"About that. The pinky promise is a big deal in our family. Annabel's going to take that very seriously."

"It's a good thing I plan to keep it."

She smiled. "You're very good with kids."

My brow furrowed. "Am I?"

"Yeah, you're so sweet with Annabel. Doesn't it come naturally?"

"Not at all. Until my niece was born, I'd never really been around children."

"Well, it seems very natural. The Santa hats were a nice touch."

I grinned. "I'm glad you approve."

"At the risk of stroking your ego, tonight was probably the best date I've ever been on."

Normally, I would have said something like, *"Of course it was, darling, it was with me."* But the cocky retort died on my lips. It was the strangest thing. Hearing that felt good, but not because I was pleased with myself. I liked that I'd made her happy.

Instead of ruining the moment with a stupid line—or worse, by giving words to the inexplicable feelings trying to work their way to the surface—I put our wineglasses on the coffee table and leaned in to kiss her.

That first kiss in the hospital had awoken a craving—an

insatiable hunger for more. I'd been holding back all evening, but alone in the flat, I could finally indulge.

Careful not to hurt her, I ran my fingers through her hair as my tongue slid into her mouth. She tasted like red wine and smelled like vanilla and sugar—like Christmas cookies. Delicious. I kissed her deep and slow, savoring her like a good meal. Enjoying the softness of her lips and the warm wetness of her mouth tangled with mine.

She shifted closer, and I gently pulled her into my lap, her legs straddling me.

"I don't want to hurt you," I said between kisses.

"I'm fine."

"Are you sure? Show me where it hurts."

"Mostly my back and shoulder on my left side."

I ran my hands up her thighs and caressed her hips. "What about here?"

"I might have some bruising on the left, but it feels okay."

"What if I do this?" Gripping her hips, I slid her up my lap so my hardness nestled between her thighs.

Her answering moan was music to my ears, and when she spoke, her voice was breathy. "That's good."

"You like that?" I moved my hips, rubbing myself against her.

She gasped, and her eyes fluttered closed. Wrapping my hand around the back of her neck, I brought her lips to mine. Her mouth was hungry, and little whimpers rose from her throat as she rocked against me.

Still kissing her, I grabbed her hips and moved her up and down in a steady rhythm. As much as I would have loved to be inside her, I wasn't in a rush. Although as good as she felt, I was a bit concerned she'd make me come in the Christmas pajamas.

How was she doing that to me?

She moaned into my mouth and moved her hands to grip the back of the couch.

"You want to come, don't you?"

"Yes." She stopped, breathing hard. "I don't know if I can. It's not easy for me."

I kissed her neck. "Don't worry, darling. I'm going to take such good care of you."

Gently, I helped her take her clothes off and ditched my pajamas, tossing them on the floor. If she hadn't been hurt, I would have happily done all kinds of dirty things to her on the couch. But she was, so I led her to the bedroom.

I laid her on the bed but didn't climb on top of her and left my underwear on. I propped myself up beside her and softly kissed her neck and shoulder while my hand trailed down her body. She tipped her legs open for me, and I slid my fingers inside.

Her hips jumped, and she arched her back. She was hot—ready to burst.

I put my mouth close to her ear. "That's it, beautiful. Show me what you want."

She moaned as she moved against my hand. I found a rhythm she liked and kept going, relentlessly chasing her orgasm.

I grinned as I felt her start to spasm. She grabbed my hand with hers and closed her eyes, her mouth falling open as her climax overtook her. I watched her come with awe, listening to her breathy moans, feeling her body writhe.

She was so fucking beautiful, I could hardly stand it.

When she finished, I slid my fingers out.

Her eyes fluttered open. "How did you do that?" she asked, still breathing hard.

"I told you I was going to take good care of you." I put my fingers in my mouth and sucked off her taste. "Mm. So good."

"Do you want—"

"Shh. No rush. If you want me inside you, I'll happily oblige. But if that was enough for you, I won't push."

"But you just—"

I touched my finger to her lips. "Darling, that was all for you."

"Are you real?"

One corner of my mouth lifted. "I believe so."

"And if I said I wanted to get dressed, you'd be fine with that?"

My brow furrowed. "Quite honestly, with everything you've been through today, I didn't think you'd be in my bed at all. Watching you come was exquisite."

She smiled. "It felt exquisite. It's been a long time."

Nestling in next to her, I pulled her close, facing me. I did want to be inside her, but she was hurt. And still so guarded. The orgasm I'd given her felt like a triumph.

She reached up and trailed her fingers along my jaw. Leaning in, I kissed her, and the taste of her mouth sent a pulse of heat through my veins.

"Jensen?" she whispered.

"Yes, darling?"

"I want more."

"Are you sure?" I kissed her again. "I don't want to hurt you."

"You won't."

Her yes made my groin ache with need. I rolled off the bed and finished undressing, then got a condom and slid it on.

Back on the bed, I braced myself over her, leaning down to kiss her again. "Tell me how you want me to fuck you. I'd get on top and drive you into the headboard, but I'm worried I'll hurt you."

"What do you want?"

"Just you, Natalie. Any way I can have you."

Sitting up, she smiled and nudged me onto my back. She

straddled me, and it was all I could do not to come as soon as she sank down.

"Fuck," I groaned, taking in the sight of her. "You're so fucking beautiful. I'm the luckiest bloke in the world tonight."

She moved her hips, and I groaned again. With a wicked smile, she stopped, then lifted herself up and sank down slowly. Her head leaned back, and she moaned.

The woman was going to be the death of me.

I grabbed her hips. "Can I hold you here?"

"Yes."

"Brace yourself. I'm done waiting."

She put her hands on my chest. Holding her hips, I thrust up into her. Her eyes rolled back, and her fingers dug into my skin. She was on top, but she gave me control.

I moved harder. Faster. Driving myself in deep as the pressure built. Our bodies moved together, increasingly frantic, and I growled with each thrust, loving every second. She was perfect.

Her moans intensified, and I could feel her start to clench around me. It was too much. I came unglued, exploding inside her with a groan. She threw her head back, rolling her hips against me as we came together.

She slowed as we both came down the other side. I slid my hands through her tousled hair and brought her mouth to mine, kissing her deeply.

"Wow," she breathed.

"How do you feel?"

"Impossibly good."

Grinning, I kissed her again. "Me too."

And that was the strange thing. I did feel impossibly good.

She got up to use the bathroom, and I disposed of the condom, all the while wondering what was happening. I was no stranger to good sex, but that had been something else. Something different.

Something surprising.

Through a small gap in the curtain, I could see the snow falling outside. With no intention of letting her go anywhere for the night, I pulled her back into bed with me. Her body was soft and warm, and as I drifted off to sleep, I had a startling realization.

I wanted to keep her.

CHAPTER 18

Natalie

J ensen's hand slipped around my waist, and he pulled me against him, my back to his front. I was already half awake, and daylight peeked through the gap in the curtains. Nestling into him, I breathed deeply, enjoying the feel of his body pressed against mine.

Had the previous night really happened?

His lips touched my neck in a lazy kiss. "Hello, darling."

"Morning."

"How do you feel?"

I shifted a little, rolling my shoulder. "Sore. But also so good."

He kissed my neck again.

We lay in bed together for a while, and the silence was surprisingly comfortable. My body was languid and relaxed, my mind calm. I knew there were so many things to do—so many problems to solve—but somehow, lying with Jensen while a light snow fell outside chased those worries away. For the moment, at least.

"You feel so good," he said low in my ear. "I could do this all day."

His voice sent a tingle down my spine. "So could I. Although I think biological necessities will get the best of me soon."

"Fair enough." He shifted, propping himself up on his elbow, and I rolled over to face him. His eyes swept up and down, taking me in, and his mouth hooked in a subtle smile. "Fucking gorgeous."

Tracing up his chest, I wrapped my hand around the back of his neck and brought him in for a kiss before moving to get up. "I'll be right back."

"I miss you already."

I went to the bathroom, and when I came out, he did the same.

"Don't you dare put your clothes back on," he said through the closed door. "I'm not done with you yet."

Thank goodness for that.

I got back in bed, and when he emerged, he paused in the doorway. His expression wasn't just hungry, it was ravenous.

He climbed on the bed, tore off the sheet, and licking his lips like he was going to have me for dessert, he buried his face between my legs.

❄

An hour later, I lay sprawled across Jensen's chest, utterly spent. He was a man of many talents, and he'd unleashed them on me. I was warm and sated, and not entirely sure my legs would be of any use if I tried to stand.

He kissed my hair. "I'd make you breakfast, but I don't have any food."

"That's okay. I should probably get up. I need to figure out what's going on with my car. And find my phone. And see if we're still on strike. For all I know, it ended yesterday, and I'm supposed to work tonight."

"I don't like any of that." He tightened his arm around me. "Stay here."

His use of the word *stay* added a sting of pain. Telling myself not to worry about that, I pushed it aside and rolled off him.

"We can't stay in bed all day. Besides, we have a mission to complete."

"That we do. And I couldn't think of a better way to start the day."

Bracing himself over me, he brought his mouth to mine in a luxurious kiss. No longer a kiss of hunger, it was slow and deep. A kiss of contentment, with the promise of more to come.

I got up and dressed while he playfully tried to stop me from putting my clothes back on. After untangling myself from him one last time, I stepped out into the snowy daylight and went over to my house.

Nina stood at the kitchen sink, rinsing out dishes. As soon as I stepped inside, her face lit up with an excited smile. "Oh my god, you're just coming home?" Her voice was just shy of a squeal. "I didn't even realize you weren't in the house. You slept over? Tell me everything."

With a dramatic exhale, I gestured for her to follow me. I went to the living room and sank onto the couch. "I don't even know what's happening."

She sat next to me. "Please tell me he's not all show, and it was the best night of your life."

"Oh, it was absolutely the best night of my life. No contest."

"I'm so happy for you. I knew this was a good idea."

I leaned back against the cushion. "Except he ruined me. I'm surprised I can walk."

"Okay, now you're making me jealous."

"Sorry," I said with a laugh. "Don't worry, you and I both know this isn't going to last."

"You don't know that."

I raised my eyebrows. "Yes, I do. You heard him say he's not the type to settle down."

"Come on, Natalie. You never know."

"It's okay. I know what this is. It's a fling. A Christmas fling. I'll enjoy it while it lasts. It's just like the holidays. There's all this fun and anticipation, and before you know it, it's January, the holidays are over, and we're back to hanging on until spring."

"Is it an older sister trait to be so reasonable? Because I'd be fantasy shopping for a wedding dress."

"Probably." I rubbed my hands up and down my face. "I need to get back to real life."

"Speaking of, I have good news and bad news."

"What's the bad news?"

"Deputy Haven stopped by a little while ago."

"Garrett Haven?"

She nodded. "He's so nice. Anyway, he said your car is probably totaled. He asked his brother to look at it to make sure, and he agrees."

I groaned. "What's the good news?"

"He brought your phone." She pulled it out of her pocket and handed it to me. "He found it on the floor and figured you probably needed it, so he brought it by since he was out on patrol."

"Wow. That was nice of him."

"Told you, super nice guy."

I opened my phone to check my messages. I had missed calls from Jensen, but I knew about those, and there wasn't anything about the strike. As much as I wanted it to end for everyone's sake, I was glad I didn't have to worry about pulling a twelve-hour shift that night.

"Do you have to work today?" I asked.

"No, I'm off today, so I'll pick up Annabel." She paused. "It sure was nice of Jensen to take you to pick her up yesterday."

"I know. He was a lifesaver."

"And the whole pajama thing, with the Santa hats? So cute."

I smiled. "Yeah, it was."

Glancing up like she was thinking, she tapped her lips. "Not really hot-guy-who's-only-a-holiday-fling behavior, though."

I grabbed a throw pillow and smacked her with it. "Stop. Even if this was more than a fling to him, which it isn't, what makes you think I want something else? My life is complicated enough. I don't need a man complicating it more."

"Not all men will complicate your life."

"I seem to be very good at attracting the ones who do."

"Okay, but if I'm right about him, I'm going to say I told you so."

"Don't hold your breath."

She took a deep breath and puffed out her cheeks. I rolled my eyes, and a second later, she let it go.

"Cute, Nina."

With a laugh, she stood. "Do you mind if I shower first? I have lunch plans."

"Go ahead. Wait. Lunch plans with who?"

Smiling, she bit her lip. "Dylan."

"And Dylan is the hot single dad?"

Still smiling, she nodded enthusiastically.

"Nina! He asked you out?"

"Yesterday. I was going to tell you, but a lot was going on."

"I'm so excited for you." I got up and grabbed her hand. "Come on. Let's go pick your outfit."

Hand in hand, we went up the stairs. Her infectious

excitement mingled with the euphoria of my mind-blowing night with Jensen to elevate my mood even more. I helped her choose the perfect lunch-date-with-a-hot-single-dad outfit—a super cute boatneck sweater with jeans and boots—and left her to get ready.

While I was waiting for my turn to shower, I went back to the kitchen to make coffee. My phone buzzed with a text.

Jensen: Operation Julian commencing in one hour.

Me: I'll be ready.

Jensen: Last night was amazing. I hope we can do it again soon.

I couldn't help the smile that crossed my face, nor the tingly butterflies in my stomach. It had been amazing, and the fact that he came right out and said it felt refreshing. For a man who'd called what he did for a living "playing the game," he didn't seem to be playing one with me.

Me: It was amazing for me too.

Jensen: See you soon, darling.

I put my phone down and finished making coffee, buzzing with anticipation for what the day would hold.

CHAPTER 19
Jensen

Natalie looked good enough to eat, even in her winter coat. I could see the memory of our night together flash through her eyes when I picked her up. It was almost as satisfying as the multiple orgasms I'd given her.

We got in my car, and I turned my thoughts to the business at hand.

"Maple did some digging for us," I began. "I have his address, as well as some initial findings."

"What did she find out?"

"On social media, he says he's in finance. He owns a home here and one in the Seattle area. He travels extensively and appears to have an interest in art as well as history. Lots of trips to museums when he's abroad. Obviously, that makes him very interesting to us."

"Wait, finance? That's so weird."

"Why?"

"There's this woman here in town, Louise Haven. She's like an amateur matchmaker. I ran into her not that long ago, and she was trying to talk me into letting her set me up with her friend's grandson. She said he works in finance and doesn't live here full-time. I wonder if that was Julian."

"Certainly possible. If he has a grandmother here, it might explain why he chose Tilikum."

"I did wonder why a guy who can afford a ten-thousand-dollar suit would move here. Although he wouldn't be the first wealthy person to relocate to the mountains. Some do it for the scenery. Others like the small town because they can be a big fish in a small pond."

"I'm interested in how he can afford that ten-thousand-dollar suit. And his imported statues, and whatever other luxuries are making him the subject of town gossip."

"Don't people in finance make good money?"

"Not all of them, and it depends on what 'finance' means. He also might have another, less reputable, source of income."

"Do you think he's the thief? Or the money behind the thief?"

"At this point, he could be either. The right buyer would pay a considerable amount for the necklace. And if that wasn't his first score, perhaps that's why he's strutting around in a Brioni."

"Or maybe he's the one who wanted the necklace, and he had the money to hire someone to get it for him."

"Precisely."

"So what's the plan?"

I smirked at her. "You like plans, don't you?"

"I'm a quintessential oldest child. I can't help it."

"The plan is, we take a look and go from there."

She took a deep breath and let it out through pursed lips. "Okay."

"Nervous?"

"A little."

"You're going to do great."

Julian's house wasn't far outside town. His street was filled with homes elaborately decorated for Christmas, almost as if they'd coordinated with each other. All except his. Not a sign of Christmas anywhere on his property.

What a Scrooge.

The driveway was gated, and an iron fence surrounded the front. Based on the map, it was backed by the river, although the water wasn't visible from the street. I slowed as we passed, noting security cameras at the gate and more mounted on the house.

Interesting.

"Now I see why the guys at the Timberbeast were talking about his statues," Natalie said.

So could I. It wasn't just their size, although they were quite large. They were out of place, their classical Greek style an odd contrast to the rustic luxury of his mansion.

I passed the driveway entrance and pulled over a short distance up the road.

"I don't plan to let you out of my sight, but just in case we get separated." I gave her an earpiece and placed mine in my ear.

"Thanks. This actually makes me feel better. It's like a tiny security blanket."

"You need to tell me now if you're not up for this. You were in an accident yesterday."

"I feel surprisingly good. I'm sore, but I can move around just fine."

I met her eyes. "Are you sure?"

Her lips twitched in a smile. "Jensen, after what you did to me this morning, you should know what I can handle."

I groaned at the memory. "God, that was good. I can't wait to ravage you again."

187

She playfully smacked my arm. "Focus."

"Fine. He has security cameras at the gate and more on the house. We'll have to find a way to get close without being seen."

"He doesn't have armed guards too, does he?"

"Let's hope not."

"I was kidding. Do you think he might?"

"You never know. Nothing surprises me anymore."

Except you, Natalie. You surprise me a great deal.

We got out and I glanced around, taking note of where I'd parked, the curve of the road, and the neighboring houses. They were spaced apart, on large pieces of property. Julian's house wasn't the only one with a gate, but I didn't see any others with obvious cameras. Trees, hedges, and thick landscaping hid most of the other homes from the road, which also meant it was unlikely we'd be seen on any of the neighbors' doorbell cameras.

"The gate is an obstacle I'd rather avoid," I said, scanning the trees surrounding the house. "If the whole property is fenced in, we might be out of luck in terms of getting close. But the back side faces the river. He could be counting on that as a natural barrier, giving us a place to get in."

"Lead the way."

Natalie's wardrobe selections came in handy once again. My blue flannel and jeans, with the coat and boots, were perfect for tromping through the slice of woods next to Julian's property. She was similarly dressed, with a coat over her long-sleeve shirt and jeans, and her hair spilling out beneath her knit hat.

Still delicious, despite the layers.

We darted across the road and picked our way through the accumulated snow beneath the trees. Luckily, more was falling, so it wouldn't take long to obscure our tracks. The biting cold flushed Natalie's cheeks, and I looked forward to warming her up later.

The ground sloped downward toward the river, and rushing water filled the air as we got closer. We emerged onto a rocky bluff. Ice crusted the riverbanks, but the middle still flowed by.

Following the edge, we carefully made our way toward Julian's property. As I'd hoped, it was open on the side of the river—no fence to be seen.

But that didn't mean a lack of security. There would almost certainly be cameras.

We crept closer and crouched behind a pair of trees. I could see where the fence ended. With the way the ground sloped, it wouldn't be easy to get into his yard. It was steep and rocky, and no doubt very slick.

"What do you think?" Natalie whispered. "Can we get closer?"

I glanced down at the glacial river, and my brow furrowed. Sliding down the slope and winding up in the water could be fatal. I would not take that chance with her.

"Not from here. Too steep." I pulled a small pair of binoculars from an inside pocket and looked through them. They automatically adjusted focus, sharpening my view of the house. "He has cameras on the back side as well."

"Can you tell if there are any blind spots?"

I kept looking. "There's no clear approach from here. He's awfully concerned about security."

"Is it just me, or does it seem excessive?"

"Excessive for your average Tilikum resident, probably. He either has something to protect, something to hide, or he's bloody paranoid."

"Maybe all three."

"That would be my guess." I lowered the binoculars and offered them to Natalie. "Do you want to take a look?"

The smile that lit up her face warmed me against the cold. She looked through them, first at the house, then out across the river.

"These are amazing."

"We're not supposed to have them, strictly speaking. Press the side, there, and they'll take photos."

She pressed it and gasped. "So cool."

"Take some of the house, would you? The cameras, back door, windows."

"Oh my gosh, I can see right into his window." She paused. "What is that?"

She handed me the binoculars and I took a second look. One of the ground floor windows opened into a large dining room. The binoculars refocused, zeroing in on the interior. A large painting in an ornate frame hung above a sideboard, with a vase and other decor on display.

"He certainly has interesting taste," I said. "I can't tell from here if those are originals or not. But if they are, they're expensive."

"But did you see the sparkly thing?"

"No." I looked again. That time, a fleck of light caught my eye. I tapped a button to focus on the spot. "What do we have here?"

It wasn't the Emerald Crown. But it was jewelry.

"Julian gets more interesting by the minute," I said. "It looks like a gold brooch with a large green stone—an emerald, if it's real—in a display frame. It's either an antique or made to look like one. Certainly displayed like a treasure. I wonder where he got it."

"All the cameras make more sense."

I lowered the binoculars. "Indeed they do. He certainly seems to be a collector. The question is whether he's also a thief. Or paid for one."

We couldn't do much more from where we were, so I

replaced the binoculars and gestured that we return the way we'd come. Natalie went ahead of me and retraced our steps through the snow. She got closer to the edge than I would have liked, and the hit of adrenaline at the thought of her falling down the slope and into the river made my heart rate rise.

I let out a small breath of relief when we turned back toward the road.

The view through the window had given me a glimpse, but I wasn't satisfied. Ultimately, I needed to get inside the house, but that would require more planning and preparation. Still, I didn't want to leave without getting a better idea of what we were dealing with.

Angling toward the house again, we came to the fence. From that vantage, I could see into the front. The landscaping on the back side of the house was largely natural, with the river as the focal point. But the front was intricate, even in the snow. The outline of lit paths and a large pond were visible.

I took more pictures, noting a small corridor outside the view of the cameras that might get me close to the house. Egress windows indicated a basement—and a possible way inside.

Gesturing for Natalie to follow, I made my way along the fence line. Large snowflakes fell all around us, and I hoped she wasn't too cold. The discomfort of shivering would be made worse by her bruises. I wanted to get her inside sooner rather than later.

"Are you cold?" I asked.

"No. I think the excitement is keeping me warm."

"All right. I just want one more look. Stay behind me, and I'll keep us out of sight of the cameras."

I led us closer to the road but stayed within the confines of the trees. The noise of an approaching car carried through the otherwise quiet morning. We crouched in the accumulating snow, and I pulled out the binoculars.

The gate started to open. It was quiet, probably well maintained, swinging inward with hardly a sound. A Range Rover turned into the driveway.

Expensive suit, expensive house, expensive car. He was certainly consistent.

Natalie placed her hands on my back, as if to steady herself, and the corners of my mouth lifted. My gut told me Julian was our guy, and I was almost disappointed. Once I retrieved the necklace, the job would be done.

I liked working with Natalie. I liked fucking her too, but that was just the cherry on top.

"We should probably get out of here," she whispered. "If he's home, we don't want him to see us sneaking around."

"No, we don't. As soon as we get to the road, we're just a couple out for a walk in the snow."

"Got it."

We rose and crept through the last of the trees. As soon as our feet hit the sidewalk, Natalie fell in step with me. I clasped her hand—just a man with his woman—as we made our way to my car.

"I'd call that a success," I said once we were inside and back on the road, driving away.

"Did we get enough information? We didn't even get in his yard."

"No, but we didn't need to. This confirms most of my suspicions—He's a collector. He has money. And his security is formidable."

"Maybe I should have asked this question sooner, but how exactly does this end?"

"My job is to retrieve the necklace."

"And by that, you mean steal it back."

"In a manner of speaking. I'm being paid to return the piece to its rightful owners."

"Which means you're going to steal it from the thief."

I glanced at her and raised my eyebrows. "No, darling. *We* are going to steal it from the thief."

She bit her bottom lip, and I could see her trying not to smile. She had a thirst for adventure. It made me like her even more.

"Okay, Mr. Lakes," she said. "What's our next move?"

"We need to get inside."

"How?"

"I haven't come up with a solution yet."

We were quiet for a long moment while I drove. I took it slow. I wasn't worried about my ability to drive in the increasingly heavy snow. I knew what I was doing. But it was other people one had to worry about.

"You said before that normally you'd find a way to get an invitation," she said. "You meant make friends with him and get him to invite you over?"

"More or less."

"How would you do that?"

"Find a way to be in the same place and strike up a conversation. Work in something about his interests. Make him feel like we're long-lost friends. But if he's suspicious of me in any way, it won't work."

"Do you think he'd be suspicious of me?"

"Hard to say. He did seem to want to talk to you at the Snowflake Ball. Why?"

"What if I get the invitation?"

A surge of—dare I say it—jealousy ran hot through my veins. An invitation to Julian's house would mean a date.

It was probably a brilliant suggestion. If he'd been planning to speak to her at the Snowflake Ball because he found her attractive, she was already halfway there. And what man wouldn't appreciate her attention?

But Natalie on a date with him? I hated the idea so much I wanted to rip his arms from his shoulders.

"Jensen?"

Realizing I had the steering wheel in a death grip and my teeth were clenched, I tried to relax. "Sorry. I was thinking about how that would work."

"He saw me at the Snowflake Ball with you, so he might have suspicions about me, too. But what if I could convince him we just met. It's not even a lie, we basically did. If I needed to, I could convince him I have no idea what you do. That I was just arm candy. Maybe I'm even furious with you because I thought you were interested in me, but you blew me off."

My brow furrowed. I hated that plan. But she was right, it was a good one.

"I need to think it through."

"Okay. But I really think I can do it. I know all I've done so far is follow you around and do what you tell me. But I bet I could get him to invite me over. And once I was inside…" She trailed off for a moment. "I admit, I'm not sure what I'd do once I was inside."

"Get me in," I said reluctantly. "You'd find a moment to slip out of sight and unlock a door or a window."

"But all those cameras."

"I can deal with them."

From the corner of my eye, I could see her excited smile. "Then let's do it. Jensen, I promise, I can do this. You can trust me."

I did trust her. Whether or not it made any sense, I did. And her plan was solid. Despite my misgivings, I was impressed. She was thinking like I did. Working through the problem to find a creative solution.

But I still hated it.

"We just need to figure out how to put me in his way," she said. "And make sure I look good when it happens."

"That part won't be a problem."

The problem was going to be me. And it wasn't just the

raging jealousy. Could I allow her to walk into danger? I'd need to coordinate with Maple—make sure we knew as much as we could. I didn't want to get into something worse than it seemed. Not when she was the one at risk.

And as for her fake date with another man, when it was over, I'd make sure she knew she was mine.

CHAPTER 20
Jensen

Mine.

The word ran through my mind on repeat as I paced around the flat. Maple had the audacity to be busy—having dinner with her bloody husband. But despite my restless energy, it wasn't an emergency. I could wait.

I needed her to find everything—literally everything—about Julian Myers. If Natalie was going in without me to keep her safe, I couldn't risk a single surprise.

Did he own firearms? Had he ever hired security? Did any of his artistic acquisitions imply an interest in binding, torture, or captivity? Were there any missing women with a connection to him?

She wasn't his. She was mine.

Natalie wasn't mine, strictly speaking. Not outside my bedroom, at least. And why was that a problem? I'd never laid claim to a woman. Why would I? That wasn't how my life worked.

It wasn't how I worked.

Maple finally rang.

"It's about time."

"I'm allowed to eat," she said, not bothering to mask the irritation in her voice.

"Fine, of course you are. Julian Myers is a solid possibility. I need everything we can find on him."

"You have what I dug up already."

"I need more."

"More what? You're the one on the ground. What more do you expect me to find from here?"

"I'm sending you photos. He has a painting in the dining room along with some other art pieces, including what might be an antique brooch on display. I want to know what else he has. What are his tastes? His interests? What else has he acquired?"

"I'll look into it, but I didn't find records of purchases at major auctions."

"If he's working with an art dealer, I want to know who it is."

"I said I'll look into it. What else did you find?"

"Security cameras. More than typical for this area. I can deal with those, so they won't be a problem. But they paint a picture."

"I'm not sure that tracing his art dealer, if he has one, is going to be more valuable than what you can discover there. If you think he's our thief, you need to get in that house."

"I know. But I think he might have recognized me."

"What? How on earth would he know who you are?"

"No bloody idea. I certainly don't know him."

"So what's your plan?"

I pinched the bridge of my nose. "Natalie. She's my plan."

"Sorry?"

"We're going to get her in. She'll get me access from the inside."

"I thought you were using her for information, not as an operative."

"I'm not *using* her for anything," I said through gritted teeth.

She paused. "You need to tell me what's really going on. This doesn't work if you're withholding things from me."

"I'm not withholding anything."

"Why don't I believe that?"

I took a deep breath. "I'm telling you everything you need to know."

"Oh, Jensen," she said, her voice laced with frustration. "I realize your dalliances are none of my concern, but in this case, I have to ask. What do you think you're doing?"

It was a bloody good question. And one for which I didn't have a good answer.

When I didn't respond, she continued. "Is she the reason you didn't go to Paris?"

"No."

"Be honest."

"I thought she was in danger."

"All right." She paused again. "And now you're willing to put her in danger?"

"Believe me, I don't like it. But it's a good plan. He was watching her at the event the other night. He might have spoken to her, but her fucking ex interrupted."

"What?"

"Never mind. The ex isn't important. Although if Natalie lets me, I'd love to ruin his life."

"Focus, Jensen."

"Sorry. You know I'd prefer to handle it myself. I'd become his bloody best friend. Get him to hand me the necklace, even just to show it off. But if he even suspects I'm a danger to him, I'll never get in."

"Or if you did, it would be a trap. And maybe the trap that finally catches you."

"Indeed."

"But if you were at the event with Natalie, surely he saw you together."

"He did. But she'll use that—act ignorant of who I really am and heartbroken after I loved her and left her behind."

"That's likely to work. And not too far from reality, either."

"What's that supposed to mean?"

"I've known you for too long not to be very aware of how you are with women."

I rolled my eyes. "Now you sound like my sister. And you know me too well to believe I'm half the manwhore I pretend to be."

"I didn't say anything about you being a whore. I simply meant your relationships are always fleeting. I'm not judging you for that. I can't fathom you settling down with a woman. Not with your life."

That stuck like a barb in my chest. I rubbed across my sternum as if the wound had been physical.

But she was right.

And that meant Natalie was not mine.

"Jensen?"

Seamlessly, I stepped into a persona. One that didn't let inconvenient feelings get the better of him—who hardly had feelings at all.

"My dalliance, as you say, is irrelevant. The plan is for Natalie to coax him into a dinner invitation at his house. And I'm confident she can pull it off. Once she's inside, all she has to do is unlock a door or a window. It's a risk, but she understands that."

"I have my misgivings, but it's your call. I'll see if I can find anything else that will be helpful."

"Thank you."

I ended the call and dropped my phone on the couch.

Maple's question ran through my mind. What did I think I was doing?

I was simply enjoying the company of a beautiful woman. That sounded so reasonable. So easy. So like me.

I could tell myself she was a temporary diversion. That our night together had been a perk of the job. A mutually desired and mutually satisfying liaison, not meant to last.

But eating pizza with her niece while wearing a Santa hat was not simply enjoying the company of a beautiful woman. Neither was abandoning the chance to catch my longtime nemesis or using a word like mine, whether or not I'd said it aloud.

The problem was, I was getting too close. Crossing an invisible and unspoken line I'd drawn in the sand of my life years ago. That line existed for a reason. Not only to protect her, but to protect myself. I didn't live a life that had room for someone else. So I made sure it was never an option.

A week in Tilikum—a fucking week—and I was in danger of not just crossing that line but erasing it completely.

I couldn't let that happen. It wouldn't be fair to her. And I couldn't let someone in. She'd have the power to destroy me.

A knock on the door broke me from my thoughts. The pain in my chest tried to flare, but I buried it as deep as I could and answered the door.

Natalie smiled. I returned it, but it wasn't real. There was no familiarity in mine. I'd given the same look to dozens of people over the years, and nearly all of them believed it.

She didn't. That woman could see right through me.

"Sorry if you were busy," she said, her smile fading. "We're going to Christmas Village to get a tree, and I thought you might want to come."

Christmas tree shopping with Natalie and her family. Yet another thing that was not me enjoying the company of a beautiful woman. It was over the line.

"I'm afraid not," I said. "I have things I have to see to this afternoon."

"Yeah, of course." Her eyebrows drew in, even as she kept her tone light. "No big deal. I assume we're not going after Julian tonight, so it's fine if I'm gone."

"Right, I won't be needing you tonight. I need time to solidify the plan."

The flash of disappointment that crossed her features dug the barb deeper into my chest like a giant, rusty fishhook.

"I'll leave you to it, then." She turned and started back down the stairs.

I wanted to say something else, but everything fell flat.

Text me when you're back, and I'll ravage you again.

Idiotic. She wasn't a toy I could take out when I wanted and put away when I was finished with her.

Pick out the biggest tree, and I'll pay for it.

Even worse. I couldn't buy her affection. Or her forgiveness.

She reached the bottom of the stairs, and I still stood in the cold air. The snowfall had slowed, but small flakes drifted from the low-hanging clouds.

I wish I were the man who could give you what you need.

It would have been the honest response. But I couldn't make myself say it.

Without looking back at me, she crossed to her house and went inside.

Clutching my chest, I stepped back into the flat and closed the door. What was happening to me? Was I having a heart attack?

I staggered to the bedroom and, with a groan, fell face-first onto the bed.

✳

Half an hour later, I hadn't moved. It was ridiculous. Idiotic. I was lying on the bed like a dramatic child. Like a man who couldn't handle himself.

I was Jensen Lakes. I could handle anything.

Even this.

Pulling myself together, I stood and straightened my shirt. I stepped into the bathroom to use the mirror and fixed my hair. Dressed in a flannel and jeans, I didn't exactly look like myself. Or maybe I looked more like myself than I ever had.

I checked every persona I'd ever used at the door and strode out to my car, calm and confident. I liked Natalie Thatcher. More than I'd ever liked anyone. I was in uncharted territory. But I lived for adventure. And what could be more adventurous than following my heart?

Which meant the line I'd drawn in the sand of my life could go fuck itself.

CHAPTER 21

Natalie

W hy were we wandering around the shops at Christmas Village? It wasn't like we could afford anything.

I stood in one of the small stores, my arms crossed, half glaring at a display tree filled with wooden ornaments. Little trees, chestnuts, squirrels, stockings, bears. Some had red buffalo-plaid bows tied on top. Others had the year or cheerful Christmas greetings.

Happy Holidays! Seasons Greetings! Merry Christmas!

What was so merry about it, anyway?

And why had Nina veered in the direction of the shops instead of going straight to the tree lot?

Christmas Village was cute, I could admit that. It was like walking through the North Pole in a Christmas movie. Lights, wreaths, candy canes, elves peeking out from behind trees. Shops made to look like gingerbread houses. And an endless supply of ornaments, decorations, and every kind of sugary treat imaginable.

But we could barely afford a tree. Why tempt ourselves—

and Annabel—with all the glitter and sparkle and cinnamon and sugar?

"Isn't this cute?" Nina asked, holding up a red-and-white candy cane ornament.

I gave it a half-hearted glance and shrugged. "Sure."

"What's wrong? You look mad. Are you hungry? When was the last time you ate?"

"I'm not hungry."

"Are you sure? You and I both get hangry, and it's not pretty. Let's go get a snack."

Leaning closer, I lowered my voice to a whisper. "With what money? In case you forgot, I'm out of work, and my car is totaled."

"You have insurance."

"But I don't know what it will actually cover. And did you forget the giant fans in the basement? And the fact that our furnace might die at any moment?"

"Wow." She hung the ornament back on the tree. "Someone needs a little more Christmas spirit."

I rolled my eyes. "I don't need Christmas anything. I need to go back to work."

"I know things are tough, but why are you stressing about it right now? At this moment, there's nothing you can do." She glanced around the displays. "Annabel, careful with that."

She was right. I didn't need to be grumpy about our financial situation when I could be enjoying an afternoon with my family.

But it wasn't our financial situation that was bothering me. Not really.

The fact that Jensen had declined my very casual invitation to join us should not have hurt my feelings. We weren't dating. He wasn't my boyfriend. A night of mind-blowing sex did not mean we suddenly had to do everything together.

It was probably better that he'd stayed behind. Not just

because he was obviously busy with something more important. Because my heart was as tangled as a bundle of Christmas tree lights.

His "no" had hurt. And it shouldn't have.

We left the shop and moved on down the path. A few snowflakes drifted down, enough to catch the glimmer of Christmas lights and sparkle in the air. "Sleigh Ride" played in the background, and people wandered, shopped, sipped hot cocoa, and feasted on sugar cookies and gingerbread.

"Where to next?" Nina asked.

"Let's go see Horace!" Annabel exclaimed

"Again? We saw Horace last time we were here. Don't you want to go look at trees?"

"Horace first. Please?"

Nina smiled at her. "Since you asked so nicely."

They walked ahead, hand in hand, and I followed at a slow shuffle. As much as I didn't want to subject Nina and Annabel to my sour mood, I couldn't quite muster the enthusiasm to keep up with them.

One of Christmas Village's main attractions was its reindeer farm. As fascinating—and festive—as the animals were, Annabel had always loved Horace, the guard donkey.

We found him in the large enclosure. Dark brown with a white muzzle, he had big black eyes and, like all donkeys, large teeth. I stayed back from the fence while Nina and Annabel approached.

"Hi, Horace!" Annabel waved.

The donkey brayed, making Annabel laugh. He stomped through the snow and came closer.

Annabel's glee that the donkey had apparently noticed her and was coming to say hello cut through the edges of my bad mood. I even smiled a little, watching her hold still, as if that would tempt him closer.

"Hello, darling."

Gasping, I spun around to come face-to-face with Jensen. "You scared me."

My hurt feelings flared, and I was about to snap at him. But I lifted my eyes to meet his gaze, and his expression was like a warm fire on a cold day. It reminded me of the way he'd looked at the hospital, without quite so much concern.

No cocky grin. No smolder. Just him.

"I'm sorry," he said, without preamble. "When you asked me to come, I was distracted and stressed. I immediately regretted declining your offer, and would love to join you, if you'll still have me."

A part of me still wanted to fire back. To stay angry. Because anger was easier. It was a shield. And maybe if he hadn't been looking down at me with so much vulnerability in his eyes, I would have.

"I was probably more disappointed than I ought to be," I said, my voice quiet. It was hard to admit. "I know we're not..."

He gently caressed my cheek. "I'm not sure what we are. Is that all right to admit?"

Leaning in to his hand, I nodded. "I don't know either."

"Here's what I do know." His thumb caressed my cheek. "I like you. Quite a lot, in fact."

That made me smile. "I like you too."

"So we go from there?"

"Yeah, we go from there."

His eyes flicked toward Nina and Annabel, and one corner of his mouth lifted. Leaning in, he kissed me—soft, but with a brush of his tongue that sent a rush of heat through me.

A chorus of childish squeals pulled me back to reality. Another little girl in a thick winter coat rushed toward Annabel. They collided in an exuberant embrace.

I didn't have to see the parent approaching to know who it was. Nina's face said it all.

It was Dylan, her hot single dad.

He was cute, with dark blond hair peeking out beneath his hat and a nice smile—especially with the way he smiled at my sister.

"Hi," Nina said. "I didn't know you'd be here today."

"You said you might be picking up a tree," Dylan said. "I thought I'd see if you need help."

Jensen met my eyes and gave me a slight nod. He clearly approved of Dylan's move.

"Thank you."

I cleared my throat to grab my sister's attention.

Her cheeks flushed. "Oh. Sorry. Dylan, this is my sister, Natalie, and her, um, friend, Jensen."

I lifted my hand in a wave. "Hi."

Jensen stepped in to shake his hand. "Pleasure."

"Nice to meet you." He gestured to the little girl. "This is my daughter, Lucy. She's in Annabel's class."

"We've heard," I said.

Nina shot me a look.

"We were about to head over to the tree lot," Nina said. "Do you want to join us?"

The last vestiges of my bad mood evaporated when I saw the way Dylan looked at my sister. He smiled like her invitation to walk across Christmas Village to look at trees was the best thing that had ever happened to him.

That man was smitten. And I was there for it.

"Let's do it," Dylan said. "Come on, Lucy Lou Who. We're going to go with Annabel to find a tree."

The girls held hands and skipped ahead while Dylan fell in step beside Nina. Jensen and I walked behind, and I watched with growing anticipation as Dylan almost held Nina's hand.

Then Jensen surprised me by clasping mine.

I glanced up at him as we walked. He squeezed my hand. I

squeezed back. And somehow, it was the most intimate thing he could have done.

We followed the path toward the tree farm, letting Nina and Dylan get ahead of us while they tried to keep up with the girls. Finally, Dylan slipped Nina's hand in his.

"About time," Jensen muttered.

I laughed. "I know, right? Come on, Dylan. She likes you. Make a move."

"I was about to stop them and tell him to quit being so hesitant."

"I'm glad it didn't come to that. They're both single parents, though. They have reason to be cautious."

"Fair enough. He seems like a decent bloke. Do we like him?"

"I don't know him very well, but he seems like a good guy. I think we can like him."

"If he hurts your sister, I'll have to ruin him."

"Not before I do."

He met my eyes, and we nodded once. We understood each other.

Was that what it was like to have a partner? Not just a date, or even a boyfriend, but a companion? Because dating and boyfriends didn't hold much appeal anymore. I'd been burned one too many times. But what if there was something else? A different way a relationship could be.

Would it be possible to have that with Jensen? Or was I kidding myself? Hoping for something that could never be?

I didn't know.

Besides, I was getting ahead of myself. I liked him, and he liked me. For the time being, it was enough.

I knew he'd stay for Christmas. After that? I didn't know what to expect. And maybe for the first time in my life, I was okay with that. No plan. No certainty. Just the possibility of... something.

Maybe even a new adventure.

CHAPTER 22

Jensen

N atalie lay with her head on my shoulder, her arm draped across my bare chest. Morning light filtered through the curtains, and I traced slow circles across her skin while I drifted in sated bliss.

She'd spent the last several nights in my bed, and I wouldn't have had it any other way. I was quickly becoming addicted to her—to her scent, the feel of her skin. To her presence.

That probably should have alarmed me, but it didn't. Nothing had ever felt so right.

I was getting a taste of small-town domestic life and found it surprisingly pleasant. Charming, even. Strolling through Christmas Village, watching Annabel's excitement, picking out a tree. I wouldn't have thought those things would appeal to me. But with Natalie and her little family, they did.

We'd spent an afternoon decorating said tree. It had been so fucking wholesome, with Christmas music playing and the scent of baking cookies in the air. And I'd loved it.

I even decorated the outside of their house. Most of their lights had been defective, so I'd taken the liberty of buying more, largely under Annabel's direction. She'd wanted it to look like a gingerbread house in the snow—multicolored lights on the house and white lights in the yard. Never one to do anything halfway, I'd added candy canes along the driveway and lit gingerbread people in front of the house.

Apparently, I did have some Christmas spirit.

Natalie shifted, letting out a slow breath. With a slight grin, I kissed her hair.

She'd been busy the past several days securing a rental car, dealing with her insurance company, and doing her part on the picket line with her fellow nurses. As much as I wanted to step in and fix everything for her—or at least the things I could— my gut told me to tread lightly. I was in uncharted territory with her, but I was good at reading people. Swooping in with a brand-new car, paying all her bills, and stuffing the space beneath the Christmas tree with an outrageous number of presents might have seemed like the heroic thing to do. And a very Jensen Lakes thing to do. But she was still guarded. I had a feeling she'd take it the wrong way.

I still wanted to do it—all that and more. But how and when were important.

"I feel like I could fall asleep," she said. "You took everything out of me. Again."

I kissed her hair.

She propped herself up and caressed my chest. "I almost don't want to bring this up because part of me wants to drag this out as long as possible. But we probably need to get moving on Julian."

"Hmm, business or pleasure?" I slid my fingers through her hair and brought her in for a lazy kiss.

"I know, I know. But we don't want to miss our chance. What if he has it and he's planning to sell it?"

"Don't worry. I haven't been idle."

We sat up, and as she slipped her tank top back on, I

grabbed my phone from the side table and opened an app. It displayed a map with a series of lines tracing routes through town.

"What's that?" she asked.

"I put a tracker on his car."

She looked at me in surprise. "How did you manage that?"

"It was easy. I followed him until he left his vehicle unattended. It's been recording his movements for the last few days." I pointed at a spot on the map. "He goes to this gym daily, always around the same time."

"Is that red dot where he is now?"

"Yes. He's at home."

"The gym is perfect. I could go and pretend to be there for a workout. I'll find a way to get him to talk to me. Should be a piece of cake."

I still had my misgivings about the plan as a whole, but she was right. Planting her at the gym would work well.

"There's a problem, though," she said.

"What's that?"

"I need to get a membership. And I hate to be blunt, but gyms are not cheap, and I'm not working."

"You won't need a membership."

"I doubt they'll let me work out for free."

"No, but you'll only need to get in once. Don't need a membership for that."

"True, I can probably get a guest pass. But have you ever been through the gym tour and sales pitch cycle? It takes forever. They'll have some big muscly guy or super fit girl show me around and talk about all the different equipment. Then sit me at a desk like I'm there to buy a house or something and try to up-sell me on their personal training and nutrition program. By the time I got my pass, Julian would be long gone."

"Why would you go through all that nonsense?"

"To get in."

"You don't have to do that."

"Okay, but how am I getting in the gym when I don't have a membership or a guest pass?"

"You just walk in."

She looked at me like she had no idea what I was talking about. "You can't just walk in."

"Sure you can."

"Someone at the front desk would stop me."

"That depends on how you handle yourself. If you walk in as if you belong there, and no one could possibly question you, they won't."

"You want me to just walk in like I own the place?"

"Yes."

"I don't know if I can pull that off."

"Why not? You've done it already." My mouth turned up in a smile. "Did you think I had tickets to the Snowflake Ball?"

Her lips parted. "I was wondering about that. I didn't think about it until later, but we didn't check in when we arrived."

"Of course not. People see what they expect to see. If your body language tells them you belong there, they'll believe you. And if not, just pretend you can't hear them and keep walking."

She took a deep breath. "I guess the worst thing they could do is ask me to leave."

"Exactly. And I don't think they will."

"I should probably get dressed. If he goes today, we should be ready."

"You getting dressed is the worst news." I leaned over and kissed her.

"What time does he usually go?"

"Typically around ten."

Biting her bottom lip, she climbed on, her legs straddling me. "Then we have some time."

I groaned. "You dirty girl, you're insatiable."

"Maybe."

"Good. So am I."

❄

True to his routine, Julian left for the gym shortly before ten. Natalie was ready, dressed in a cropped tank top and leggings. Instead of bundling up in her winter coat, she'd put on a hooded sweatshirt. I was concerned she'd be too cold, but she reassured me she was acclimated to the mountain winters and she'd only be going from the car to the building.

A buzz of anticipation pulsed through me as we drove across town. She tracked Julian's route, noting when he arrived at the gym a few minutes ahead of us. By the time we arrived, he was already inside.

I parked on the side of the lot, away from his Range Rover, where I had a clear view through the large windows. I got out the earpieces and handed one to Natalie.

"Take a few deep breaths," I said. "Walk in like a model on a runway. Back straight, chin lifted. It's your gym. It belongs to you, and no one needs to raise a bloody eyebrow about it."

She nodded and inserted her earpiece. "Can you hear me?"

"Loud and clear."

"Okay, so I'll walk in and position myself where he'll notice me. Then I guess see what he does."

"Try to let him come to you. Eye contact is good but keep it coy. A little smile, glance away. Then look again, like you're trying to catch him watching. You're enjoying the attention."

"What if he ignores me?"

"He won't."

She rolled her eyes. "But what if he does? I need to think this through. Actually, I'll just ask him to spot me."

A low growl rolled through my throat. "I don't want him touching you."

"He doesn't have to touch me."

I growled again.

She laughed. "Jensen, I'm trying to get this man to ask me out. Not just ask me out, but invite me to his house. I'm going to have to flirt and be a bit aggressive about it."

"I know. But I don't have to like it."

"I probably shouldn't say this to you, but this possessive thing you're doing is so hot."

I scowled, and my voice had a hint of sarcasm. "I'm glad you're enjoying it."

She leaned across and planted a firm kiss on my lips. "Wish me luck."

"We make our own luck. And you're going to be magnificent."

With a smile, she took another deep breath and got out of the car.

Tension rippled through my back and shoulders as I watched her walk in the front door. This was the least dangerous part of our plan, and my stomach was already in a knot.

And at the same time, I knew she could do it.

A moment later, she whispered to me, "You were right. I walked in, and no one said anything."

"I told you."

"That was a rush. Anyway, I don't see him. Oh wait, there he is. He just came out of the locker room."

"Go get him, darling."

"My heart is beating so fast. He's going over to the weights. He hasn't looked my direction yet."

"Be patient."

"Okay."

I heard movement but no voices. Lifting the binoculars, I took a brief look through the windows. It was difficult to see past the line of cardio equipment, but I located Julian racking weights on a bench. Natalie came into view, moving closer to him, as if she were looking for the dumbbells she needed.

He did a double take.

"I think he saw me," she whispered.

"He did. Relax, darling."

I heard her deep breath, and I checked with the binoculars again. He finished his set and got up, his attention clearly on her.

Lowering the binoculars, I waited, my ears sharp. I could hear the music playing in the background, but not well enough to place the song. Except... was that Christmas music? In the gym?

So very Tilikum.

A male voice made my back straighten.

"Hey. Sorry, I don't mean to bug you while you're working out."

I lifted the binoculars. He'd approached her.

"That's okay," Natalie said. "Do we know each other? You look familiar."

"I don't think we've met." He held out a hand and she took it. "Julian Myers."

"Natalie Thatcher."

"You are Natalie," he said. "I thought you must be."

"How did you know?"

"Sorry, that sounded creepy. My grandma keeps trying to set me up on dates. A couple weeks ago, she started going on and on about, well, you. She showed me a picture. And now I sound creepy again. It was from your social media. My grandma isn't a stalker."

"She must know Louise Haven," Natalie said. "She's the one who always wears a velour tracksuit."

"I think they've been conspiring against us."

"I think you're right."

My back tightened at the flirtatiousness in Natalie's voice. Fucking Julian. What a prick.

"I saw you at the Snowflake Ball," he said. "I was going to introduce myself, but it looked like you were with someone."

Natalie groaned. "That was a very brief, and I mean extremely temporary, mistake."

I bit the inside of my lower lip to keep from commenting.

"Oh really?" Julian asked, and even through the earpiece, I could hear the hopefulness in his tone.

"Really. He's just this guy from out of town. He's not even here anymore. That was the one and only time we ever went out."

"That's, um... that's good to hear."

"You have him in the palm of your hand," I said quietly.

She sighed. "Yeah, I don't know. I keep thinking I should give up on dating. Or maybe just give in and let Louise Haven set me up with someone."

"That's not the worst idea," he said. "Depending on who he is."

"It would definitely depend on who he is," she said, her tone laced with suggestion.

"Tell me this," he said. "What are you looking for?"

"Bloody hell, he just handed it to you," I said. "Remember what we know about him."

We'd discussed the summary of Maple's findings at length, as well as pored over his social media accounts together. We knew his interests—things like art, history, travel—and we also knew he liked attention. He was a man quite concerned with appearing sophisticated.

The light flirtation in her laugh was perfection. "What am

I looking for? That's actually a good question. I guess I'm looking for someone smart and interesting. Successful, but not so he can wine and dine me. Someone who likes to talk about things besides sports and cars. Who's willing to let me get to know him. Share what fascinates and interests him."

"You're fucking brilliant," I said. "Subtle but leading him in the right direction."

"Wow, that was a lot," she said. "You probably didn't mean for me to get that deep. Especially while we're standing here in the gym."

"No," he said, his voice emphatic. "That's exactly what I meant. And you should know what you want. I love that."

"Thanks."

"So maybe we don't need to wait for the town match-makers to do their thing," he said.

"No?"

I looked through the binoculars again. He was leaning in, closing the distance between them. My lip curled in a sneer.

"I'd like to have dinner with you," he said. "Actually, I'd like to cook for you. No wining and dining. Just two people getting to know each other."

She hesitated. "We just met. You can't blame me if I'm a little hesitant to come to your house."

"I understand. But there'd be no pressure. Besides, Louise Haven thinks you should go out with me, so..."

"That's true. She does." She hesitated again. "Okay, Julian. I'll have dinner with you. But so we're clear, just dinner."

"Absolutely. Just dinner. Are you free tomorrow?"

"I am, as a matter of fact."

"Great."

I waited while they exchanged numbers and made a date for six the following evening. I was torn between triumph and indignation. Natalie had performed beautifully, her suggestion so subtle he thought having dinner at his place was his idea.

"There's a gate," he said. "Just pull up, and I'll buzz you in."

"Okay."

"I should let you get back to your workout," he said.

"Yes, my workout," she said. "I'm just here for a short one today."

"All right. I'll see you tomorrow night."

"It's a date," she said.

I looked again and watched her move to the cardio area and get on a treadmill.

"I want to get out of here, but I guess I have to work out now," she whispered.

"Unfortunately, you're about to get a phone call and have to leave."

"Perfect."

I picked up my phone and called.

"Hey," she answered.

"Hello, darling. There's a dire emergency here in the parking lot."

"Oh no, what's going on?"

"I had to listen to you flirt with another man. Now I'm incensed."

"Don't worry. I'll be right there."

"I wouldn't want to interrupt."

"No, it's fine." She got off the treadmill and started toward the door. "I'm on my way."

She emerged from the building. I ended the call as she hurried toward me, leaping over a hill of plowed snow. She got in and smiled, her eyes shining with excitement.

"I did it. I can't believe I did it."

"You were brilliant." I pulled out of the parking spot and drove onto the street. "I knew you would be."

She let out a breath. "I thought for sure he was going to ask me to coffee or something."

"No, you planted the perfect seed. Besides, he wants to show off. If I had to bet, he's thinking he'll be the one to wine and dine you the right way."

"That's what I was thinking too."

"You have good instincts."

"Thanks. Let's hope I can pull off the next step. Having dinner at his house is going to be a much bigger deal than flirting at the gym. And I don't want to have to do this twice. If he's not involved with the necklace, I don't want to lead him on."

"You won't have to. I only need one shot. I'll find out the truth."

She smiled. "Okay. Is it bad that that was kind of fun?"

"Not bad at all. You're good at this." I glanced at her. "I'm glad I have you as my partner."

Her smile was like the sun breaking through the clouds on an icy cold day. "Me too."

The trap was set. Soon, it would be time to spring it.

CHAPTER 23

Natalie

I was surprisingly calm as I drove to Julian's. I did feel a bit more like I was on the way to the dentist than to a date, fake or otherwise, but I wasn't afraid.

In fact, I was a little bit excited.

Houses sparkled with Christmas lights, and I turned on a playlist of soothing instrumental Christmas music. Nina had caught me leaving, but I'd explained my outfit—a shimmery silver blouse, black pants, and heels—by telling her I was going out with Jensen. It wasn't a lie, exactly. We were both going out, and to the same place.

It was going to be fun to tell her the entire story once the necklace was back with its rightful owner. She was hardly going to believe it.

"I'm in position," Jensen said quietly through the earpiece. "How are you feeling? Ready for this?"

"I'm ready." I turned onto Julian's street. "A little nervous, but not as much as I thought I'd be."

"Good. You look beautiful."

I smiled. "Thank you."

"I hate that another man gets to spend time with you tonight."

"Don't worry," I said, recalling what he'd said to me at the Snowflake Ball. "It's all part of the game."

"Indeed. Once you're inside, I'll try not to interfere unless I'm needed. And darling, if he does anything to make you feel unsafe, leave. We can always come up with a new plan."

"I will." I turned onto his driveway. "I'm here."

"Brilliant. Go get him, beautiful."

With a deep breath, I stopped in front of the gate. A second later, it swung open, and I drove in.

It was easy to see why Julian had become the object of town gossip. The house itself was built with the sort of rustic luxury style that was common in the mountains. Large beams, big windows, wrought-iron embellishments. But the statues flanking the front looked like something out of Renaissance Italy.

I was no art expert, but they looked like white marble. One was a man, the other a woman, both standing with one arm raised, as if reaching for each other across the driveway. Lighting illuminated them from below, making them seem to glow in the evening darkness.

The driveway curved, making a loop, so I parked in front of the house. The gate closed behind me, making me feel a bit trapped, and I was well aware of the numerous cameras. It was eerie.

My heart beat faster as I got out and walked to the front door. Strangely, my heightened nervousness didn't make me want to leave. It made me want to succeed.

I knocked, and a moment later, Julian answered.

He wore a dark gray suit, no tie, and the top button of his shirt was undone. Not a hair was out of place, and his formality made me glad I'd dressed up. This wasn't a casual, hang-out-and-eat-dinner-on-the-couch-while-watching-a-movie sort of date.

"Hi," he said with a confident smile. "You look beautiful."

Jensen growled in my ear.

"Thank you."

He stepped aside. "Come in out of the cold."

I went in, and he shut the heavy door behind me. He helped me slip off my coat and hung it in a closet near the door.

"Can I get you a glass of wine?" he asked.

"Yes, please."

A large iron chandelier hung from the high ceiling, and a curved stairway with a polished wood banister led to the second floor. A water feature with a Renaissance-style sculpture—this one a cherub with wings—stood in the center of the foyer, and another statue perched on the landing above.

"Look for cameras," Jensen whispered.

I glanced around but didn't see any. If he had indoor cameras, they were hidden.

"This is lovely," I said, gesturing to the fountain. "The water is so soothing."

"It was sculpted by an artist in France. I had to have the entire floor torn up to get the plumbing put in, but it was worth it. Feel free to look around. I'll be right back."

While he went to the kitchen to pour the wine, I took slow steps through the first floor and tried to memorize the layout as best I could. Windows, doors, hallways, rooms. The formal living room at the front of the house featured a fireplace with a stone front that reached the high ceiling. That led to a dining area—the room Jensen and I had looked into from outside.

"Looks like a collector to me," I said quietly. "Paintings, sculptures, vases, all kinds of things. He has art on the walls everywhere, and at least three glass display cases. No cameras that I can see."

"Good," Jensen answered. "You're doing wonderful."

I wandered into the kitchen, and Julian handed me a glass of white wine. It pricked that he hadn't asked whether I liked white or red, but I accepted it with a smile.

"Your house is so beautiful," I said. "I love how you've decorated."

"Let me give you the grand tour."

I followed him from the kitchen into an open great room with floor-to-ceiling windows facing the river. Although it was dark, soft lighting illuminated the landscape, giving it a dreamy winter wonderland ambiance.

Interestingly, however, he didn't point out the view.

"This is late nineteenth-century Russian." He gestured to a glass case with a bronze statue of a man in uniform on a horse.

"It's beautiful."

"And rare." I didn't miss the hint of self-satisfaction in his voice. "Probably the only one in North America that isn't in a museum."

Without waiting for me to reply, he continued moving slowly through the room and gestured to a large painting of a woman in a fancy white dress posing in a plush red armchair. "The painting is also Russian, same time period."

"You must have a love for Russian art."

"I have a love for pieces that are rare or...difficult to obtain."

I hope you're hearing this, Jensen.

"This is fascinating," I said. "I saw some things when I walked in. Can you show me?"

"I'd love to."

I sipped my wine as he showed me around the first floor, highlighting the various art pieces he had on display. They were from all over the world. Statues from Italy and France. A painting from Spain. A glass case filled with artifacts from Columbia and Brazil. A colorful tapestry from South Africa.

"Have you traveled to all these places?" I asked. "These don't seem like the sorts of things you can find at regular art galleries."

"I acquired some of them personally. But I also have some associates in the art world who procured certain pieces for me."

A necklace displayed in a glass case caught my eye. It was gold strung with two layers of diamonds and pearls. It wasn't *the* necklace, of course, but I hoped I could get him talking about his jewelry.

"This is beautiful. Do you collect jewelry as well?"

"Some. Especially antique jewelry. I'm not interested in diamonds for their own sake, but when they're crafted into something like this, they're worth having."

"It tells a story. I can almost imagine the woman who wore it. Do you have more like this?"

"I do. It's in the dining room."

On the way, he pointed out a few more paintings, hinting each time that they were rare, and therefore expensive.

"He's sure trying to impress you," Jensen said quietly in my ear.

It wasn't working.

The dining room had an ornate table and chairs with a matching cabinet on one wall. The windows Jensen and I had looked through opened to the side of the property. The shadowy outline of the iron fence was visible, as were the snow-covered trees beyond.

"This is one of my favorite pieces." He picked up the glass case with the brooch. It had a large square-cut emerald in the center surrounded by a starburst pattern of gold-set diamonds.

I touched my hand to my chest, emphasizing my awe. "It's so beautiful. Is it an antique?"

"Victorian era. It belonged to a British noblewoman."

"Stolen," Jensen whispered.

"Where did you get it?"

He smiled. "This one was a bit of an adventure to acquire. It came from the UK."

I waited, but he didn't elaborate. He set it back on the cabinet, and I didn't miss the hint of a smirk that crossed his features.

"Ready for dinner?" He gestured to the table, already set with two place settings across from each other, including wineglasses. "Have a seat. I'll bring everything in."

"Are you sure you don't need help?"

"Absolutely. I'll be right back."

"I hope he's our thief," Jensen said. "I very much want to screw him over."

I pressed my lips together, trying not to laugh, and took a seat.

A moment later, Julian returned with a large white serving dish. He set it down and removed the cover. "Beef bourguignon."

Interesting that at no point had he asked me about my food preferences.

"It smells delicious."

"I have a soft spot for French cooking."

He left again and returned with a plate of bread and an open bottle of red wine.

Apparently, we were drinking red now.

I hadn't finished my white, but I moved the glass aside. He poured me some red before pouring a glass for himself.

He sat at the head of the table and lifted his glass. "To new acquaintances."

I held my glass up and clinked it against his. "Cheers."

Julian kept the conversation going as we dished up and started eating—conversation that centered squarely on him.

His business. His main residence on Mercer Island, just outside Seattle. His even more extensive collection of art housed there.

The more he talked, the more I disliked him. We got through the entire meal, and he hadn't asked a single question about me. He didn't know what I did for a living, where I lived, whether or not I had any family, or what I liked to do in my free time. Literally nothing.

And something else was off about the situation. I glanced around a few times, wondering what it was. While he was back in the kitchen preparing our dessert, it hit me.

No Christmas decorations.

He didn't have a single nod to the holiday season. No Christmas tree, no lights, no wreaths or garlands. Not a candle, candy cane, evergreen bough, or sprig of holly.

I shifted in my seat. I still needed to find a door or window to unlock so Jensen could get in.

"Julian," I called. "If you'll excuse me, I need to use the restroom."

"Down the hallway and to the left."

"Thanks."

I rose, and it felt like I'd been injected with a shot of adrenaline. My heart raced, and nervous energy thrummed through me. I found the bathroom—a full bath with a glass-enclosed shower—but peeked farther down the hall.

Walking carefully so my footsteps wouldn't make a sound, I checked the next door. It opened into a study lined with bookshelves and a leather armchair. The snowy landscape gleamed through the large windows, and a set of French doors led onto a patio outside.

"I'm in a study. Must be the corner of the house. Windows on one side. I can see the fence. French doors lead to a patio."

"Brilliant. Have you seen any indoor cameras?"

Tiptoeing across the hardwood, I made for the door. "No. Maybe I'm just not seeing them, but I haven't noticed anything."

"Good."

My heart raced, and for a second, my stomach roiled with a sudden surge of nausea.

Don't throw up, Natalie. Don't throw up.

Blowing out a small breath, I reached for the door handle and unlocked it.

"It's unlocked."

"You're a goddess. Get out of there as soon as you can."

I crept back to the bathroom and shut the door as quietly as I could manage. Letting out another breath, I took stock of myself in the mirror, hoping my cheeks weren't flushed or my eyes wide with terror.

Who was that woman looking back at me? She was cool and composed, without a hint of fear in her expression.

I liked her.

When I went back to the dining room, I found Julian waiting with slices of chocolate cheesecake at our places. I smiled and took my seat.

"Did you really cook all this?" I asked.

"I did. I told you I wanted to cook for you."

"You're very good at it." I took a bite of the cheesecake. To his credit, the food was delicious, and the rich, smooth dessert was a nice complement to the meal.

I ate a little, debating my next move. I'd done my job. Jensen had a way in. But how was he going to find the necklace? Was it even there? Julian didn't have it on display, at least not on the ground floor. There was an entire upstairs we hadn't explored, but the last thing I was going to do was suggest he show me the bedrooms. That would give him the wrong impression and might even put me in danger.

But I still wanted to know if he had it. Was it even worth the risk for Jensen to break in?

I turned my gaze to the brooch. "I'm still so fascinated by that brooch. I was thinking the necklace in the other room tells a story, and this one does too."

"Careful, darling," Jensen whispered, as if he knew exactly where I was trying to take the conversation.

He was right. I did need to be careful. If Julian knew who Jensen was, he'd have to suspect why he was in town. And if he caught the slightest whiff of my real reason for being there—became even mildly suspicious that I'd been sent in by Jensen to locate the stolen necklace—I had no idea what he might do.

"That's exactly why I wanted it. It's not even important to me what it's worth. Well, it's a little bit important." He winked.

"It must be exciting to get your hands on a treasure with real history behind it."

"Believe me, it is. There's nothing like the rush of finally acquiring a rare piece."

"I can only imagine. Is this one new to you?"

"No. I acquired that a few years ago."

"What's your most recent find?" I met his eyes and lifted the corners of my mouth in a subtle smile. "I want to hear about your latest adventure."

Jensen groaned. "Fuck, you're good at this."

Julian watched me for a moment, his mouth curling in a grin. I held his gaze, lifting my eyebrows.

I dare you, Julian.

"All right." He rose from his chair. "I'll be right back."

"Bloody hell, he's going to show it to you," Jensen said. "Where's he going? Can you tell?"

"Upstairs."

"Are you sure?"

"Positive." I paused, listening. "I can hear his footsteps."

A moment later, Julian returned carrying a square wooden box with hinges on one side. He sat and set it on the table, turning it so the front faced me.

"Are you ready for this?" he asked.

I set down my wineglass. "Yes. What is it?"

"Everything else I showed you? Nothing compared to this." He slowly raised the lid.

There it was. A crown-like net of gold and diamonds, set with rubies and a large teardrop emerald in the center.

My gasp wasn't feigned. "Oh, Julian. This is incredible."

"Isn't it?"

"Where did you get it?"

"The UK. It took quite a bit of work to get my hands on it."

"I've never seen anything like it. I love the red and green. It's very Christmassy."

"Oh." He furrowed his brow like that had never occurred to him. "I suppose it is."

If I'd been on a real date with him, I would have used that to ask about his lack of Christmas decorations. But I didn't really care. Maybe he wasn't planning to spend Christmas in Tilikum, so he hadn't bothered to decorate. Or maybe he didn't celebrate Christmas. None of it mattered to me.

And since he'd asked zero questions about me or my life, he didn't know I was on strike. Therefore, needing to work in the morning was a valid excuse to leave.

"I almost hate to say this, but I should get home. I have to work early tomorrow."

"Are you sure I can't persuade you to have another glass of wine? Maybe a cocktail?"

"Tempting, but maybe another time."

He hesitated, and I got the distinct impression he was sizing me up—deciding whether he was going to push harder for me to stay. A ripple of tension tightened my shoulders. I hoped he wouldn't make it difficult to leave.

"Let her go, you prick," Jensen whispered.

"Understandable," he said, finally. "This was great. I hope we can do it again."

I smiled. Not likely, Mr. Jewelry Thief.

To make it clear I wasn't playing some sort of game and trying to get him to coax me into staying longer, I rose from my chair and went directly to the foyer. Without waiting for him to get my coat, I opened the closet door and took it off the hanger myself. He stepped in to help me slip it on, and I did my best not to shudder.

Something about him made my skin crawl. Maybe because the dinner conversation reminded me of my ex. He'd been excellent at talking about himself, too.

Julian walked me to the door, and when he stepped in for a kiss, I turned my cheek. *No mouth kisses, thank you very much.* Jensen seemed to be able to hear what had just happened. He growled in my ear again.

"Thanks again for dinner," I said.

"Anytime. I'm looking forward to showing you more cuisines."

I'm sure you are.

"I'll call you," he said.

"Sounds good. Have a nice evening."

I walked outside, and my shoulders loosened as soon as I heard the large door close behind me.

"I'm out. Going to my car."

"You were fucking magnificent."

"Thanks." I opened my car door, my heart racing again. I wanted past that gate. "Do you think he's really going to let me go?"

"Seems so."

"What if it's a ruse? What if he knows why I was here?"

"I think you fooled him."

I drove around the circular driveway to the gate and waited. It didn't move.

"Jensen, it's not opening."

"It's all right, darling. There's probably a sensor. Give it a moment."

My eyes flicked to the rearview mirror. I was half expecting to see Julian walking down the driveway, but no one was there.

The gate started to open.

"There it goes. It's opening." As soon as it was wide enough for my car, I went through. "I'm out."

I heard Jensen's long exhale. "Good. Go straight to the flat. Keep the door locked. I'm switching over to Maple while I finish the job, so I'll see you there, all right?"

My heart jumped again. "This is going to be the longest wait of my life."

"Don't worry, darling. This is what I do. I'll see you soon."

"Be safe."

"I will."

The earpiece went dead. He was gone.

"Be careful, Jensen," I whispered into the night. "Come home soon."

CHAPTER 24

Jensen

Once Natalie's rental car faded as she drove away, I finally allowed myself to feel relief. She was safe.

I'd hated every moment she'd spent in Julian's house. Partly because of the ruse. He thought it was a date, and the mere idea of Natalie on a date with another man was abhorrent.

But she'd also been in danger. Julian's invitation could have been a trap.

I'd been prepared for that. At the first hint that her safety was compromised, I would have intervened. But my gut had told me Julian didn't suspect her. Whether it was his ego, and he couldn't fathom that her interest wouldn't be real, or the fact that his matchmaking grandmother had already planted the idea of Natalie in his head, he'd believed her.

She'd played her part perfectly. Now it was up to me to finish the job.

I'd left my car up the road, out of sight of any doorbell cameras, and slipped into the trees next to Julian's property. The large dining room windows had given me a mostly unobstructed view during dinner. And I'd managed to get a few pictures of the necklace itself. No doubt about it. He was our thief, and the necklace was in his possession.

I connected to Maple.

"There you are," she said. "I was getting concerned. What's happening?"

"Natalie just left. She unlocked a door for me, but that's not even the half of it. She got him to show it to her."

"Fuck off."

"I told you she could do it. A few hints and suggestions and he brought it out."

"I doubt you'll be lucky enough to find that he hasn't put it away."

"No, I'm sure it's locked up already."

"Do you think he's the one who stole it? Or did he pay for it?"

"I think he did it. How he had the resources to pull it off is another question. But that's not my immediate concern."

"Do you want me to arrange for security for Natalie until we can be sure she's not a target? Once he realizes you've taken the necklace back, it's unlikely he won't suspect her."

"I'll handle it for now."

"All right. I have a floorplan ready. Where are you planning to enter?"

"There's a study located at the back corner with an exterior door."

"Got it. That leads into a short hallway. There's an upper floor and a basement. Where do you think he's keeping it?"

"Natalie heard him go upstairs to retrieve it. I'll look there first."

"You'll have to cross a fairly large foyer to get to the stairs."

"Shouldn't be a problem."

"Then get to work."

"Yes, ma'am."

The snow blanketing the ground reflected the light and

absorbed sound, making the landscape unnaturally bright and quiet. I made my way toward the river, choosing my footing carefully.

Balancing against the pitch of the slope, I leaned forward and used my hands, practically crawling across the bluff, past his fence line, and into his property. My foot slipped, and for a second, I thought I might slide all the way into the glacial water below.

"Fuck," I muttered.

"You all right?" Maple asked.

"Just trying to avoid falling into an icy river."

I picked my footing carefully and got past the fence line.

"Disabling the cameras." I pulled a jammer from my pocket and activated it. The device sent a signal that would temporarily overpower the frequency the cameras were using. There was a chance he'd notice, but it was a risk I was willing to take.

With that done, I crept across the open ground to what I hoped was still an unlocked door. I couldn't do much about the footprints I left in the snow. Considering Julian had stolen the necklace, I doubted he'd involve local law enforcement. No one was going to be processing the scene for evidence.

I approached the dark study and peered inside. Empty. I tried the handle, and sure enough, it was unlocked.

Quickly slipping inside, I closed it behind me.

"I'm in."

"Short hallway. You'll see the main foyer when you come out."

I paused to listen but didn't hear anything—no sign that Julian was in that part of the house. My shoes were wet from the snow, so I took a second to wipe them on the mat at the door—more to avoid them squeaking than for any concern about his flooring—then crept out of the study and down the hall.

CLAIRE KINGSLEY

He'd turned off the lights in the entryway, and the trickle of water in the fountain would be a good cover for my footsteps. Hugging the wall, I made sure to get a good look at the dining room. Finding the necklace sitting out would have been shocking, but one never knew when that kind of luck would strike.

Not that time. He'd already cleared the dishes, and the table was empty.

I didn't like not knowing where he was. I took a few steps toward the stairs and ducked behind the fountain. Hesitating there, I strained to listen.

After a moment, I heard him walking around upstairs.

I could find a place to hide and wait until he came down. Or risk the open staircase and hide upstairs.

My gut said upstairs.

"Where's the main bedroom?" I asked Maple.

"Far left from the top of the stairs."

Moving like a shadow, I padded up the stairs and turned right. Julian emerged just as I passed the gaudy statue looking down from the landing.

I slipped into another bedroom unseen and peeked out. He paused at the top of the stairs and looked around as if he'd heard something.

Holding my breath, I waited.

Instead of going downstairs, he went back to the bedroom. A moment later, I heard his voice, and he came out, talking on his phone.

"Sorry, I had a date," he said. "Not very well, considering she left."

Damn right, she left. As if you ever had a chance with her.

He started down the stairs. My jealous and irrational side wanted to follow so I could listen in on his conversation. If he said a single bad thing about my Natalie, I'd make him regret ever laying eyes on her.

But I wasn't there to eavesdrop on his post-date musings. I needed to get the necklace and get out, or everything Natalie had accomplished would have been for nothing.

I couldn't let her down.

His voice faded. The phone call was fortuitous. He was occupied and less likely to hear anything going on upstairs.

I left my cover, moved across the landing, and slipped into his bedroom.

It was dark. No lights left on and the curtains were closed, blocking even the outdoor lighting. I couldn't make out details, but he had a king-size bed and a large dresser against one wall.

No closet doors in the bedroom itself, so I went to the en suite bathroom. I assumed he was keeping the necklace in a safe, and closets were often where those would be found.

Moving as quietly as I could manage, I searched for a safe. It wasn't in plain sight, and I began to wonder if it was built into the wall or hidden behind a false panel of some kind.

Finally, I found it, tucked away behind a suitcase. It was built into the wall with an electronic lock.

"Found the safe," I whispered to Maple. "Electronic."

"Can you crack it?"

"Of course I can crack it. Who do you think you're talking to?"

I pulled my code cracker out of an inside pocket and set to work. It was yet another tool I wasn't technically supposed to have. Obviously, I was a man who took those sorts of legalities as suggestions that applied to others rather than to myself. I fastened it to the lock and began the process of resetting the code.

It only took a moment, and the new code flashed on the screen. I plugged it in, and the lock released.

"I'm in."

CLAIRE KINGSLEY

"That took a while," Maple teased. "You must be getting rusty."

In the interest of staying quiet, I didn't fire back, but my mouth turned up in a subtle grin.

Inside the safe, I found a wooden box. Lifting the lid, my smile grew. There it was.

"I have it."

"Get out of there."

The box would be cumbersome, so I gently removed the necklace and put it in an inside pocket that zipped shut. Then I closed the safe and detached the device, returning it to another pocket.

I crept out of his bedroom and paused in the doorway to listen. The faint sound of his voice carried from another part of the house. The kitchen, perhaps.

Ideally, I'd leave the way I'd come. But I wasn't sure if I could get past him to the study.

"Where are my exits?"

"Front door, study door, another double door at the back."

The front door was closest. And there was something audacious about walking out his front door with the necklace he'd stolen. I liked it.

I made my way quickly and silently down the stairs, once again glad he'd decided to put a water feature in his entryway. It covered the sound of me leaving. I slipped out the door and closed it softly behind me.

"I'm outside."

"Still on property, I assume."

"I went out the front door."

"Jensen Lakes," she scolded.

I grinned as I stole around the corner of the house and ducked below the dining room windows. There was almost no snow along the perimeter of the house, but he'd probably still be able to follow my tracks if he looked for them.

Didn't matter. I had the necklace.

Pausing at the edge of the house, I looked to make sure he wasn't near the windows. I didn't see any movement or shadows, so I darted for the bluff above the river and retraced my path along the rocky edge.

It was precarious, but I managed to get by without slipping and, moments later, emerged into the trees. Veering in the direction of my car, I picked up speed, jogging through the snow.

As soon as I got to my car, I scrambled in, turned on the engine, and got out of there.

"It's done. I'm on the road."

"Nice work. I assume you'll bring it back yourself?"

"I will, but we need to hold them off for a couple days."

"Why? They want it for Christmas."

"I promised someone I'd be here for Christmas."

"Jensen, what on earth are you talking about?"

"If they want it now, you'll need to send another operative to Tilikum to retrieve it."

"I suppose I can arrange that. Deacon is still in the region. He could fly in tomorrow morning."

"He'll do."

"But... why are you spending Christmas there? Wait. You're spending the holiday with Natalie, aren't you?"

"And her family. Shocking turn of events, isn't it?"

"Are you serious?"

"Completely."

"I'm not quite sure what to say."

"How about 'Merry Christmas, Jensen, your fee will be in your account by tomorrow.'"

"Your fee will be in your account once the client has their property."

"Fine. But get Deacon here early. Tomorrow is Christmas Eve, and I have an outrageous amount of shopping to do."

She laughed. "I'll see what I can do."

"Give my apologies to Mr. Exton for keeping you on so late."

"Don't worry. He'll make me pay for it when I come to bed."

"Good man."

She laughed, and we disconnected.

I drove back to the flat with a smile on my face. I'd hand off the necklace to Deacon in the morning. He'd take it the rest of the way home. Mission accomplished.

As for me, I'd finished the job just in time for Christmas. And it was going to be one to remember.

CHAPTER 25

Natalie

I spent the rest of the evening pacing around the apartment, waiting for Jensen.

Sitting still wasn't an option. Neither was going over to the house. I wouldn't have been able to keep quiet, and I wasn't ready to tell Nina what Jensen and I had been up to.

So I walked, and wandered, and paced, more anxious than I'd been when I was the one who could have been in danger. I'd been much more calm at Julian's than I was knowing that Jensen was in the midst of breaking in to steal the necklace back.

Would he find it? Would he stay hidden? He'd been so vague about how he was going to accomplish his task. There were cameras and home security to contend with, not to mention the fact that Julian was home.

The timing made sense. The longer he waited, the more chance there was of Julian locking the study door. He needed to act while the window of opportunity—or the door, to be precise—was open.

And I understood why he hadn't told me the details of his plan. Sure, he did this for a living, but he wasn't law enforcement. He was breaking in as sure as any thief. The less I knew, the better.

He was protecting me.

Finally, I heard a car outside. With my heart in my throat, I stood in front of the door, practically bouncing with anticipation. A moment later, Jensen walked in and shut the door behind him.

I threw myself at him, jumping into his arms, and wrapped my legs around his waist. He held me tight and spun me around, pushing me up against the wall. Our mouths met in a deep, frenzied kiss as if we'd been parted for months and couldn't get enough.

"I'm so glad you're back," I breathed. "I've been a wreck."

"You didn't need to worry about me."

"I did anyway." I kissed him again, reveling in the feel of his velvety-soft tongue sliding against mine.

As he pulled away, the corners of his mouth lifted. "Ask me if I got it."

"Did you get it?"

He set me down, and with a smirk, reached into his coat and gently pulled out the necklace.

I covered my mouth with my hands. "You did it."

"We did it. I couldn't have done it without you."

"How long do you think it'll take for him to realize it's gone?"

"Hard to say. It depends on how soon he tries to take it out of the safe." He touched my face. "He's going to realize you were involved."

"I know. Do you think he's dangerous?"

He hesitated. "Yes and no. My impression is that he's a collector, not a black market art dealer. He stole it for himself, and he won't be happy about losing it. I'll make sure he doesn't get anywhere near you." He smirked. "But I doubt he'll ask you for a second date."

I laughed. "He'll just be saving me the trouble of telling him no."

"Indeed." He pushed me against the wall and kissed me. "I hated every minute you were in his house. I didn't even want his eyes on you."

Biting my lip, I wiggled against him a little. "I like it when you get possessive. Besides, he was a jerk. All he did was talk about himself."

"I noticed. Prick."

I laughed again. "What happens now?"

"My organization is sending one of my colleagues to retrieve the necklace. We'll meet him at the airport in the morning."

"This is going to be the best Christmas."

"It is, isn't it?"

He kissed me again, and it was triumphant and decadent. We'd done it. We'd won. And we'd done it together.

❄

By the time we woke up Christmas Eve morning, it was snowing heavily. Jensen wrapped and boxed the necklace with care and off we went. Together.

Visibility was low, and the drive to the airport to meet Jensen's colleague was a bit treacherous. He was in a rush—his pilot in a hurry to take off again before the incoming storm got worse—but the handoff went smoothly. We waited there until we saw the private plane take off.

And just like that, my first—and certainly only—operation to re-steal stolen jewelry was over.

I spent the drive back into town feeling a little giddy and suddenly very excited for Christmas morning. Considering the state of my bank account, I was grateful to be earning a cut of

Jensen's fee for the necklace's recovery. I intended to use at least some of it to make Christmas magical.

The heavily falling snow added to Tilikum's holiday charm. Lights gleamed even in the daylight, and the wreaths and garlands were even prettier with a dusting of white.

"Will stores be open in this weather?" Jensen asked as we turned onto Main Street.

"Definitely. It would take a record-breaking blizzard to get this town to close, especially on Christmas Eve."

"Brilliant. I don't know about you, but I have shopping to do."

"Me too," I said, smiling with excitement.

He found a parking spot on the street, right in the center of the little downtown corridor. Despite the weather, people walked up and down the sidewalks, bundled against the cold, carrying shopping bags.

"Shall we start with Miss Annabel?" he asked.

"You know you don't have to—"

He put a finger to my lips. "Darling, I plan to spoil the three of you absolutely rotten, and nothing you can say will stop me."

"Okay, I'll let you. Just this once." I paused. "And you have to let me get you something."

With a slight grin, he rolled his eyes. "Now you're taking things a bit too far."

"Why can't I get you something for Christmas?"

His eyes met mine, and his expression turned serious. "Because I already have everything I want."

Warmth spread through me, and I smiled. "So do I. But I'm still getting you something."

He started to protest, so I put my finger on his lips.

"How about something we can both enjoy?" I bit my lower lip. "Something sexy."

"Mmm," he hummed like he was tasting something delicious, "I like that."

"I thought you might."

We got out and, hunkering against the wind, hurried into the toy store. Although my first thought was to stop him from buying Annabel too many presents, it didn't take long for me to throw out my responsible-older-sister-and-sometimes-second-mom role and take on the role of coolest aunt ever.

Dress-up clothes, fairy wands, fancy markers, coloring books, puzzles, dolls, and a giant teddy bear that would probably not fit in her bedroom all got stuffed into Jensen's car.

Nina was a little harder to shop for. But considering her fledgling relationship with Dylan, I knew she'd love some date-night attire. And since we wore the same size, it was easy to find things that would fit. We got her a gorgeous little black dress, a blouse and skirt, and two pairs of very splurgy high heels.

Jensen also insisted on buying her a long wool coat so she wouldn't freeze on her date nights.

We stopped for a quick bite to eat, then resumed our shopping. I had a feeling Jensen was sneaking presents for me between purchases for Annabel and Nina. I pretended not to notice and did my best not to look. I didn't want to ruin his surprises.

I still hadn't found anything for him, but I knew just the place to look.

The snow was starting to pile up as we made our way to a boutique up the street that carried pretty lingerie. It was a short walk, but my cheeks and nose tingled with cold, and I was glad to get in out of the wind.

The clerk—a young woman with long blond hair and thick eyelashes—sat on a stool behind the counter. She looked up from her phone. "Welcome in."

"Thanks." I brushed the snow from the front of my hair.

The store was busy, with a group of women who appeared to be shopping together walking around and talking as they browsed. The clerk stayed on her stool and went back to her phone.

"How about you go get some coffee or something while I shop?"

Jensen's brow furrowed. "No. It's too soon to leave you alone."

"Even here?" I gestured toward the other customers. "It's just a bunch of ladies."

"How about I turn around? I won't peek."

"All right. I won't be long." I handed him my coat and purse. "Do you mind holding these?"

"Not at all." He took them and draped my coat over his arm.

Loud laughter erupted from several of the women. They were certainly having fun. The clerk remained on her stool behind the counter, glued to her phone.

The front of the store featured clothing—dresses, blouses, pants, skirts. One wall had a small display of earrings, belts, and other accessories, with a shelf of shoes below. I found what I was interested in at the back of the store.

They didn't have an extensive lingerie selection—it wasn't a large store—but at a glance, I had a feeling I'd find something. I wanted to look like a present for Jensen to unwrap, and they had a whole rack of sexy Christmas pieces.

I glanced toward the front of the store. Jensen stood with his back facing me, his posture casual and relaxed. I knew he wasn't in any hurry, but I didn't want to make him stand there for too long, so I picked a red bra with sheer cups and a lacy white negligee with red ribbons.

The women had congregated around the single dressing room. One of them came through the curtain wearing a sparkly green dress, and her friends clapped and squealed with excitement.

I went to the counter, and it took a second for the clerk to look up from her phone.

"Are you ready to check out?" she asked.

"Actually, I'd like to try these on. Is there just the one dressing room?"

She nodded. "Yeah, sorry."

I glanced at Jensen again. "Do you have a restroom? Could I maybe try them on in there?"

"Sure," she said with a shrug. "It's down the hall, last door on the right."

"Thank you."

I took the lingerie down the hall and found the bathroom, but the door was locked.

"Occupied!" called a woman's voice from behind the door.

"Sorry!"

As I stepped back to wait, a sudden cold breeze made my cheeks and nose tingle again. Before I could turn to see where it had come from, someone grabbed me, jerking me to the side.

A large hand clamped over my mouth. I tried to struggle, but a strong arm wrapped around me. I dropped the hangers and threw my body weight forward, trying to break his hold. But he was too strong. In seconds, I was dragged out a door into the falling snow.

CHAPTER 26
Jensen

S tanding in front of the store window, idly watching the snow fall, I listened to the women cackling behind me. They were certainly having a good time. A little loud, but I figured it was Christmas. If they'd enjoyed a few drinks with lunch before going shopping, who could blame them?

My phone buzzed. Maple. I wasn't going to be able to hear a thing, so I stepped outside into the cold.

"Go ahead," I answered.

"Necklace is en route, and the client has been notified. They're thrilled, by the way."

"Good. Shouldn't you be off celebrating?"

"I am, in fact. But I wanted to keep you updated. And to let you know you'll have another crack at Archer Prince. He didn't show in Paris. Your hunch to stay where you are was apparently a good one."

"He wasn't there? Did he send someone else?"

"No. They must have called it off before the meeting happened."

"Or it wasn't in Paris."

"That's possible. At this point, we simply don't know."

"All right. Merry Christmas, Mrs. Exton."

"Merry Christmas, Mr. Lakes. Good work."

A gust of wind blew the snow sideways as I ended the call, and I shivered, hunkering down in my coat against the cold. Natalie and I probably needed to get back to her place before the storm got any worse.

After pocketing my phone, I stepped back into the shop and the cacophony of tipsy women. I cast a glance around but didn't see Natalie. She was probably in one of the fitting rooms.

To keep my no-peeking promise, I turned toward the window again. But something bothered me, like the pinch of a splinter I couldn't get out. Why hadn't Archer Prince been in Paris?

There were any number of explanations. It could have been a ruse, and the sale could have occurred elsewhere. Or he could have gotten wind that my organization knew. Perhaps it was bad information to begin with. After all, it seemed unlikely that the man I'd been chasing for years was actually in possession of one of the most famous stolen works of art in modern history.

Another minute went by, and the laughing began to grate on my nerves. My shoulders grew tense, and I couldn't shake the feeling that I was missing something.

Where was Natalie?

I glanced back into the store again, this time looking carefully. The other women still congregated around the fitting room. Natalie was nowhere to be seen. I'd promised I wouldn't look, but I couldn't ignore my gut any longer.

The fitting room was in one corner of the shop, and I made my way over there first. A woman threw the curtain aside as I approached, striking a pose in a bright red dress to the cheers of her friends.

"Excuse me, ladies," I said. "Is this the only fitting room?"

Two of the women gaped at me as if I'd spoken a foreign language. Another looked around but didn't answer my question.

Finally, the woman in the red dress spoke up. "I think this is it."

One of the women might have said something else, but I turned, my sense of alarm growing. The shop wasn't that large. Where could Natalie have gone?

I went to the clerk, sitting behind the counter with her eyes on her phone.

"Excuse me."

She looked up. "Can I help you?"

"I'm here with my…" The need for a label tripped me up. What was I supposed to call her? Maybe girlfriend wasn't right, but I didn't care. "My girlfriend. Long dark hair, hauntingly beautiful eyes. Do you know where she could have gone?"

The clerk shrugged.

"Are there more fitting rooms? In the back, perhaps?"

"No. Oh, there's a restroom. I think she went in there."

"Brilliant."

That answered the question. She was in the restroom.

So why were my instincts still telling me something was wrong?

I went down the hall that led toward the back of the shop. A door stood ajar, leading into a stockroom. Another looked like it led outside, and a third had a restroom sign affixed to it.

"Natalie?" I called through the restroom door. "Darling, are you in there?"

"Occupied!" a voice rang out.

A voice that was not Natalie's.

Shifting back a step, my foot caught on something. A red bra and a red-and-white negligee lay on the ground, both still on their hangers.

I checked the stockroom, but it was empty. No sign of Natalie. The restroom door opened, and a woman came out. She hiccuped, then giggled as she went to join her friends. I glanced into the restroom, but it was for a single occupant.

Where the fuck was Natalie?

Pushing the hangers aside with my foot, I tried the third door. A blast of cold air and whirling snow hit me. It led to a narrow alley between buildings.

The tracks were quickly filling, but I could make out a set of footprints and two troughs in the snow, like something—or someone—had been dragged outside. Fresh tire tracks led away.

Panic flashed through me. It was like being kicked in the stomach. The air rushed from my lungs, and for a second, I couldn't breathe.

A second later, one thought solidified, consuming my entire being. *Find her.*

I couldn't chase them down on foot, so I flew back through the shop and out the front door. Ignoring the freezing air and the thick snow on the sidewalk, I hurried down the street to my car.

Hoping against hope that Julian hadn't discovered the tracker I'd put on his car, I brought up his location. He was moving, not far from downtown, heading toward the highway.

Did he have her?

It was the only thing that made sense.

My tires spun as I pulled out onto the street. As much as I wanted to race to catch up with them, visibility was shit, and the snow was accumulating quickly. I couldn't save her if I was in a ditch.

Keeping an eye on the moving dot on the map, I followed. The wind gusted, blowing drifts of snow across the road.

Twice I had to stop until the wind died down again when I couldn't see past the front end of the car.

The dot kept moving away from town. Where the fuck was he taking her? Not to his house. That was in the opposite direction.

Doubt crept in. Was the tracker still on his car? He could have found it and put it on another vehicle. Was I chasing a decoy?

A car pulled out in front of me, losing control as it made the turn. I had to stop as it spun almost in a full circle. Gritting my teeth, I growled in frustration, and my eyes flicked to the dot on the map again.

I couldn't be in two places at once. It was either follow the tracker or head straight for Julian's house.

The driver in front of me righted their car and started moving again. I made my decision. Follow the tracker. If I was wrong, I'd never forgive myself. But my instincts said that dot would lead me to her.

Although there wasn't anything she could do, I rang Maple to keep her apprised of the situation.

"Yes?" she answered.

"Julian took Natalie."

"What?"

"She disappeared out the back of a shop. Dragged. There were tracks in the snow."

"Obviously, I'm not in my office, but—"

"No need. I'm in pursuit. In a fucking snowstorm."

"The tracker is still on his vehicle?"

"I hope it is."

"Jensen, there are about a thousand ways this could go wrong."

"I'm aware. Doesn't matter. I'm going to find her. And I'm going to rip that bloody prick to shreds."

"Jensen—"

I ended the call.

A second later, my phone rang again. I was about to tell Maple not to try to talk me out of anything, but it was an unknown number.

"Hello?"

"Jensen Lakes."

The voice on the other end sent an icy chill through my veins. "Archer Prince."

"It's been a while. Shall we catch up?"

The tires slipped, but I kept the car on the road. "I'm a bit busy at the moment."

"I'm sure you are. I'd be looking for her too."

My blood turned to ice in my veins. "Where is she?"

He clicked his tongue a few times. "Patience, old friend."

"If you touch her, I'll rip your fucking face off."

"It hurts when someone steals from us, doesn't it? I'd say this is no less than you deserve."

"What are you talking about? You can't mean the Emerald Crown?"

"Why not?"

"When did you become a jewelry thief?"

"You know me. I like beautiful things. Like your lovely lady."

Rage seared through me, and I growled through clenched teeth. "I'll fucking kill you."

"So angry. I take it you like this one. Good. That makes our game much more fun."

"This isn't a game."

"Isn't it? But I'm having such a good time."

"Why her? Why not come after me?"

"I told you. You took something from me. I'm simply returning the favor."

The dot on the map picked up speed. Was Natalie with Julian? Or did Archer have her?

The wind gusted, and the snow filled my field of vision. I had to stop; I couldn't see where I was going.

"Let me talk to her."

"No, we're not going to do that."

"What the fuck do you want?"

"I want you to know that I beat you. You thought you won this round, but you didn't."

The line went dead.

In an instant, I realized what was happening. Not only was Archer Prince behind the heist of the Emerald Crown but he also had Natalie. And it was a trap.

He knew I'd come for her. He was using her to get to me. To kill me, most likely. Prevent me from interfering in any more of his carefully planned endeavors.

My eyes narrowed, and I gripped the steering wheel. I was going to spring his trap. I had no choice. Saving Natalie was paramount. Nothing else mattered.

But that bastard had no idea who he was dealing with. I was walking straight into an ambush. He knew it. I knew it.

And I was still going to win.

CHAPTER 27
Natalie

eing grabbed in the back of a boutique and shoved into a car at gunpoint had not been on my holiday Bingo card. But there I was.

I lay across the back seat, zip-tied at the wrists and ankles, not wearing a seat belt. You'd think that last one wouldn't have worried me as much as it did, considering I'd just been abducted. And there was a gun. But the storm made it almost impossible to see, and I didn't care how fancy Julian's car was. If we crashed, I was dead.

The so-called self-defense class I'd taken in college had been useless. The whole thing had happened too fast. One second, I was waiting for the restroom, and the next, I was being dragged outside into the cold.

He'd hit me upside the head before I had the chance to scream or fight back. He hadn't knocked me unconscious, but the blow had stunned me enough that he'd been able to get me in the back of his car. While I was still in a daze, he'd brandished the gun and zip-tied my feet and ankles.

Maybe I had blacked out for a minute because I couldn't remember him closing the door or getting in the driver's seat.

The next thing I knew, I was lying across the back seat of a moving car with a brutal headache.

"Where are we going?" I asked, my voice hoarse from the pain.

"You're awake," Julian answered. "You know, you're not a bad actress. You actually had me fooled for a while."

I didn't reply.

"Stupid mistake on my part. I knew you were with Lakes. I actually bought your story about being his already forgotten one-night stand. I felt sorry for you. What the hell is that?"

"The necklace is gone."

"I'm sure it is. Doesn't matter. I'm still getting paid."

The windows looked like they were covered in a white sheet. How could he see where he was going? I felt the tires slip and wondered how he was managing to stay on the road.

"All we did is take something you had no right to in the first place," I said. "That necklace wasn't yours. You stole it."

"So?"

"Why are you retaliating like this?"

"I'm not retaliating."

"You grabbed me, hit me, tied me up, and shoved me in your car. How is that not retaliation?"

"I didn't do it to get back at you. Although I should. You almost fucked me over more than you know."

"Then why?"

"To fix what you screwed up."

"What are you talking about?"

Shaking his head a little, he chuckled again. "The necklace wasn't the prize, sweetheart. It was bait. I counted on Lakes coming for it. That's why I was hired to steal it. What I didn't count on was you. You're not here because I'm pissed at you, although I am. Now, you're the bait."

My mind raced to put the pieces together—to make sense

of it all. Julian had been hired to steal the necklace to trap Jensen? And it hadn't worked, so now I was the bait?

"What were you going to do to him?"

"I wasn't going to do anything to him except hand him over to the guy who hired me."

"Who hired you?"

"Don't worry about it."

"What is he going to do to me?"

"Hopefully nothing."

I glanced up and caught his eyes in the rearview mirror.

"But don't worry," he said, his voice taking on a hard edge. "I'm not finished with you."

"But..." The car swerved, and I almost rolled off the seat. "You can't do this. It's Christmas."

"What?" he asked with a derisive laugh. "What does that have to do with anything?"

I wasn't sure, but somehow it made my situation a thousand times worse. I couldn't be abducted on Christmas Eve. I'd promised Annabel I'd be home. I'd *pinky* promised.

His phone rang, and he answered. "Yeah."

I strained to listen, but I couldn't hear what the other person was saying.

"In case you didn't notice, we're in the middle of a snowstorm. I'll get there as soon as I can."

He paused again.

"I told you the storm would be a problem... I know... If you say so."

He ended the call.

I didn't bother asking questions. Tears welled in my eyes. Maybe it was silly to be upset about missing Christmas when I had much bigger and probably life-threatening problems. But I couldn't help it. The sudden realization that I was zip-tied in a car headed who knows where on Christmas Eve and might not make it home in time for Christmas with my niece was devastating.

Or maybe my brain focused on the holiday as a means of keeping my sanity, considering it was possible I wasn't going to make it home at all.

I felt the car turn, and the back end slid. Wincing, I sat up and looked out the windows. Heavy snow fell all around us, and I had no idea where we were. There was nothing but snow and the faint outline of trees.

We climbed a hill, and the trees encroached on either side. Where were we? Not on the highway or any of the main roads. There was hardly enough room for one car to pass through.

Finally, a single light came into view up ahead. Julian slowed, and when he stopped, I could see the vague shape of a house or cabin through the swirling snow.

Without a word, Julian held up the gun—a clear threat. He got out and opened the door, pointing it at me.

Staring down my imminent death, I scooted across the seat. With my ankles tied, I wasn't going to be able to walk— especially in the snow. Still holding the gun, he manhandled me onto his shoulder.

Pain from my car accident injuries exploded through me. The wind whipped through my hair and stung my cheeks as he carried me to the cabin. His shoulder dug into my stomach, but I refused to make a sound. Although I was terrified and in pain—who wouldn't have been—something else bloomed inside me.

Defiance.

Screw that pompous ass. He was not going to take me out.

He opened the door and went inside. It was slightly warmer out of the storm, but not much.

"About time," a man's voice said.

Julian set me on my feet and gestured with the gun for me

to sit in a threadbare armchair. I sank down, my gaze darting around.

The rustic cabin was small—just one open room with what was probably a bathroom at the back. The walls and floor were wood, with a few mismatched rugs strewn around, and several pairs of old snowshoes hung on the wall. A black wood stove stood in the tiny kitchen area, and a four-poster king-size bed took up much of the space.

"In case you didn't notice, the weather is shit," Julian said.

The second man stood with his hands casually clasped behind his back, looking out a paned glass window. He was dressed all in black, from his ski jacket to his boots, and the way they fit made them look sleek and expensive.

He turned, and his eyes swept over me. Nothing in his expression changed, but something about his gaze made my skin crawl.

"Which is why time is of the essence," he replied, still looking at me.

"I don't know what you expect," Julian said, irritation plain in his tone. "I had to wait for an opportunity and improvise the hell out of it. I got lucky when they went in that shop and the back door was unlocked."

The other man came closer. He reached out, and I flinched when he touched my chin, angling my face to the side.

"You hit her."

"Look, if you could have done a better job, you should have done it yourself."

The man's eyes flashed with anger, but when he spoke, his voice was even. "Let's not forget that she's here because of you. This is your fault."

Julian's jaw tightened, and it took him a second to reply. "No. It's her fault."

"Have it your way." He waved his hand as if the issue was no longer important.

"Who are you?" I asked.

"Where are my manners?" He took my bound hands and lifted my fingers to his lips. "Archer Prince."

I snatched my hands away. Archer Prince? The art thief Jensen had been hunting?

He scrutinized me again and seemed to come to a decision. He reached into an inside pocket and pulled out a pocketknife.

"I don't think we'll be needing these. You're not going anywhere in that storm." He crouched and cut through the zip ties at my ankles, then freed my wrists. "And if you try, I'll just kill you."

His matter-of-fact tone was clear. He wasn't kidding.

"This was all a setup, wasn't it?" I asked.

Pocketing his knife, he shot an irritated glance at Julian. "What did you tell her?"

"Nothing," he said. "Does it matter? I still don't get why we're out here. Lakes might not even find us."

Archer took a few slow steps. Something about his relaxed and unhurried body language was unnerving. I didn't like his confidence.

"That was your real mistake," he said. "You underestimated him. And we're here because it suits my purposes."

"You're out here alone. How is that not underestimating him? You should have snipers out there to take him out before he even gets close."

The smirk that crossed Archer's face sent another chill down my spine. "Oh no. Lakes deserves much better than that. I respect him too much not to see to it personally."

"Suit yourself." Julian tucked the gun in the waistband of his pants. "While we're waiting, we need to renegotiate."

The fury that crossed Archer's face made my blood run

cold. Julian seemed oblivious. Maybe he wasn't worried because he was armed, but I had the distinct feeling Julian had not only underestimated Jensen but he was underestimating Archer, too.

"I don't renegotiate," Archer said. "The terms are set."

"What about her?"

"What about her?"

"I want her when we're done." Julian took a step toward him. "She owes me."

Archer didn't answer. Just watched Julian through slightly narrowed eyes.

"You get Lakes," Julian continued. "Once you have him, you don't need her. Besides, what's she to you? She's just a lying bitch."

My stomach roiled with dread. There was no question what Julian meant or what he planned to do to me. It was unspeakable.

Archer hesitated and cast a glance at me before replying. "Let's talk outside."

Julian nodded and followed him to the door. His eyes lingered on me as he passed, undisguised anger—and lust— plain on his face.

The wind howled and snow blew inside when the two men walked out the door. Julian shut it, and the world seemed to fall quiet again.

My heart beat furiously, and I stood, wondering if I could use anything in the cabin as a weapon. Panic rose, sucking the air from my lungs.

A gunshot rang out, and I froze with terror.

I watched, wide-eyed, as the door opened again, ushering in a fresh blast of snow and frigid air. Archer calmly came in and closed it behind him.

"I should probably thank you," he said, his voice smooth and even. "For giving me an excuse to get rid of him. He had promise, but his ego was always going to get him killed."

With no idea how to reply, I gaped at him.

He checked his watch. "You might as well have a seat. I don't know how long we'll be here."

I sank into the chair, my body trembling with fear and cold.

Would Jensen come? And if he did, how would he avoid falling into Archer's trap?

How were we going to get out of this?

CHAPTER 28

Jensen

The dot on the map had stopped. Whatever Julian's destination was, he'd arrived.

Eventually, I came to the turn he'd taken. It was probably a dirt road and nearly impossible to see in the storm. My car bumped over something, but a gap in the trees indicated where the road should be.

With the snow falling so heavily, I vaguely wondered if I'd be able to get out again. I'd have to hurry, or we risked getting stuck out there.

But one problem at a time.

I followed the road—or what I hoped was a road—gradually closing the distance between myself and the tracker. The snow deepened, and when I came to a slight hill, I almost got stuck. Fighting back frustration, I coaxed the car forward until I started to move again.

Since I couldn't drive up and announce myself, I stopped at a flat spot a short distance from the dot on the map. If I had any chance of rescuing Natalie and getting out alive, I had to spring the trap—on my terms, not theirs. Stealth was imperative.

I grabbed a few things I might need from the center console—a pocketknife, a lock picking tool, and a few small explosives I typically used as a last resort if there was a lock I couldn't crack. And thank goodness for Natalie and her insistence I get Tilikum clothes. I stashed everything in my inside pockets, zipped my winter coat, and donned the hat and gloves she'd pressed me to purchase.

Snow blew into the car as soon as I opened the door. I had to push against the wind to get out, and the cold stung my face. Ignoring the discomfort and squinting into the blizzard, I got off the road and took to the trees.

Wary of the possibility that Archer had brought snipers, or at least henchmen, I looked for any sign of them. It was hard to tell in the storm, but I had a feeling Archer was on his own. He always worked alone. Just like me.

Still, despite the frigid temperature, I was careful and glad for the cover of the biting wind and swirling snow.

Finally, a light came into view. I could see the vague outline of two vehicles parked in front of what seemed to be a small cabin.

There was the trap. Now, I had to figure out how to spring it without getting myself killed.

All in a day's work.

While I didn't know for sure that Natalie was there, my gut told me she was. I could practically feel her presence calling to me.

Don't worry, darling. I'll be there soon.

Creeping closer, I spotted the front door. Still no sign of henchmen. Good. Once I got rid of Julian, it would just be me and Archer. Man to man, as it had always been meant to be.

I picked my way through the snow, using the trees as cover, and made my way around the cabin. Just the one door. Several windows. A stack of wood in the back. The roof had a high pitch to allow the snow to slide off, and the wood stack was similarly protected.

I couldn't see much through the small windows, even with my binoculars. Possibly a bit of movement—was someone walking around in there?—but the glare was too strong and the snow too thick to make out anything useful. I moved positions and paused again, looking at the landscape around me.

A bulge in the snow a short distance from the cabin caught my attention. It looked human shaped, like a person lying prone on the ground. I focused on the far end, and sure enough, there was blood in the snow.

No. Not Natalie. It couldn't be my Natalie.

Forcing away the panic that tried to seize me, I crept toward the body and brushed away the accumulated snow. It was Julian.

Relief washed over me as I darted back behind a tree for cover. The bullet wound in Julian's head meant Archer was armed. I was not. My work didn't usually require that sort of direct confrontation. I was sent in to woo and flatter. To sneak in and get out without being suspected.

I needed to lure Archer outside. And use the storm to my advantage.

Reaching into one of my inside pockets—Natalie really had chosen the perfect coat—I drew out the small explosives. They weren't strong enough to do a great deal of damage, but hopefully a few together would be loud enough to draw Archer outside.

I affixed them to a tree, set them to detonate, then circled around so I could see the cabin door and approach from a different direction.

A few seconds later, the blast filled the air. The sound echoed off the nearby mountain slopes, rumbling through the air like thunder.

I held my breath. Would he come out?

The door opened. Archer stepped out.

And he had Natalie.

He held her in front of himself, his arm wrapped around her upper body, and he brandished a gun in his other hand. The fear on her face cut me to the core.

"Lakes?" he called. "Is that you?"

If I answered, I'd give away my position. He turned to face me as if he somehow knew, so I backed up until I could hardly see them through the blizzard and circled a short distance in the other direction.

"Come out, Jensen," he taunted. "I know you're here."

He turned so his back was to me. I darted closer, then froze when he called out again.

"I so enjoy our games, old friend. But we've reached the final round." Still taking slow steps in a circle, he raised the gun to Natalie's temple.

Rage burst through me like a torrent of fire. He was not going to hurt her.

In a few steps, I was there. I slammed into him and grabbed his elbow. The gun went flying and his grip on Natalie loosened enough that she fell forward into the snow.

Archer spun into me, landing a blow to my jaw. I took it— hardly even flinched—and returned the favor.

From the corner of my eye, I saw Natalie crawling away. Knowing she was out of his reach, I turned my full attention to Archer.

He staggered against the force of my strike, and I took advantage of his lack of balance, smashing into him. We hit the ground, each struggling for control. My hands slipped against the slick surface of his jacket. I couldn't get a grip on him.

He wrestled me to my back and was about to land another blow when I grabbed a handful of snow and shoved it in his face. I hit him while he was blinded, but not hard enough to knock him off me. He came for me again, and we grappled, rolling through the freezing snow. He tried to get me on my back again, but I threw him off and surged to my feet.

He got up and wiped his arm across his face. I tasted the metallic tang of blood, and his nose bled freely. His shoulders were hunched, and an angry sneer distorted his features.

"You piece of shit," he spat. "You can't beat me."

Maybe this was all a game to him, but it wasn't to me. Gritting my teeth, I was about to charge again when he moved, reaching into his pocket. The strangest thought went through my mind. He was going to shoot me. And I was too far away to stop him.

My eyes darted for Natalie. I was about to throw myself on top of her in case he decided to point the gun at her instead, when several shots rang out. I looked down at myself, expecting to see bullet holes and splashes of blood dripping into the snow.

But I hadn't been shot.

Archer crumpled to the ground in a heap. Natalie stood to the side, the gun still raised. The gun Archer had dropped.

She let go of the weapon, and it fell into the snow.

In an instant, I rushed to her, wrapping her in my arms while her body shook.

I held her for a long moment, but she was shivering violently.

"Is there anyone else here?" I asked.

"Don't think so."

"Let's get you inside."

She nodded against my chest.

I led her into the cabin and shut the door. It wasn't much warmer, although at least there wasn't any wind. I ripped the quilt off the bed and put it around her.

"There you go."

"I'm so cold," she said through chattering teeth.

"Your clothes are wet. We have to get you dry." I glanced at the wood stove. "Give me a minute. I'll get a fire going."

Buried in the large quilt, she sat in an armchair.

With a sense of clarity born of our crisis, I got to work. Luckily, there was a stack of faded newspapers and a few sticks of kindling. I crumpled the paper and added it to the stove, along with the kindling to get the fire started. The box of matches was nearly empty, but the first one lit, and I touched it to the edges of the paper.

The flames began to spread, licking the kindling.

"There's wood outside."

I rushed out and grabbed an armful. Despite the storm, it seemed dry. Filled with urgency, I rushed back in and shut the door on the storm. Natalie smiled at me.

And it hit me harder than the force of the wind. I was in love with her.

The shock was so deep, I almost dropped the wood. I loved that woman. I loved her with everything I had. There was nothing I wouldn't do for her.

With no idea how that could have happened—or how I hadn't realized it before—I took the wood to the stove and put a piece in.

"Are you hurt?" she asked through chattering teeth.

"No." My jaw would probably be sore later, as would my knuckles, but at that moment, all I cared about was her. "Are you?"

"I don't think so. Just cold."

"It'll warm up fast once the fire gets going." I put in another piece of wood and blew on the flames. "We need to get you out of those wet clothes."

Although she still shivered, she smiled. "I'm sure that's very disappointing."

"Darling, I'm happy to take your clothes off anytime you want me to. But I really do want to get you warm."

"Body heat works best."

Still bewildered by my realization—because what was I supposed to do with that—I took off my boots and stripped down to my boxer briefs. Natalie peeled off her wet clothes, and I quickly laid them out in front of the fire to dry.

We climbed onto the bed, and I covered us with the quilt. Her skin was cold to the touch. I rolled her onto her back and settled on top of her, careful not to put too much weight on her. She wrapped her arms and legs around me and tucked her face against my neck.

"I don't know why I got cold so fast," she said. "I guess sitting in here without a coat and then getting wet outside was enough."

"It's bloody freezing out there."

We lay together for long moments, just breathing. Her body gradually relaxed and stopped shivering as warmth seeped back into her.

"Jensen?"

"Yes?"

"He was going to kill you."

I propped myself up so I could look her in the eyes. "He was. And then he would have killed you. But you stopped him."

"I didn't even think about it. I just pulled the trigger. I couldn't let him hurt you."

The corners of my mouth lifted. "You were amazing."

"The whole thing was a setup. Archer hired Julian to steal the necklace, and it was all a trap to get you here."

"He certainly went to a lot of trouble, didn't he?"

She laughed softly. "How did he know you'd be the one sent to steal it back?"

"Proximity, I suppose. I don't live far from here. It's probably why Archer chose Julian."

"But it's over." She reached up and touched my face. "You did it. You beat him, and you saved me."

"We did it." I leaned in and captured her mouth in a deep kiss. "I never could have done this without you."

And it was true. I'd always worked alone, but without Natalie—without someone I could trust—I would have failed. And Archer would have won.

I kissed her again, savoring her. This wasn't just a partnership. And it wasn't just sex. It was something deep and profound. A feeling I'd never experienced before.

Struck with awe, I pulled away and stared at her.

"What's wrong?" she asked. "Are you okay?"

Looking deep into her beautiful, dark eyes, I smiled. "Yes."

"Then why are you looking at me like that?"

"Because I just realized something."

"What? That we're stuck in a cabin in a blizzard with two dead men outside?"

"No." I chuckled softly. "I love you."

Her lips parted, but she didn't reply.

"Natalie, I love you. I love you so much I hardly know what to do with myself."

"Are you serious?"

"Absolutely. Darling, I love you, and the more times I say it, the more true it feels. I love you." I kissed her. "I love you." I kissed her again. "I love you."

"I love you, too. It's crazy, but I don't care. I love you so much."

"Well, isn't this the best Christmas I've ever had."

With our bodies pressed close and a fire crackling in the background, I kissed her again. Kissed her and loved her— hard but gentle, slow but deep. I poured myself into her, loving every inch of her. Showing her with all I had how much she meant to me.

CHAPTER 29

Jensen

The fire warmed the small cabin, and the flames provided a source of light as the sun went down. Under different circumstances, it would have been rather cozy. But as I lay with Natalie in my arms, I knew we weren't out of the woods yet. Quite literally.

We were stuck in a cabin in the middle of nowhere in a raging blizzard, and I didn't know how we were going to get out.

Natalie shifted, propping herself up on one arm. "Are you thinking what I'm thinking?"

I caressed her face. "That you're the most beautiful woman in the world?"

She smiled. "No. That we're stuck in a snowstorm."

The wind howled, rattling the windows.

"At least we have shelter for the night."

The firelight flickered, illuminating her sad eyes. "It's Christmas Eve."

"We can't go out in that." My gaze moved to the dark window. As if to emphasize my point, the wind howled again. "Not until the sun comes up at least."

"I know. I don't suppose your phone has a signal?"

"No. Nothing."

"I think my phone is still in your car, but I doubt it would work out here anyway."

"Unlikely." I brushed her hair back. "Listen, I'm going to get us out of here."

She nodded, but the sadness didn't leave her expression. "Nina is probably freaking out, wondering where we are."

"She might be, but there isn't anything we can do about that tonight."

"I promised Annabel I'd be home for Christmas. I didn't just promise—I pinky promised."

"As did I. And we're going to keep those promises. We might be late, but we'll get home for Christmas." I brought her in for a soft kiss. "For now, let's focus on the fact that we're safe from the storm. We'll see what daylight brings."

"Okay."

She settled against me, and I held her until we both drifted off to sleep.

※

The cold woke me before dawn. The fire had died down during the night, leaving a chill in the air. Natalie nestled against me, her body soft and warm. I held her for a while, letting her sleep, and enjoyed the feel of her in my arms.

We had a difficult day ahead. I harbored no illusions that we were driving out. There was far too much snow. I wondered if we'd even find my car in the drifts. Although we had to. Natalie wasn't dressed for a long trek through the woods. Her coat was in my car, as were the extra hat and gloves she'd insisted I purchase.

The pale light of dawn began to filter through the windows, and Natalie stirred.

"Morning," she said.

"Merry Christmas, darling."

She smiled. "Merry Christmas."

I kissed her. But as delicious as she was, it wasn't the time to linger in bed.

"First things first," I said. "We need water. And then a way out."

"We can use snow, but we need to melt it first. If there's a pot or something, we could do that over the stove."

I gestured to the old snowshoes on the wall. "And those might get us out of here."

"They look ancient. They must be for decoration, not use."

"As long as they hold together, they'll help. My car isn't far. I don't think there's any chance of driving it, but you need warmer clothes. We'll go there first, then hike out until we get a signal and can call for help."

"Is it still snowing?"

It was hard to tell in the dim light, but at least the wind was no longer shrieking.

"It might be. If we have any luck, the worst of the storm is over."

"I guess we just hope for a Christmas miracle."

Leaning in, I gave her a quick kiss. I felt like I'd already been given one.

One thing I knew—I was going to get her home for Christmas. No matter what.

We moved quickly, getting dressed and adding more wood to the fire. Natalie found a pot and cleaned it out with snow, then set some to melt on the stove. Fat flakes drifted down peacefully outside, settling on the thick accumulation of fresh snow from the storm, but at least it was no longer the blizzard of the previous day.

The cabin didn't have much more that would help us. We

took down the snowshoes, and they seemed sturdy enough to use. I insisted Natalie wear my coat, hat, and gloves. It occurred to me that there were two fully dressed bodies outside, and we could probably use some of what they were wearing. But I decided I'd rather hike to my car without a coat than dig out the bodies of Archer and Julian.

When we were hydrated and bundled as much as possible, with snowshoes on our feet, we ventured out.

Snow spilled inside when we opened the door. The wind had built up a tall drift in front of the cabin, and we had to climb out. Even with snowshoes, we sank to our knees, and the frigid air bit into me.

I narrowed my eyes, peering through the early dawn light. The road had disappeared. The only sign of its existence was the space between the trees.

"Can you manage?" I asked.

She nodded. "You must be freezing."

"I'll be all right once we get moving."

We set out, past the mostly buried vehicles, toward the road. The fresh snow was soft and the drifts uneven, making it hard to keep a straight path. Although the howling wind of the previous night had died down, gusts still whistled through the trees and bit at my exposed skin.

It didn't take long for our legs to ache from both exertion and the cold. The snowfall grew heavier, making it hard to see very far ahead or keep track of the road. I had to stop and squint, looking around to make sure I didn't lose our way.

Finally, we spotted it. The top half of my car stuck out in the midst of all the white. As I'd suspected, it was too buried to get us anywhere. It was going to be difficult enough just getting inside.

"I wish there'd been something in the cabin to help us dig," she said. "Although I guess I should be grateful for the snowshoes."

"Indeed. I'll need the gloves if I'm going to do this without frostbite. Just keep your hands tucked in your pockets."

She gave me the gloves, and I set to work, digging my way through the snow.

Movement kept me warm, although it was impossible not to get wet. But I wasn't worried about myself. Natalie hadn't uttered a word of complaint, but I knew she was sore and cold. Concern for her and determination to get her to safety edged out everything else. I didn't care if I broke my body doing it. I was going to get her home.

After what felt like an eternity of digging, I was able to wedge the driver's side door open. Since Natalie was smaller, she crawled in and retrieved her coat, plus another hat and set of gloves. She found her phone, although it didn't have a signal any more than mine did.

"All those presents," she said with a laugh as we traded coats. "They seemed so important yesterday. Now I just want to get home."

I gave her the dry set of gloves and tried to ignore the fact that the wind was increasing again. "It won't be long, now."

"I hope not. And I hope the highway is open once we get there."

"One thing at a time." I gave her a quick kiss, although my lips were numb. "Ready?"

"Let's do this."

Leaving my car behind, we headed out again. Hunkered against the wind, we trudged along. Sometimes our snowshoes kept us on top of the snow. Other times, we'd step and be up to our thighs in a powdery drift. More than once, I had to help Natalie climb out of a deep spot.

I glanced at her regularly as we hiked, making sure she could keep up. I could see the toll it was taking on her. She was still injured from the bloody car accident, and I had no doubt Julian had been rough when he'd shoved her in his car.

Fucker.

At least he was dead.

The wind picked up, blasting snow in our faces. Natalie stumbled forward, and I reached out, catching her before she fell.

"Sorry," she said through chattering teeth. "My legs are so numb."

I checked my phone, but still no signal. "Just a little farther, darling. You can make it."

She nodded. Snowflakes clung to her eyelashes, and her cheeks were pink from the cold. I'd never wanted anything more than I wanted to bring her home.

I held out my arm, and she took it. With her clinging to me, we kept going. Our existence was reduced to the struggle to lift each leg and put it in front of us, one step at a time.

Natalie's foot sank into soft snow, and she tumbled forward, almost taking me down with her. I crouched and scooped her up, helping her to her feet.

She didn't say anything, but tears gathered in her eyes.

My chest felt like it might burst with determination and rage. And something else. Something bigger than both combined.

Love.

I loved this woman, and I was going to save her. No matter the cost.

"Come on." I turned and put my back to her. "Climb on."

"You can't carry me."

"Of course I can. Get on."

She managed to get on my back, and I held her legs while she clung to my shoulders. The added weight made me sink deeper into the snow, but I didn't care. Every step, no matter how painful, brought us closer to safety.

My legs screamed at me, my back ached, and the wind tore through my clothes. But I kept on putting one foot in front of the other. I couldn't give up. Natalie needed me, and I wouldn't fail her.

Besides, it was Christmas. That had to count for something.

The forest seemed endless, and it was hard to estimate distance, but the land gradually descended. I kept near the trees along what I hoped was the road. The more numb and tired I became, the harder it was to tell. I leaned forward, trudging through the snow, sheer force of will the only thing keeping me upright.

Finally, when I was starting to worry that my legs might buckle beneath me, we emerged from the trees onto what had to be the highway, covered in snow.

I set Natalie down and paused to catch my breath.

"I don't have a signal," she said. "Do you?"

I checked my phone. "It's coming in and out, but it might be enough. I'll—" A noise in the distance made me pause. "Do you hear that, or am I hallucinating?"

"Hear what?"

Maybe I was hallucinating. But there it was again. It sounded like music.

"Wait," she said. "I do hear something."

A deep rumbling grew, and for a moment, I thought the music had been a hallucination.

"I think I hear a vehicle, but..." She leaned one ear toward the direction of the sound. "Are those bells?"

It did sound like bells. Open-mouthed, she and I stared at each other as the noise grew—the roar of an engine accompanied by the tinkle of bells.

What was happening?

Through the falling snow, headlights appeared. At that point, half delirious with exhaustion and cold, I wouldn't have been surprised to see a sleigh pulled by bloody reindeer.

It was bright red, but it wasn't a sleigh. It was a vintage fire truck with a wide snowplow mounted to the front—the one we'd seen outside the farm store. "Jingle Bells" blared from speakers mounted to the top, and the entire thing was decked out in blinking lights.

"Oh my gosh!" Natalie exclaimed, waving to the driver. "Woody! Stop! Woody!"

The fire engine slowed and pulled to a stop a short distance away. The music cut off, and a man with a thick white beard and a Santa hat leaned out.

"You've got to be kidding me," I muttered. Santa Claus had just come to our rescue?

"Woody!" Natalie called again. "Oh my gosh, I'm so happy to see you!"

"Natalie Thatcher? What in the name of Christmas Day are you doing out here?"

"It's a long story. Can you give us a ride?"

"Of course I can. You're lucky I saw you in all this mess."

"Who is that man, and why does he look like Santa Claus?" I asked.

Natalie laughed. "Woody Blankenship. He's the one I told you about who plays Santa every year. Because of the beard."

"Naturally."

In a daze, I helped Natalie up into the truck and got in with her. She settled onto my lap, and the relief of not dragging myself through the snow was overwhelming. Woody turned up the heat before making a U-turn across the highway.

"What are you doing out here?" Natalie asked.

"Plowing," Woody replied. "The county guys are doing their best, but I figured they could use some help. Gotta be a lot of folks out there trying to get into town for Christmas. But what were you doing out there?"

"Would you believe I was abducted by a jewelry thief and

taken to a remote cabin as bait to lure him into a showdown with his longtime nemesis?" She gestured to me.

"Huh." Woody nodded as if that didn't sound the least bit implausible. "Glad you made it out all right. And just in time for Christmas."

Natalie laughed. "Just in time."

"Should I take you home, then?" Woody asked.

"Yes, please. Thank you so much."

"You're quite welcome." He turned the music on again, and "White Christmas" filled the air around us.

Of course. It was our song.

CHAPTER 30
Natalie

Woody's old fire truck rumbled into town, pushing snow aside as it went. His Christmas music filled the air, and he waved to the townspeople who came outside to see where the noise was coming from.

I sat in Jensen's lap, my head tucked against his shoulder, his arms around me. The heat coming from the vent helped, but I wouldn't be able to get truly warm until I changed out of my wet clothes. But even as a few shivers still overtook me, Jensen was there, and I knew we were safe.

We turned onto our street just as "I'll Be Home For Christmas" began. It was as if we'd planned the playlist.

I sat up and looked out the window. Snow blanketed the neighborhood, hanging heavily on the trees and covering the ground. Christmas lights twinkled through the white, and a few more flakes drifted through the air, the last vestiges of the previous night's snowstorm.

Woody pulled up next to my house and parked. The front door flew open, and Annabel came tearing out into the snow, still dressed in her pajamas.

"Santa?" She stopped in the middle of the yard. "Is that you?"

Nina appeared in the doorway. "Annabel, you don't have—"

She was probably about to say "shoes," but her mouth dropped open, and she stared in disbelief as the three of us got out of the fire engine.

Annabel squealed. "It is you! And you brought them home!"

Nina kept gaping while Jensen and I finished climbing out of the truck. My legs were wobbly, almost crumpling beneath me, but Jensen kept me steady.

"Merry Christmas, Anna-banana," I said. "Sorry we're late."

She rushed over and grabbed us both. A moment later, Nina joined the group hug.

"Where have you been?" Nina asked. "I thought you were next door. I've been saying all morning that of course you'll be here, you pinky promised, but I went over to the apartment, and no one was there and I was about to call 911."

"Breathe," I said. "It's such a long story. And I'm freezing."

Annabel didn't seem to want to let go, so Jensen reached down and picked her up. I was surprised he had it in him, after carrying me through the woods.

"Woody... I mean, Santa," I said. "You're a Christmas miracle. You saved our lives. Literally."

"Ho, ho, ho," he said, playing up his character. "Happy to help. You all have a very Merry Christmas."

"Thank you, Santa," Annabel said. "See, Mom. I told you Santa would bring them home."

"I don't really know what's happening, but thank you," Nina said. "Merry Christmas."

Jensen carried Annabel inside while Nina and I followed.

Dry clothes were the first order of business, so Jensen went to the apartment, and I went upstairs to change. After donning my holiday pajamas, plus two pairs of socks, and a hat—it felt like I might never be warm again—I went downstairs and curled up on the couch with a blanket.

Nina had obviously let Annabel open some of her presents. The floor in front of the tree was littered with bows and torn wrapping paper. Her stocking had been unceremoniously dumped out, leaving a pile of candy and trinkets on the floor, and more than a few discarded wrappers indicated she'd already eaten a lot of chocolate.

Because Nina was the best sister ever, she brought me a hot cup of coffee, and when I took the first sip, I grinned at the added splash of Irish Cream. Nothing had ever tasted so good.

Understandably, she was not willing to wait for a better time to find out what had happened. She put on a Christmas movie for Annabel, and in a quiet voice, I told her everything. From Jensen's job and the stolen necklace to agreeing to help and our adventures tracking down the thief, all the way to my abduction in the boutique and being held as bait by Jensen's longtime nemesis.

She gasped when I told her what had happened to Julian and gaped at me in awe when I described how I'd ended it when Archer had been about to kill Jensen.

"You are such a badass," she said, just above a whisper. "Oh my gosh, I can't believe this. I mean, I can. I totally believe you. And I already knew you were amazing, but this is all so wild."

"I know. I'm not quite sure how this is all real, but here we are."

"Do you need anything else? Are you getting warm?"

"I'm fine for now. I think I'm finally starting to thaw."

"I feel like such an idiot for not realizing you were gone sooner. I knew you weren't here last night, but I figured you were just spending the night with Jensen. And this morning I thought you were sleeping in. Annabel kept asking if she could go wake you and finally I said yes. I went over there with her, and of course, no one was there."

"I'm so sorry. We were stuck in the blizzard with no signal."

"It's okay. I'm just so glad you're all right."

"I'm so glad Woody came along with his plow. I don't know what we would have done."

"Half the roads must be closed. That storm was no joke." Her eyes widened. "Speaking of, I need to check my phone. I invited Dylan and Lucy to come over, but I wonder if he can even get out of his driveway."

"Aw, you invited them for Christmas?"

"I know, it probably seems too soon to spend a holiday together."

"Not at all. Sometimes things are so right, they have to move fast."

Her smile said it all. "Yes. Exactly. I knew you'd get it. I'll be right back."

I did get it. Jensen and I hadn't known each other for very long, but what was happening between us was still very real. And it was right.

Maybe even a Christmas miracle.

He came in dressed in his holiday pajamas, his hair damp beneath his Santa hat. I lifted the blanket so he could snuggle in next to me. He sat and covered us both, then pulled me almost into his lap with his arms around me.

"Merry Christmas, darling," he whispered in my ear.

"Merry Christmas. Did you let Maple know we're okay?"

"Of course. She sends her best."

"What's going to happen with the, um... bodies?"

"They're buried in snow. No one will discover them until spring."

My mouth dropped open.

"I'm kidding," he said with a grin. "No need to worry. My organization will handle it."

I let out a relieved breath. But for some reason—past experience, probably—a pang of doubt hit me. It was like stepping on something sharp.

What if I was wrong? What if it wasn't real?

After all, we'd been through a lot. Facing death could make people say or do things they wouldn't have otherwise. When Jensen had said he loved me, had it been genuine? Or just relief that we were still alive?

Annabel was still occupied with her movie, and I could hear Nina in the kitchen, talking to Dylan on the phone.

I had to know, even if it ruined my Christmas.

"Jensen..." My voice was soft and tentative. "Last night was a lot. And now that we're back, and we didn't die, I'm wondering... We said a lot of things, and..."

Placing a knuckle beneath my chin, he lifted my gaze to his. "I meant what I said."

"You did?"

With the hint of a grin, he nodded.

"You still mean it?"

The corners of his mouth lifted a little more. "I still mean it."

"We're talking about the same thing, right?"

Leaning down, he kissed me, and when he spoke again, his voice was low and quiet—just for me. "I love you. I have no idea how this happened to me. I thought I was immune. But I'm not immune to you, nor do I want to be. I'm in love with you, my beautiful Natalie. So fucking in love. And I wouldn't have it any other way."

"I love you, too. So much. But this is crazy, right?"

"Not at all. Falling in love with you is the most sane thing I've ever done."

"What's going to happen? You have a life. I have a life. Are we going to try to do things long distance? How will this work?"

"You think I'd leave you?"

"No, I don't think you'd leave. Not like that. But we live hours apart. I'm just trying to be practical."

"I can live wherever I like. And where I like is with you. I'll stay if you'll have me."

Reaching up, I ran my hand along the stubble on his jaw. "Yes. Stay."

He kissed me again—deep and slow. Fortunately, Annabel's eyes were still glued to the TV, or she probably would have groaned and called us gross.

"Besides," he said when he pulled away, "I could use a partner. Hunting art thieves isn't exactly as glamorous as nursing in the emergency department, but..."

I laughed.

"You've gone and spoiled me," he continued. "I can't imagine doing my job without you."

"You want me to hunt art thieves with you?"

"It's not a bad way to make a living. Speaking of, once my fee comes through, we'll have to make arrangements to transfer your half. It might be a day or two because of the holidays."

"How much is it?"

"Half a million pounds."

Stunned, I gaped at him. "They paid you half a million pounds to get the necklace back?"

"No, they paid me a million pounds. Well, a bit more than that. My organization takes their cut, of course. Your portion is half a million."

Shock reverberated through me. I had no idea what to say. When he'd offered me a portion of his fee, it hadn't occurred to me that it would be so much money. Even with the conversion from pounds to dollars, it was more than I could have dreamed.

"Is that not enough?" he asked. "It's quite standard for this type of job."

I laughed, and tears gathered in the corners of my eyes. "No, it's so much. You have no idea what this means. There was a flood in the basement, and the furnace could go out any minute, and my car, and all the bills. I don't know what to say."

"How about, 'Jensen, I'm madly in love with you, and you're the best Christmas present I could have asked for.'"

"That's the thing. I wouldn't have thought to ask for you. Or for this. I didn't think it was possible."

"Neither did I. But here we are."

Annabel's cheerful voice carried over the sound of the TV. "Mr. Jensen, I have a present for you!"

Raising his eyebrows, he looked at me. I shrugged. I didn't know what it was.

She dug through the wrapping paper beneath the tree and produced a thick sheet of paper. With a bright smile, she brought it over and handed it to him. It was a crayon drawing of two people, a man and a woman. The man had dark hair, a scribbled beard, and he was dressed in what was probably meant to be a black suit. The woman wore a white dress, and a flush crept across my cheeks when I realized what it was.

"That's you," Annabel said, pointing at the man. "And that's Auntie Natalie."

"And what is Auntie Natalie wearing, Miss Annabel?"

"A wedding dress!"

"Is she, now?" Jensen grinned. "It's a beautiful present. Thank you."

"You're welcome. Merry Christmas!"

"Merry Christmas," he said.

I wanted to bury myself in the blanket. She'd drawn me as

a bride with Jensen as the groom. That had to be freaking him out.

But he just smiled at me, then turned back to Annabel.

"I'm afraid our presents to you are going to be a little late," he said. "We got caught in the snowstorm, and my car is stuck. Santa couldn't manage to get it out."

"That's okay." Annabel climbed into our laps. "Mommy got me presents. And then we can just do Christmas again."

"I like the way you think," he said.

Annabel stayed on our lap and told us all about the presents she'd opened that morning. Nina was busy in the kitchen making pancakes. I felt a little bad that she was doing all the work, although pancakes weren't really a two-person job.

And I had survived an abduction and a blizzard.

It wasn't long before there was a knock on the door. Annabel bounded out of our laps and hurried to answer it.

She jumped up and down with excitement as her little friend Lucy ran in, followed closely by Dylan. He had an armful of presents, and Nina came out to greet him with a kiss.

Jensen leaned in and spoke quietly in my ear. "I'm all for staying, but we'll need to find a new place to live. I predict this house is going to get crowded very soon."

I had a feeling he was right.

Dylan and Lucy joined us in the living room, and the girls opened their presents. Wrapping paper went flying, and the air was filled with giggles and exclamations of glee. I nestled against Jensen, enjoying the Christmas chaos and the warmth of his body snuggled with mine.

When the last of the presents had been torn open, we all crowded around the dining table for the Thatcher family Christmas morning tradition of pancakes with red and green sprinkles.

Sitting at the table, surrounded by the people I loved, I realized something. Nina and I weren't alone anymore.

We'd been on our own for so long, it hadn't occurred to me that things would ever be different. And sure, her relationship with Dylan was new, and there was no guarantee they'd wind up together in the long run, but it wouldn't surprise me if they did. And while what I had with Jensen had only just begun, I knew it was something special.

He was mine, and I was his. Those were our real Christmas presents. Each other.

And it was the best Christmas ever.

Epilogue: Natalie

O ne year later...

Snow fell softly outside, illuminated by the elaborate Christmas lights Jensen had strung on our new house and in the yard. It looked peaceful, the large flakes drifting lazily through the air. Nothing like the snowstorm last Christmas.

Thinking about that made me smile as I finished cleaning up the kitchen. It had been a harrowing experience. But also an adventure. And one that had changed the course of my life.

The nurse's strike had ended the day after Christmas. And the day after that, I'd put in my notice. I still took shifts when they needed coverage, and working part-time at the hospital was great. I could keep up my skills and help out my coworkers. But only when I was in town.

Sometimes I was out hunting art thieves.

Jensen and I had successfully recovered several pieces that year, including an oil painting that had made its way to New

Mexico, a statue in Prague, and several vases that we got by posing as buyers in Turkey.

I never knew where the next job would take us. And I absolutely loved it.

Jensen sidled up behind me and slipped his hands around my waist as I dried my hands on a dish towel. Leaning in, he placed a soft kiss on my neck.

"Merry Christmas, darling."

I hummed with pleasure as his lips traced across my skin. "Merry Christmas."

"Champagne?"

"I'd love some."

After one last kiss, he got out a bottle and popped the cork.

We'd spent Christmas Eve with Jensen's sister and her family, then come back to Tilikum for Christmas Day. Nina and Dylan had been married for a few months—their wedding had been on a gorgeous sunny day in September—and it was their first holiday season as a family. The girls had woken them up before five, so after our big breakfast of pancakes with sprinkles, we'd taken over so Nina and Dylan could nap.

After a leisurely day with my family, full of presents, food, Christmas movies, and lots of hugs from our excited nieces, we'd come home for a quiet dinner. The holiday had lacked the excitement—and danger—of last year, but it had been a wonderful couple of days.

Jensen handed me a champagne flute, then held his up. "Cheers."

"Cheers. Merry Christmas."

Taking my hand, he led me into the living room. The Christmas tree illuminated the room, and a fire flickered in the gas fireplace. Holiday music played softly, and while we had our own present mess to clean up, it was nothing compared to the chaos at Nina and Dylan's.

Jensen pushed the wrapping paper aside with his foot, set our champagne on the coffee table, and gathered me in his arms. With one hand on the small of my back, he drew me close and took my other hand in his. We swayed to the music, and he leaned in to brush my lips with a kiss.

"You're still the best Christmas present I've ever had," he said.

"So are you."

"Have you had a nice day?"

"It's been great."

"Did you get everything you wanted this year?"

I smiled. "I did. Although I never really made a list. How about you?"

"Not quite."

"No? Did I miss something you wanted?"

"Not exactly." He kissed the tip of my nose. "There's one more thing I have for you."

The song ended, and "White Christmas" began. We kept dancing for a moment until he released my hand and reached behind his back. Whatever he had for me must have been tucked into his pants.

He produced a small black box. There was only one thing that could be.

I gasped. Jensen grinned.

"Natalie, my love." He opened the box as he lowered himself onto one knee. It held a vintage-style diamond ring. "Will you be my wife and make me the happiest man alive?"

Pressing my lips together so I wouldn't cry, I nodded. I couldn't seem to get a word out. Finally, my yes broke free. "Yes. Yes, I'll marry you."

With that sexy grin that still made my stomach flutter, he took out the ring and slipped it on my finger.

"You didn't steal this, did you?"

He laughed a little as he stood. "No."

I threw my arms around his neck. He held me close, pressing me against him as he leaned in to kiss me deeply. He tasted like champagne and adventure and love.

It wasn't long before the only thing I was wearing was his ring. Our bodies came together in the soft light of the Christmas tree, and it was every bit as incredible as our first time. Maybe even better.

Because now, we had more. We were madly in love and fiercely dedicated to each other.

I never would have guessed that the sexy and mysterious stranger I'd met the year before would turn out to be the love of my life. I'd more or less given up on that ever happening. But Jensen had blown into my life like a storm, and nothing would ever be the same.

He was mine, and I was his. We were lovers, partners, and best friends. And we were going to spend the rest of our lives together.

He was truly the best Christmas present ever.

Bonus Epilogue: Jensen

T *en years later*

Snow swirled around me and the wind bit through my coat as I made my way across the drifts in the dark. A storm had blown in on Christmas Eve, dumping snow and sending the temperature plummeting.

Not unlike another Christmas I'd spent in Tilikum. Fortunately, this year I was not being lured to my death by my long-time nemesis.

Still, the cold was brutal, and it wouldn't be long before Natalie would realize I'd slipped out of our bed. I didn't want to risk a light, so I chose my steps carefully, following a small noise that carried through the predawn air.

"Don't worry, love. I'm coming."

Hurrying around the fence, I tried the gate. Unlocked, just as we'd planned.

It was impossible to see the path in the snow, but partially buried footprints made the way clear, even in the dark. I heard the noise again and picked up the pace until I came to a small building.

I opened the door and ducked inside, closing it behind me so the heat wouldn't escape.

"There you are, pretty girl."

The golden retriever puppy's tail wagged furiously as I crouched to let her out of her crate. She hadn't been there long. I'd picked her up late on Christmas Eve and made sure she'd be comfortable in my neighbor's shed—with a heater—until morning.

She jumped up, planting her front paws on me, and licked my face.

"I'm happy to see you, too." I clipped a leash to her collar and picked her up. "Let's go potty. And be quick about it. It's bloody cold out there."

Holding the soft bundle of fur, I went outside and waded through the snow, looking for a suitable spot to set her down. She wiggled against me until I settled on a place near my neighbor's house where the snow wasn't quite so deep.

"Go on. There's a good girl."

After a few tentative steps, she pranced through the snow, sniffing as she went. I walked her around a bit, hoping she'd do her business. She didn't.

"It's not playtime. It's still dark."

Why I was talking to her like she could understand me, I had no idea. Habit, I suppose. I'd done the same when my two daughters were babies.

Finally, the puppy circled a few times and peed. I scooped her up and she happily licked my face again.

"All right, good girl. Let's go back to bed."

With a quick glance around to make sure I hadn't been seen, I brought her to the shed and tucked her in her crate.

"There you go. It'll only be a little longer. Promise."

She tried to break my heart by yelping as soon as I left. I hesitated outside the shed. The wind picked up again, but I knew she'd be fine. She was warm, and it was almost morning.

After a few more yelps, she settled down, and I crept away.

The Christmas lights were off, leaving the house shrouded in darkness. I made my way to the back door, eased it open, and slipped inside.

Pausing for a moment, I listened for any signs of life. It was Christmas morning, so my girls would be up well before dawn. But all was quiet. They were still asleep.

I took off my coat and boots and set them aside. Then I crept up the stairs, silent as a shadow, and opened my bedroom door.

The room was dark, but I could make out Natalie's form in our bed. My mouth lifted in a subtle smile. My wife. I loved her so much.

It had been almost a decade since I'd done what had once been unthinkable and walked down the aisle as a groom. And it was the best decision I'd ever made. I'd thought I was immune to falling in love. But it turned out I hadn't been immune at all. I'd just been waiting for my wife.

She didn't make a sound when I slid into bed. The sheet settled over us, and I was about to close my eyes when hers opened.

"Where have you been?" she whispered.

"Right here, darling."

Her lips turned up in a smile. "No, you haven't. You got up twenty minutes ago."

"You heard me?"

"Of course I did."

I'd never been able to get anything past her. "Just a little Christmas surprise for the girls."

I moved closer and gathered her in my arms. She settled against me and draped her arm across my chest.

"Merry Christmas." I kissed her head.

"Merry Christmas."

Her body was warm and soft against mine, and she smelled like sugar and vanilla. If I hadn't known we were liable to get caught—having children had created interesting challenges to our sex life—I'd have rolled her onto her back and buried myself deep inside her.

There'd be time for that later. Behind a locked door.

My eyes closed and I drifted for a while, enjoying the feel of my wife in my arms. It was a rare moment of quiet before the hustle and bustle of the holiday ahead. Soon we'd be immersed in the chaos of presents and treats and family.

And a puppy.

It was a good life.

Natalie and I still went on several "business trips" every year. We were selective about the jobs we accepted, working around our daughters' schedules. Nina and Dylan took care of the girls while we were gone, and the reunions when we returned had become my favorite part of the job.

Nothing quite like two precious girls running into your arms with shouts of, "Daddy!"

The door swished open, and I grinned. Christmas was about to begin.

"They're sleeping," Kayla, our eight-year-old, whispered to her sister.

Five-year-old Maizie lacked her big sister's finesse, and her voice was laced with excitement. "Can we wake them up?"

A second later, my precious girls jumped onto the end of the bed.

"Mommy! Daddy! It's Christmas!"

Natalie rolled away and we both sat up.

"Merry Christmas, loves." I held my arms open, and my daughters barreled into me, nearly knocking me over.

I kissed their heads, and Natalie's arms wound around

us. Despite their excitement, they gave me the gift of a moment of stillness. I closed my eyes, surrounded by the best Christmas present I could ever have received. My family.

But it was Christmas morning, and their anticipation couldn't be contained. We got up and went downstairs to gasps and squeals of joy at the full stockings and presents beneath the tree. I turned on the Christmas lights, and their soft glow filled the room while Natalie started our holiday playlist, adding to the festive ambiance.

My mind was on the waiting puppy as Natalie and I settled on the couch and the girls dug into their stockings, dumping out trinkets and candy. I couldn't wait to see the looks on their faces. They'd been asking for a dog for months, and although Natalie had agreed to it, I'd put it off, claiming it wasn't the right time.

"Did you hear that?" I asked, tilting my head in the direction of the back door.

"No," Natalie said.

I hadn't heard anything either, but I needed a quick excuse to go outside. I stood. "How could you have missed it? It sounded like something hitting the roof."

"I didn't hear anything."

"I better check."

Natalie started to ask where I was going, but I hurried to where I'd left my boots and coat and put them on. A second later, I was out the door.

The sun hadn't risen, but I retraced my steps into my neighbor's yard. The puppy seemed to hear me coming and began yelping before I opened the shed door.

"You're all right." I went in and opened her crate. She burst out, tail wagging, and I scooped her up. "Let's go meet your family."

I took her out for a potty break, then tucked her into my

CLAIRE KINGSLEY

coat. She happily licked my chin while I hurried through the cold. I went in through the back door and shut it behind me.

"Is everything okay?" Natalie called from the other room.

"Yes, fine."

I coaxed the puppy deeper into my coat and zipped it so she was somewhat hidden. Natalie's eyebrows drew together as soon as I emerged into the living room. The girls looked up, but didn't seem to notice the bulge in my coat.

"Darlings, it seems that Santa left you something outside."

Kayla and Maizie gasped, their eyes widening. Natalie's lips parted. I winked at her and unzipped my coat enough that the puppy poked her head out.

Maizie jumped up, her face shining with excitement. Kayla immediately burst into tears.

"A puppy?" Maizie asked. "Is it for us?"

"She is."

Crouching down, I scooped the puppy out of my coat and set her on the floor. Maizie crumpled in a fit of giggles as the puppy jumped on her.

"She's so cute," Kayla sobbed.

I stood, and Natalie rose from the couch. She slipped her arms around my waist, and I held her against me.

"So that's why you were sneaking off last night," she said quietly.

"I told you, just a little Christmas surprise. Do you like her?"

The puppy happily bounded around the girls while Maizie laughed and Kayla cried.

"She's adorable," Natalie said. "I thought you didn't want a dog."

"I was just stalling for time."

"Oh, Kayla," Natalie said. "Are you okay?"

With tears running down her face, she nodded and scooped the puppy into her arms. "I just love her so much."

316

"What shall we name her?" I asked.

"Doggie!" Maizie shouted.

"No, not doggie." Kayla sniffled and seemed to pull herself together. "How about Poppy?"

"Poppy." With my arms still around my wife, I glanced at her. "I quite like that. What do you think, darling?"

"I like Poppy. It fits her."

"Poppy it is."

The girls were distracted, so I leaned down and kissed my wife. Her lips were soft against mine, and I lingered for a long moment, savoring her.

I never would have thought I'd go from perpetual bachelor to small-town husband and girl dad—now with a dog. It was all so bloody wholesome.

And better than I could have imagined.

Natalie and our girls were my everything. My life, my love, my greatest adventure.

❄

Dear reader

Dear reader,

I have to be honest, the entire time I was writing this book, I kept thinking, what the heck am I doing?

A small-town, romcom, romantic suspense, Christmas romance? What *is* that? Will anyone even want this book?

Whatever happens, I wanted to write it, so here we are!

If you've read the Dirty Martini Running Club series, you might remember Jensen Lakes. He's Nora's handsome half-brother with a charming British accent. He's known for shamelessly flirting with Nora's friends. And admittedly, his persona is a little over the top.

When I first introduced Jensen, I'd planned to write him as a hero in his own book. But after the unexpected loss of my husband in 2021, most of my plans fell by the wayside. I decided to let Jensen go, and if he ever spoke up, I'd revisit his story.

And what do you know, speak up he did!

I found myself with a gap in my schedule, and rather than go an entire year without releasing a book, I decided a

Christmas romance was just the thing. Setting it in Tilikum was an easy call. I love our quirky, squirrel-infested town. It's the perfect place for more Christmas romance goodness.

And then I thought, could I add some suspense? Is a romantic suspense Christmas romance a thing? And if it's in Tilikum, that naturally means a dash of humor too. So, also romcom?

As if that wasn't enough, what if I brought in a sexy, suit-wearing side character from another series. Jensen Lakes in Tilikum? Why not!

At that point, my creativity was running wild, which probably explains most of this book. But I have to tell you, it was so much fun. Jensen the secretive high-end thief hunter with Natalie the sweet, tough, and a little down on her luck nurse. It's a bit insta-love, a bit silly small-town, a bit adventure, and a lot romantic. Plus, Christmas!

For me, this book was delightful and invigorating to write. I hope you enjoyed this slightly chaotic mix of romance genres. Who doesn't love a little Christmas adventure with a happy ending!

Love,

Claire

Acknowledgments

Thank you to everyone who helped make this book a reality!

To TeamCK, for cheering me on and reassuring me, for your helpful feedback, and for all your hard work behind the scenes.

To Lori for figuring out what a small-town/romcom/romantic suspense/Christmas romance cover should look like and making it gorgeous.

To Michelle and Jenny for cleaning up my words (and commas!).

And to all my readers for your love, support, and sweet Christmas wishes.

Happy holidays!

Also by Claire Kingsley

For a full and up-to-date listing of Claire Kingsley books visit
www.clairekingsleybooks.com/books/

For comprehensive reading order, visit

www.clairekingsleybooks.com/reading-order/

❄

Sleigh Bells and Snowstorms (Jensen and Natalie)

A stand-alone small-town/romcom/romantic suspense/Christmas
romance.

❄

The Haven Brothers

Small-town romantic suspense with CK's signature endearing
characters and heartwarming happily ever afters. Can be read as
stand-alones.

Obsession Falls (Josiah and Audrey)

Storms and Secrets (Zachary and Marigold)

Temptation Trails (Garrett and Harper)

Whispers and Wildfire (Luke and Melanie)

Captivation Creek - coming April 2026

The final Haven Brother - coming September 2026

❄

How the Grump Saved Christmas (Elias and Isabelle)

A stand-alone, small-town Christmas romance.

❄

The Bailey Brothers

Steamy, small-town family series with a dash of suspense. Five unruly brothers. Epic pranks. A quirky, feuding town. Big HEAs. Best read in order.

Protecting You (Asher and Grace part 1)

Fighting for Us (Asher and Grace part 2)

Unraveling Him (Evan and Fiona)

Rushing In (Gavin and Skylar)

Chasing Her Fire (Logan and Cara)

Rewriting the Stars (Levi and Annika)

❄

The Miles Family

Sexy, sweet, funny, and heartfelt family series with a dash of suspense. Messy family. Epic bromance. Super romantic. Best read in order.

Broken Miles (Roland and Zoe)

Forbidden Miles (Brynn and Chase)

Reckless Miles (Cooper and Amelia)

Hidden Miles (Leo and Hannah)

Gaining Miles: A Miles Family Novella (Ben and Shannon)

❄

Dirty Martini Running Club

Sexy, fun, feel-good romantic comedies with huge... hearts. Can be read as stand-alones.

Everly Dalton's Dating Disasters (Prequel with Everly, Hazel, and Nora)

Faking Ms. Right (Everly and Shepherd)

Falling for My Enemy (Hazel and Corban)

Marrying Mr. Wrong (Sophie and Cox)

Flirting with Forever (Nora and Dex)

❄

Bluewater Billionaires

Hot romantic comedies. Lady billionaire BFFs and the badass heroes who love them. Can be read as stand-alones.

The Mogul and the Muscle (Cameron and Jude)

The Price of Scandal, Wild Open Hearts, and Crazy for Loving You

More Bluewater Billionaire shared-world romantic comedies by Lucy Score, Kathryn Nolan, and Pippa Grant

❄

Bootleg Springs
by Claire Kingsley and Lucy Score

Hot and hilarious small-town romcom series with a dash of mystery and suspense. Best read in order.

Whiskey Chaser (Scarlett and Devlin)

Sidecar Crush (Jameson and Leah Mae)

Moonshine Kiss (Bowie and Cassidy)

Bourbon Bliss (June and George)

Gin Fling (Jonah and Shelby)

Highball Rush (Gibson and I can't tell you)

✳

Book Boyfriends

Hot romcoms that will make you laugh and make you swoon. Can be read as stand-alones.

Book Boyfriend (Alex and Mia)

Cocky Roommate (Weston and Kendra)

Hot Single Dad (Caleb and Linnea)

✳

Finding Ivy (William and Ivy)

A unique contemporary romance with a hint of mystery. Stand-alone.

✳

His Heart (Sebastian and Brooke)

A poignant and emotionally intense story about grief, loss, and the transcendent power of love. Stand-alone.

✳

The Always Series

Smoking hot, dirty talking bad boys with some angsty intensity. Can be read as stand-alones.

Always Have (Braxton and Kylie)

Always Will (Selene and Ronan)

Always Ever After (Braxton and Kylie)

❄

The Jetty Beach Series

Sexy small-town romance series with swoony heroes, romantic HEAs, and lots of big feels. Can be read as stand-alones.

Behind His Eyes (Ryan and Nicole)

One Crazy Week (Melissa and Jackson)

Messy Perfect Love (Cody and Clover)

Operation Get Her Back (Hunter and Emma)

Weekend Fling (Finn and Juliet)

Good Girl Next Door (Lucas and Becca)

The Path to You (Gabriel and Sadie)

About the Author

Claire Kingsley is a USA Today and #1 Amazon bestselling author of sexy, heartwarming contemporary romance, romantic comedies, and small-town romantic suspense. She writes sassy, quirky heroines, swoony heroes who love big, romantic happily ever afters, and all the big feels.

She can't imagine life without coffee, great books, and the characters who inhabit her imagination. She lives in the inland Pacific Northwest with her three kids.

www.clairekingsleybooks.com

www.ingramcontent.com/pod-product-compliance
Ingram Content Group UK Ltd.
Pitfield, Milton Keynes, MK11 3LW, UK
UKHW040128141025
8371UKWH00003B/342